THE TRAPEZE ARTIST

WILL DAVIS is the author of two novels, *My Side of the Story*, which won the Betty Trask Prize 2007, and *Dream Machine*. He has trained as an aerialist and specialises in corde lisse (rope), tissu (silks) and static trapeze. He lives in London.

THE TRAPEZE ARTIST

WILL DAVIS

BLOOMSBURY
LONDON · NEW DELHI · NEW YORK · SYDNEY

First published in Great Britain 2012
This paperback edition published in 2013

Copyright © Will Davis 2012

The moral right of the author has been asserted

Bloomsbury Publishing Plc
50 Bedford Square, London WC1B 3DP

www.bloomsbury.com

Bloomsbury Publishing, London, New Delhi, New York and Sydney
A CIP catalogue record for this book is available from the British Library

ISBN 978 1 4088 3162 5

10 9 8 7 6 5 4 3 2 1

Typeset by Hewer Text UK Ltd, Edinburgh
Printed and bound in Great Britain by CPI Group (UK) Ltd, Croydon CR0 4YY

MIX
Paper from
responsible sources
FSC® C020471

To the many talented people I have met and been inspired by in the world of circus – you showed me a new level of discipline and purpose, thank you.

IN THE NIGHT he will sink down onto his bed, that same bed he has slept in his whole life, which has been both a shelter and a prison and which now feels like neither of these things. There he will lie, staring into nothingness and listening to the sound of his own breath, heavy and strained. He will think with strange detachment of the extraordinary effort required in order to live, effort the body applies without any instruction from the mind. He will wonder if it is possible to overthrow the mysterious ongoing labours of the body, to overwrite the mechanical secretions of glands and the functions of organs – if the ending of a life could ever come down to a simple matter of willpower alone.

In the darkness above him, space that in the dread light of day will take on the familiar dull properties of his room, there will float two possibilities. They are either to lie here until daybreak, and remain lying beyond it, until weakness overthrows his body's natural resilience, or else to rise and resume his life, pick up the pieces and somehow force them back together in such a way as will allow him to carry on. But he will want neither possibility, and so there on the bed he will remain, cocooned within a state of suspended reality, not forever but until a time when he will have gained the insight he desperately needs in order to choose for himself a new future, one that he will be able to endure and commit to.

He was six years old when he decided he wanted to be gay. It was his uncle Dan's fault, for crashing his parents' New Year's Eve party.

His parents were obsessed with cleanliness and order, things he hated because he was always being sent to his room to tidy up or make the bed, or perform some similar chore that he felt couldn't possibly make any difference to anyone in the world but himself. When he went over to other boys' houses their bedrooms were always messy, the floors strewn with toys and crayons and colouring books. Their parents were too busy worrying about jobs and bills, trying to win at scratch cards, watching TV – or else drinking – to care about the state of their sons' bedrooms. When he once described one of these rooms to his mum she rolled her eyes and asked how anyone could live in such chaos, and after that he was not allowed to go over to this same boy's house again.

The party was dull because there were only adults present. Adults and him. They were all dressed in grey and brown and neutral shades of green and blue, the same colours the walls of their house were painted in. The women wore very little make-up and most had the same hairstyle, which made it hard for him to distinguish between them. They all smiled big scary smiles when they greeted him and the men all wanted to shake his hand to test out his grip.

His mum had spent a long time vacuuming and putting everything in order, and he had been given strict instructions to watch TV quietly or else he would be sent to bed. He sat cross-legged on the carpet while the adults talked and drank sickly-sweet-smelling orange punch from a big crystal bowl. The TV was showing highlights of the year and included the Queen giving a speech as well as snippets of all the major events that had been in the news. He was bored by the programme, but he couldn't change the channel because there were two adults watching it, sitting on the sofa and not talking to anyone.

His mum came and made him sit on a cushion so he didn't get dust on his trousers, and as he repositioned himself the doorbell went. She looked at the clock and said, 'Who could that be so late?' then a merry, high-pitched voice in the hall shouted out, 'Where's the booze?!' and his mum turned pale. He knew right away who it was.

Uncle Dan was big, fat, loud and always sounded like he was running out of breath. He was his mum's brother and she always frowned when his name came up. When he received birthday and Christmas cards from Uncle Dan she threw them out because she said they were inappropriate. He had once saved one of these cards from the dustbin and it showed a picture of a muscular naked man sitting on the beach holding a placard which hid his private parts saying 'Happy birthday, big boy' in golden swirly letters. On the few occasions he had seen Uncle Dan she had warned him not to pick up any bad habits or pay any attention to what he said.

Uncle Dan charged into the living room and called out, 'Happy fucking New Year's, everybody!' Then he grabbed him by the shoulders and started to do a little dance with him, right in front of the TV, obscuring the view from the adults who were watching, spinning him around while he sang, 'Let's twist again – like we did last summer!' Then his mother intervened and told Uncle Dan to calm down, but he pushed her away and shouted, 'Where's the vino?'

For the rest of the night he watched Uncle Dan instead of the TV. Uncle Dan talked loudly to everyone and then spent a long time whispering to one of the men on the sofa and touching his knee. Then Uncle Dan spilt red wine all over the sofa and his mum ran to get a cloth and some salt. But Uncle Dan only laughed about it and told his mum to relax. Her chin wobbled and he thought she was going to get angry, but then unexpectedly she smiled and let out a laugh of her own.

Suddenly it was midnight. Fireworks were going off on TV and everyone was pulling party poppers, except for Uncle Dan who was behind a curtain kissing the man he had been whispering to on the sofa. Then the man's wife was crying and the man started shouting and the next thing he had hit Uncle Dan in the face and was leaving with his wife, saying he would never come back ever again. Blood was gushing out of Uncle Dan's nose and everyone was panicking or trying to calm down the man he had kissed, but Uncle Dan was just laughing. Then Uncle Dan looked at him and gave him a wink, and right there and then he decided he loved his Uncle Dan more than anyone else in the world, including his mum and dad.

Later on when his mum came to tuck him into bed she let out a long sigh and said Uncle Dan was a liability and she hoped he had learned a lesson from his behaviour. She said that they had only invited him because they never thought he would come, and they certainly wouldn't be making the same mistake next year.

'He's wasted his life,' she said, reaching for the light switch. 'Such a pity.'

'When I grow up I'm going to be gay,' he told her.

To this his mum could only gape.

'But why?' she managed eventually.

'Because I want to enjoy myself,' he replied.

As the audience files out of the big top he remains seated, huddled up, still lost in the world he has just witnessed, a world of spectacle and illusion so alien to the one he knows it could come from another universe altogether. The two women in the emerald leotards who twisted themselves up in the strips of red fabric are now standing at the entrance bidding the crowd goodbye as they pass, and the black-and-white clown is offering children multicoloured balloon animals, created in seconds by long nimble fingers.

The last family leaves the tent and still he cannot bring himself to move. Instead he watches as the women and clown wave and pull the curtains across the entrance, their bodies visibly relaxing as they do. They have not noticed he is still here and are no longer concerned with holding themselves erect or smiling any more. The clown pulls off his white curly wig to reveal a spiky Mohican and says 'Fuck me!' loudly. Abruptly he is a clown no more. In his place stands a very different person, one scary and adult and not remotely funny or endearing. The women yawn and sigh and one of them lets out a small fart, making the other squeal with disgust. Yet even though they are no longer acting the spell is not broken. He can still feel that glow from watching their performance under the hot stage lights, can still feel the glamour like an aura that emanates from each of them. He wishes he too could possess that aura.

Suddenly he becomes aware that they are all looking at him, foreheads creased with resentment at his having observed them unaware and without their stage personas.

'Come on, you cunts, no time for gabbing!' snaps the ringmaster, appearing at the opening to the ring without his white gloves or moustache. Minus the curling antennae above his lip and the quizzical painted-on eyebrows, his face looks gaunt, his expression hard. The trio glance at him and the clown jerks his head. The ringmaster turns and sees him. He looks back at the others and then takes a few steps forward, his hands on his hips.

'Is there something we can do for you?'

The ringmaster's voice is accusing. He wishes there was some way to convey how he feels, to make this fearsome man understand that in the context of his life what he has just seen has opened his eyes to possibilities never before conceived of, and that the reason he is still sitting is because the thought of leaving the tent and returning to the drab existence that lies outside it is one he cannot bear. But there is no way to convey such a thing. He cannot even find his voice to speak. Instead, feeling his cheeks flush, he shakes his head.

'Well, in that case,' says the ringmaster curtly, 'would you mind buggering off? Show's over now.'

Shakily he stands. He goes down the steps and stumbles on the last one, ending up painfully on his knees. The man who was the clown emits a snort of derisive laughter and the ringmaster lets out an impatient sigh. He reaches for the handrail and uses it to pull himself back to his feet. As he reaches the entrance the women and clown begin to talk once more and the ringmaster bleats at them to move their arses and help him shut down. Already forgotten, he pauses to look back at them, thinking to himself, 'If only, if only, if only . . .'

He will watch as night gives way to morning, the blackness around him dissolving into a darkest shade of grey from which the outline of his room and its contents will gradually emerge. His breathing will be less heavy by this time. It will have grown silent and long as he realises that neither of the two futures he has seen are possible for him – the breathing of someone who has comfortably given himself over to despair.

Then, as if the coming light contained clarity, a third future will unexpectedly present itself. And as he thinks of it, it will seem to him the only possible future, and he will know that he has found what he has been seeking all night. For though he cannot will his body to shut down, there are other measures which he can force it to take.

Slowly, warily, lest doubt should catch him unaware and crush his resolve before he has had a chance to exert it, he will turn his body to the side and climb out of bed. He will step over to the empty space between the end of the bed and the door to his room and lower himself down, stretching out his legs on either side of him until it hurts. He will plant a hand above each kneecap and apply pressure, forcing his thigh muscles down towards the carpet.

The pain will resemble a burning and the nerves of his hamstrings will cry out for him to let go. But he will not — not until he starts to feel giddy and light-headed and the pain has become a distant throb which hardly seems connected to him any more. Only then will he release his legs and flex and point his feet, over and over until they are cramping and begging to be left alone. But he will not let them alone. Instead he will immediately push down on his thighs once again.

He will do this until the pain of stretch has begun to feel exquisite. He will do it until it feels as if his body is opening up, becoming infused with fire. And he will try another stretch too, bringing his legs together and extending his arms and reaching for his toes. His hands will be inches away and the stretch will create a jolt of agony in the small of his back. But he will take a deep breath and push and push with everything he has, until he can push no more without gasping, at which point he will slump back against the side of his bed exhausted. But as soon as he has caught his breath he will reach forward once more, extending towards his toes as though they were a ridge he must grasp in order not to fall back into a bottomless pit. Once again he will eventually start to gasp and lapse back against the bed, but he will not stop trying, not for hours.

As the greyness of his room is touched by rays of orange from the rising sun he will lie face up on the carpet soaked with sweat, his back and legs throbbing from the pain. But his mouth, which has not smiled for days, will be twisted into a triumphant grin, for he will have succeeded in brushing the nail of each big toe with the tip of each index finger.

★　　★　　★

'Hey, you!' calls a voice as he stumbles out into the night, blindly, without direction or hope.

He stops and turns. The lights that surround the perimeter of the big top have now been switched off and the moon casts a pale light across its own eerie winking depiction on the cupola of the tent. All about him the world is cast in shadow. From out of this darkness a man materialises just a couple of feet away, a glowing red ember held in one hand.

'Want one?'

It is the aerialist, the man who turned his body into an impossible spinning missile as he flew back and forth on a trapeze far, far above the heads of the audience. Amazed that such a being should actually be addressing him, he looks down and sees he is being offered a cigarette. Instinctively he shakes his head, then immediately regrets his decision as the slender hand with the packet is withdrawn, for even though he doesn't smoke had he accepted he would have created a reason to stay.

'So what did you think?'

The aerialist has an accent and he cannot help noticing its similarity to the accents of various Count Draculas he has seen in films. It sounds stagy and he has the faint sense it is put on, or else perhaps emphasised for effect. He searches for the right words to tell the aerialist how the circus has made him feel, and once again fails miserably to find them. The aerialist grins.

'You liked us? I can tell.'

'Oh yes,' he stutters. 'I thought it – I mean you – you were beautiful! All those things that you do. I could never imagine . . .'

The aerialist laughs. He can tell he is pleased, and is amazed that it should make any difference what someone like himself might think. The aerialist lets out a stream of smoke and throws down his cigarette on the wet grass. Immediately he is sorry, since it seems the conversation is over already.

'Could I buy you a drink?'

The words come from nowhere. He trembles, scarcely able to believe he has had the courage to say them, yet now that they are out he is glad, glad because no matter what the aerialist's answer at least later on he will be able to tell himself that he did not leave without trying. Though what exactly it is he is trying for he does not know – or else does not dare admit to himself.

The aerialist too appears surprised. He waits for him to look outraged and refuse, or else to laugh again, this time in scorn. But he appears to be genuinely considering it.

'I should get back,' the aerialist says, shrugging his shoulder in a vague gesture back towards the big top. From within a series of heavy thuds and the clanking of metal can be heard. 'Big Pete, he has what you call a very short fuse.'

He breathes out, unsurprised, preparing to be dismissed. Then the aerialist leans towards him and lowers his voice.

'Where can we go?'

The aerialist's use of the word 'we' thrills him to such an extent that at first he doesn't register the question. Then he realises the aerialist is waiting for him to respond and stifles his exhilaration.

'I ... well, there's the Old Mill ...'

But the idea of the local, where everybody knows him and will talk in hushed voices if he enters with another man, or else launch themselves at the aerialist with questions about the circus and take him away, is hideously unappealing.

'That little pub?' says the aerialist, seeming to share his reluctance. 'Do not take this the wrong way, but I do not particularly wish to have a drink there. Is there nowhere else?'

'Not unless you don't mind a drive,' he says, before quickly adding, 'I could drive us!'

'There is another possibility,' says the aerialist. 'Let's have a drink in my place. What do you say?'

Without waiting for an answer the aerialist nods in the direction of the dark field and begins to walk. Straight away he is swallowed up by the night. After a second of hesitation he hurries after him, unsure whether he is more afraid of losing him or of catching him up.

When he was fourteen a new boy started at school, and was placed in his set. Immediately on his arrival this boy gave out the impression that he was already bored of the school from the way he drifted into the classroom and gazed lazily at the other kids as if he had seen it all before and this time wasn't even going to bother with having expectations. The boy then took a seat near the front and sat there drumming his fingers up and down, not so much as troubling to look around again. It wasn't long before someone took a shot at him.

'Oi, newbie,' called Katy, who was one of the worst bullies. She hung out at the back of the class with the kids who came from bad families, the ones who didn't care about getting told off or put in detention. 'You a fag or what?!'

He looked at the new boy sympathetically, knowing what was coming. Katy had picked on him several times the previous year, saying he was gay and that he fancied other boys, boys who then felt compelled to confront him and warn him not to come near them. He sighed to himself, already feeling sorry for the boy as he waited for his inevitable humiliation.

'Oi, didn't you hear me?!'

The boy frowned and turned slowly as if he had heard something vaguely annoying. Katy grinned, as if assessing her prey for the weakest spot to attack.

'You a girl?' demanded Katy. She was obviously referring to the boy's longish hair, which was luxurious, dark and so curly it fell about his face in ringlets, a stark contrast to Katy's own straggly dyed-blonde mane.

The boy surveyed Katy for about two seconds, smiled pityingly and turned away. Katy made a few more remarks to the boys she sat with, deliberately audible to everyone else, culminating in the word 'poof'. At this point the new boy looked back again, puckered up his lips and blew Katy a kiss. There was a shocked intake of breath at the back, but Katy did not have the chance to react further as just then the teacher arrived.

'Ah,' said the teacher, 'you must be Edward.'

As the new boy turned back to face the teacher, for a fraction of a second their eyes met, and he had the distinct impression that despite his cool nonchalance he had been noted by the boy, a fact that made him strangely pleased, though he couldn't figure out why. He watched him for the rest of the day, trying to catch his eye again, but Edward didn't turn in his direction even once, and took off in a hurry at break time, and was mysteriously absent for the rest of the day.

★　　★　　★

'This is my grotto,' says the aerialist, switching on the light with a flourish. 'You like it?'

He peers into the caravan. Vlad's living space is tiny and so crammed full of items and clothes it is close to overflowing. Indigo, sepia and ruby fabric spills out from all directions; bronze buckles and crystal buttons gleaming in folds like the eyes of submerged reptiles. Across the little window above the counter hangs a curtain made out of strands of winking jet and a hundred diamonds of light float ethereally on the walls, the reflections of a sparkling silver mirrorball that hangs beside the light. The room resembles a cross between a thrift store and a gay disco, and it takes him a few seconds to believe that it really is in fact someone's home, with a stove in one corner, a baby fridge and cupboard in another, and a bunk containing a mattress all but buried under the hoard of gaudy riches.

'It's a little messy,' admits the aerialist, registering his expression. 'It's hard to be neat all the time when you're on the road. Things . . .' he gestures resignedly at the mess, 'have a habit of exploding!'

He realises the aerialist is waiting for him to enter and so he does, stooping under the low ceiling and standing awkwardly next to the buried bed, unsure what to do with himself. The aerialist enters after him and pulls the door shut, leaning against it and grinning at him. Instantly he feels a wave of doubt. The grin of the aerialist is sly and knowing, as if now that they are shut away from the world a veil of pretence has been lifted. They are no more than half a foot away from each other in this microscopic compartment, yet he thinks that for all they know about one another they may as well be standing observing each other from opposite precipices with a gaping chasm between them. Sweat prickles on his skin and nerves force him to sit down on the bed, even though it means sitting on what he presumes is a costume, crushing the rim of a black bowler hat with a pink silk band around its base.

'Is something wrong?' says the aerialist, stepping forward and dropping to his knees beside him. The aerialist reaches up and places his hand over his forehead, an oddly parental action that touches him even as it frightens him. The hand of the aerialist is cool and rough, and when he removes it he notices the palm is covered with calluses.

'Sorry,' he says, 'I just came over all dizzy.'

'Ah,' says the aerialist knowingly, 'you need a drink, baby.'

The word 'baby' sounds funny when pronounced in a Transylvanian accent, and he stifles a giggle as the aerialist turns and clatters around at the counter behind, turning it into a cough instead.

'So what is your name?' says the aerialist, handing him a shot glass of clear-coloured liquid.

He tells the aerialist, who repeats it to himself in a whisper; as though it is a sacred word he wishes never to forget.

'I'm pleased to meet you. And I am Vlad, as perhaps you may remember – "The Amazing Vampire Vlad!" '

The aerialist announces his circus title grandly, puffing out his chest and sweeping one hand through the air in a dramatic circle. He nods quickly. Vlad picks up another glass and touches it lightly to his, producing a faint chime, then throws his head back and drains the contents. Copying Vlad, he does likewise. An instant rush of burning sweetness blasts down his throat. Then he is giggling uncontrollably, for suddenly the situation strikes him as impossibly comical. Here he is in a tiny caravan after having been picked up by a beautiful young man, a circus performer no less, someone who cannot possibly know he lives with his mother and has never lived elsewhere, that he has not gone to bed with anyone for over twenty years, and that earlier on this very night he was on the verge of making the most important decision of his life. He clutches his arms to his stomach as the air empties out of him, unable to stem the giggling until finally it turns to coughing, this time for real, forcing him to bury his face between his knees until the fit has passed. The aerialist is laughing too, but he can tell it is mostly out of confusion. When he raises his head again Vlad is looking at him quizzically, one black eyebrow arching towards the low ceiling, waiting for him to explain the joke.

'I'm sorry,' he says lamely. 'It's just that it's been a while.'

'A while?'

'Since I . . . had a drink.'

For a second he thinks he may have somehow repulsed Vlad with this admission, because the aerialist turns away, but then he turns back, holding the bottle, and pours another measure into his glass.

'In that case, you must make sure to get drunk!'

Eventually he will wake up. The sunlight will have formed a pool about his body, and from outside will come the sounds of birds and the occasional car passing at the bottom of the street. He will sit up and immediately gasp, for his whole body will ache as though his insides have been beaten black and blue. But he will welcome this pain, because it will distract him from his emptiness, filling the void with something real and powerful, even though it makes his temples pulsate and his eyes mist over when he moves.

He will try to stand, and a wave of giddiness will pass through him. He will steady himself by reaching out and taking hold of the bedpost, and then will stagger through the door and out onto the landing. As well as the crippling in his muscles he will feel a knotted sensation in his stomach, and he will realise that it has been almost two days since he last ate.

He will limp to the bathroom, put the plug in the bath and turn on the taps. Then he will lower himself down onto the toilet seat, panting from the effort, and stare at the steam as it rises off the water. He will turn his head and look back out through the open door at the landing, and he will realise there is no need to close it or any door ever again, for the house is his and his alone.

And as he will have this thought another thought will occur to him, an idea he will mull over as he strips and lowers himself into the scalding water. That if the house is really his, this means he can do as he likes with it.

He is drunk by the time Vlad leans over and kisses him, not only on alcohol but on the romance of the situation. Life has not prepared him for romance: he has no understanding of how to act or what he should say – does not understand that the romance is sustained precisely because of such uncertainties.

Vlad's kiss deepens. It becomes urgent and forceful. He falls back against the bed and the aerialist falls with him, his hands burrowing into the mattress around his waist. He worries that he is crushing

Vlad's costumes and tries to move, but Vlad is all over him, pushing him down, hot lips against his mouth and strong limbs wrapped hungrily around his body. It is as if he is being devoured. He feels desire filling him, feels himself getting hard, and is immediately ashamed and unsure. He pulls back.

'Is something wrong?' Vlad asks, breathless, his face just inches away. He does not remember the last time he was this close to somebody, and he is astonished by the detail in the features before him. He can see imperfections he had not previously noticed. How Vlad's nose points slightly to the left, how his cheeks are pitted from tiny acne scars and the sides of his nose dotted with black-heads, how his skin is showing the beginning signs of the ravages of age and sun, tiny buds of little crow's feet bunching up at the corner of each eye, how his jaw is red in places from stubble rash, how his left ear is lower than his right and how his brutally shaved head disguises the fact that although Vlad cannot be more than thirty his hairline is fast receding. But these flaws do not matter, for within them is a greater beauty, the simple beauty of another human being, the touch of his skin, the taste of him, and the heat of his desire – all things he has denied himself for so many years it now makes him tremble to acknowledge how much he wants them.

He reaches out, gently because he is not capable of strength, and strokes Vlad's face. Vlad is amused by the tenderness of the gesture, so different from his own fierce mauling. The aerialist places his hands over the top of his fingers, smiling at him, and guides them to his lips, then takes them inside his mouth, running his tongue over them in little circles.

He moans and closes his eyes, giving himself over to what he is feeling, allowing himself to be carried away by his own desire and forgetting his shame and inhibitions. He feels the aerialist pulling at his clothes, feels that he is helping in this process, and that he is loosening the clothes of the aerialist too, his fingers undoing buttons and removing restrictive layers, throwing garments randomly on the jungle of clothing that lies about them. He hears another moan as Vlad touches his penis and then realises it comes from his own lips. He reaches down to touch Vlad in the same place and suddenly everything changes.

As if brought out of a pleasant dream by a cold slap, he comes to his senses to find himself sitting opposite Vlad who is now standing with his trousers around his ankles, staring hard at him, as if ready to take up a violent challenge. He doesn't know how to meet this stare so he looks instead at Vlad's penis, soft and only very slightly swollen, risen just a couple of inches and pointed at an angle towards the floor. His hand is still on it, his fingers still wrapped round the base, entwined with hundreds of curly dark hairs.

'It doesn't happen for me,' says Vlad tersely.

Now he looks up at him, forced to by the words, uncertain at first of what he is saying.

'Oh,' he says then, suddenly embarrassed.

He feels his own erection subside and suddenly the magic is gone, replaced by a miserable conclusion. He knows that it must be over now, and feels too that in some way this is because of his own failure. He swallows despondently.

'Sorry,' he mumbles.

He turns away, looking for his clothes. As he does he feels the pressure of the aerialist's hand on his cheek, turning him back to face him.

'It's a sad story,' Vlad says softly, kissing his ear and touching the head of his penis. It instantly rears up again. 'But we can still try to have fun, if you want ...'

He nods, desperate, ready to beg the aerialist if necessary. But he does not need to do this, for Vlad is grinning and leaning over him once more, and in any case, his words would be cut off by their mouths meeting.

It quickly became obvious that Edward should have been put into the top set. He was clever and always knew the answer when the teacher asked him a question. But Edward didn't seem interested in his own cleverness: he never raised his hand in class, and when he was called on to answer the teacher he always did so in a lazy voice that bordered on outright insolence. For this reason teachers rarely ever picked on him.

As well as being smart Edward was mysterious and self-assured. Rumour had it that his father was a famous author and his mother an actress, and that he had been expelled from his previous school for setting fire to it, but where these rumours came from no one seemed to know. Edward was easily the most fascinating person he'd ever seen. He couldn't stop watching him – and neither could anyone else. It seemed to him there was a lull in the atmosphere when Edward wandered into the room or passed by in the corridor, that people's attention was momentarily caught and fixed as if a spotlight were beaming down to follow his every step. After the mocking kiss Edward had blown Katy on his first day she hadn't come back at him, perhaps wary that he might turn the situation around and make everyone laugh at her instead. Certainly he seemed capable of it. There was real glamour to his languid walk and world-weary air, and this glamour seemed to cow the troublemakers of the class into leaving him alone, an exceptionally rare occurrence for a new kid, especially a boy.

Everyone who wasn't a troublemaker wanted to be friends with Edward, and had he desired he could easily have become very popular in a short space of time. Only Edward didn't seem to desire this. He didn't try to be friends with anybody. He gave blunt yes–no answers to questions, replied to greetings with careless shrugs, never laughed at jokes and stared blankly at the various girls who smiled meaningfully in his direction. Another rumour spread of his having psychotic episodes – sudden fits of violence that required powerful medication to keep them under control. But in the end this only added to Edward's glamour. Still he remained impenetrable and uninterested in anyone, and eventually people stopped trying to impress him and began to act as though they had never wanted to in the first place.

Within a few days he had begun to fantasise about Edward, though Edward was a far cry from the images he had recently started to masturbate to. His fantasies about Edward were not based on sex, though they often resulted in slowly stroking himself off. Instead they consisted of a series of tense and dangerous situations into which he and Edward found themselves thrown, forced to fight for their lives against rabid zombies or crazed hit men and discovering attraction and then love while in the heat of protecting one another. Sometimes the fantasies were centred around a simple everyday situation, one which he knew would never really happen, such as him stealing out on a hot summer night and wandering across the common to look at the stars and running into Edward doing the same: they would sit down together to point out constellations. Edward would tell him all about how he had burnt down his previous school and how tyrannical his famous parents really were, and he would share the tragic details of his own family – details he tailored specifically for the fantasy, in which his father became an abusive drunk and his mother sick and dying. Then, stunned by the secrets they had shared and neither one of them quite knowing what he was doing, they would find themselves drawing closer, and a moment later their lips would touch in a single passionate kiss. Although he was embarrassed by the soppiness of his fantasies he could not stop them coming. It was the most enjoyable hobby he'd ever had.

Each morning he swore to himself that he would speak to Edward, a simple hello, something to pave the way towards a future friendship and maybe more. But each time the opportunity presented itself his heart began to panic and his skin to sweat, and he found he did not dare, for he felt that were he to experience that same shrug of indifference which Edward gave to everyone else it would puncture his fantasies forever. Eventually he resolved to love Edward from afar, dreaming of a mythical day in the future when they would get to know each other.

As it turned out, that day was closer than he'd imagined. One morning roughly halfway through the term Edward paused in the doorway to the classroom, and then instead of going over to the desk where he usually sat, walked up to his, set down his bag and said in his direct yet faintly bored style, 'May I?'

He was aware of the eyes of the class on him. He knew that they were jealous, and he was thrilled to be the focus of this jealousy. Yet he was careful not to show it. Instead he nodded casually, as if Edward's sitting down was neither here nor there to him, and then for a second he waited with bated breath, terrified that Edward would change his mind, snap 'Well, fuck you then' and head over to his usual space. But instead Edward smiled, as if he knew perfectly well this was just a front, and swung himself into the seat.

He wakes up alone to the sounds of shouting and hammering coming from outside. Shots of sunlight filter in through the tiny window above the counter. He is squeezed into the little bed, half buried under all the piles of clothing and junk. The room looks even smaller and even more cluttered in the morning, almost as if he has woken up in the land of Lilliput. He inhales deeply, smelling coffee, and sees it comes from a whistling little pot over on the tiny stove.

His bladder aches but he doesn't move. Instead he breathes deeply and relaxes back into the mattress. He wants to savour this, the sensation of waking up in an unfamiliar bed after spending a night with his arms wrapped around the body of another man, and the strange and wonderful fluttering inside, something he has not felt since he was a teenager. He knows full well it cannot last, that eventually he will have to rise and resume life once more. He will have to leave the tiny room with its lovable clutter and re-enter the great gruelling world outside. He will have to stumble to his car and drive across town to his house where his mother is waiting, frantic with worry, ready with demands to know why he did not come home last night. But right now he is as close to happy as he can remember feeling and he wants to postpone life and its inevitable complications for as long as possible.

But life will not be postponed. All at once there is a great thundering from outside, as if a huge tree has fallen, and a second later the door opens and Vlad squeezes in. He is dressed in torn jeans and a shabby black T-shirt with the words 'Who the fuck is Harry Potter?' emblazoned in red across the chest. Vlad does not look at him and makes a show of trying to be quiet, somewhat unnecessarily considering all the noise coming from outside. Kneeling by the bed, Vlad starts to burrow into the mass of clothing and costumes. Suddenly his face lights up and he looks over at the other side of the bed. 'Aha!' says the aerialist. He leans across him to reach for whatever item it is he's been searching for and as he does his eyes flick down to his face and he sees he is awake. Vlad lets out a little scream and tumbles backwards, slamming into the wall on the other side and sending a shudder through the entire caravan. For a split second they stare at one another, then Vlad puts his hand on his heart.

'You terrified me!' he gasps. 'I thought you were still sleeping!'

'Sorry,' he says.

Vlad starts to laugh. He joins in and sits up. He is tangled in various sleeves and trouser legs, and reaches down to unwind them. Vlad stands up and turns to the coffee pot, pouring the contents into two mugs. He turns back and hands one of them to him.

'A chilly day,' Vlad comments.

'It is?'

He takes the mug and sips even though he doesn't drink coffee. It is bitter and black and he thinks it is the best thing he has ever tasted. He looks at the aerialist, who has turned back to the stove again, recalling the feel of his tawny skin, of the defined muscle beneath it and of his hot wet mouth. He reaches across the space and touches Vlad's behind. Vlad does not respond so he hooks his finger into his waistband and tugs gently. Vlad looks back, irritated, but then his face softens and he grins. There is another crash from outside.

'What's going on out there?' he asks. 'It sounds like an earthquake.'

'Moving,' says Vlad. 'Got to get on.'

'Moving?' he says dumbly, unable to work out what Vlad means.

'Off to next site. No audience in your little town. And that means no –'

Vlad rubs his fingers together to indicate money, then takes a mouthful of coffee, throws his head back and gargles. He has never seen anyone gargle coffee before – it seems irreverent somehow. He would like to tell Vlad this and then maybe try it himself, but he is too stunned by the fact that the circus is packing up.

'But you've only been here a day!'

Vlad finishes gargling and gulps. He lets out a small silent belch and shrugs as if he is weary of arguing a point.

'I tell this to Big Pete. I say to him we only just set up and we have contract that says we stay minimum of three days every place. It's the schedule. A lot of effort and lot of fucking time. But does he listen? Oh no. You just want to mess around with that local village tart, he says – we all saw you!'

Panic fills him, a sense of impending dread. Too fast is everything returning to the way it was. Too fast is he losing his grip on the dream of last night. Vlad steps over to him. At first he thinks his disappointment must have shown on his face, and that Vlad is going to kiss him, but instead Vlad reaches past, pulling out a small black duffle bag that was embedded between his body and the wall. He slips it over his shoulder and goes to the door.

'Does it have to be over?' he hears himself say.

Vlad pauses and turns back with one eyebrow pointed towards the ceiling.

'I mean, we like each other, don't we?' he quavers, hating how desperate he sounds.

Vlad's expression changes to one of tenderness.

'Of course,' he replies gently. 'I like you a lot. But duty and work . . . this is what I do. You get dressed and I'll see you outside.'

He wants to say no, that this is not good enough, that he will die if it is over. But he knows it is not true, that in all probability the memory of last night will sustain him for many years to come. Yet this knowledge, that he could be so pathetic as to let the fantasy of a past event keep him going long into the future, makes him almost sick with self-disgust. He searches around for his clothes, which he finally locates in a crumpled pile under the bed, and throws them on miserably.

Outside he has to shield his eyes from the morning sun which is white and brilliant and set in an empty grey sky. The field is in disarray. The big top from last night has been deflated to a pile of murky material, as though a great celestial hand had reached down with a giant pin and punctured it. All around lie long metal poles and flaps of perforated canvas. Vlad is talking to two men. One of them is stocky with lots of stubble and holds a metal bracket, the other has his arms folded and a cigarette between his lips. This man looks over at him and scowls. Although he has none of his make-up on he recognises him by his Mohican as the clown from last night. Vlad sees him and hurries over.

'Well,' says Vlad.

The aerialist holds himself stiffly and his smile is big and glassy, the smile of someone who wants to get something over with. Suddenly it is intensely awkward between them. He is aware of the eyes of the other men who stand next to the demolition of the big top, watching. He wonders now if the awkwardness was there before, back in the trailer when he woke up, and if he just failed to notice it.

'It was lovely,' says Vlad, reaching out and taking his hand.

He imagines that Vlad is glad to be getting rid of him. That he is glad that the circus is moving on and that last night, while they lay together after making love with their limbs entwined and their hearts side by side, all along Vlad was really wishing he would just leave so that this awkward morning did not have to happen.

'Yes,' he says. 'Thank you.'

And with this he walks quickly across the field, towards the little car park hidden behind a clump of trees on the edge. He doesn't dare to look back, not until he reaches the trees, for he suspects that the company will be laughing openly at him. But when he does finally turn, the stocky man and the clown are loading a pole into the back of a van, and Vlad has disappeared.

★   ★   ★

He will drag the table from across the parlour to the kitchen. It will be the same table he has eaten at all his life, which has never in this entire time had a foot placed upon its surface. Boldly he will clamber up on top, feeling some dread taboo falling away as he plants each foot squarely at the centre and stands inspecting the ceiling. Then he will take the hammer he is carrying and send it as hard as he can into the plaster above. The ceiling will explode in hundreds and thousands of tiny flecks of white, which dance on the air like snowflakes before drifting down to rest on the lino. The hammer will be withdrawn and then slammed into the ceiling again, and then again, and more flakes will dance, until it will seem that the room is filled by a snowstorm. Again and again he will attack, until a large hole has opened up directly above him. Behind it will be a wooden panel, the floor of what used to be his mother's bedroom. With an animal cry he will send the hammer hurtling into this panel, and there will be a screaming sound from the wood as it splinters and gapes open, revealing the space beyond.

He will work all day, hurling himself into the ceiling, dislodging chunk after chunk of plaster and wood, creating cloud after cloud of paint flecks, bit by bit wrenching his way through the floor above. At midday he will stop to catch his breath, his calf muscles sore and aching, and he will see that he has created a crater-like opening directly in the centre of the room. A wonderful sense of exuberance will fill him, of a change finally being wrought after years of the stagnant same. Tears will be sliding down his cheeks, baptising his face with the spirit of revolution and he will open his mouth and let out a harsh croak – a sort of war cry.

As he will stand there, letting the tears drip down his face, touching the crumbs of paint that encrust his T-shirt and pulping them into dust with his fists, he will become aware of another presence. He will look up to see a familiar face staring in through the window, her features slack from shock. He will recognise it as Mrs Goodly from next door. His mother's friend. He will cross the kitchen and open the door and stand there smiling as she looks past him with disbelieving eyes at the mounds of plaster and chunks of wood.

'What on earth are you doing?' she will breathe.

'Taking down the ceiling,' he will calmly reply.

'But . . .' For a moment it will seem Mrs Goodly is lost for words, a rare thing, but then the full force of her outrage will hit her and she will exclaim, 'But what would your ma say?!'

He will not lose his smile when he answers, 'Nothing. She can't say a word.'

And Mrs Goodly, who knows this full well and is angered because it wasn't what she meant at all, will open her mouth and find herself talking only to glass, because in the time it has taken her to process his words he will have shut the door on her. From behind it he will give a friendly wave and return to the table. As she watches, horrified, he will climb up on it, take the hammer and resume attacking the ceiling.

He will not look back at the window for a long time. When he does Mrs Goodly will have found her way out of the garden.

'Would you like to come over to mine tomorrow?' Edward asked him. Despite sitting together for the week, they hadn't spoken much, though Edward had once made a joke to him about the squeaking of the chalk on the blackboard, saying it probably resembled the sound of the combined brainpower of the class working on overdrive. He'd been surprised by the venom in the joke and had had to repeat it back to himself to make sure he'd got it right, so that by the time he smiled and nodded it was too late and Edward's attention was elsewhere. Although each morning he looked forward to sitting beside Edward, he was terrified that sooner or later Edward would realise how dull he was and move away. Worse still he couldn't concentrate on the lessons, and teachers seemed to pick on him more frequently with Edward by his side. He would stare dumbly at them, repeating their questions back to them and waiting until they gave up and told him the answer. Edward seemed to find this funny, perhaps thinking he was doing it on purpose, and always grinned at him afterwards.

'OK,' he said, careful not to sound too keen. Although he was excited by the invitation, which just over a week ago would have seemed beyond his wildest dreams, he was wary too, in case anyone else in the class had heard. A couple of other boys had cornered him outside the bus stop the day before; one had pushed him against the timetable while the other proclaimed that he and Edward were bum buddies. He had been saved by the bus arriving.

'Cool,' said Edward.

When he told his mum he would be going over to another boy's house the following morning she looked worried, since he never went to other boys' houses any more, and asked who it was.

'It's a new boy,' he said proudly. 'His name is Edward.'

At this his mother looked even more worried and asked for his surname. He told her and watched her face grow pale. It turned out Edward's parents were indeed famous – not only that, but they had moved to the town after a big scandal that had been in the papers, though his mum refused to tell him what it was.

'I'm not sure,' she murmured. 'Perhaps another time.'

'What?' he said, shocked. 'Why?!'

'And in any case, it's a Saturday.'

Saturdays he helped out at the old people's home where she worked. He hated it; that sleepy world of faded furniture and beige blankets, with its stale sour smell and snoring occupants who awoke only to gaze at you myopically and call you by a name that wasn't your own. Most of all what he hated were the sing-song voices all the carers spoke in, his mother included, as if this could somehow protect against the reality that, silent and inescapable, death stalked the building, picking off its residents one by one.

'I can hang out with whoever I want when I want,' he heard himself cry. 'You can't stop me!'

As soon as the words were out of his mouth he wished he could take them back, for he saw his mother's face tighten. He had never shouted at her before. Her eyes turned into big circles and began to glisten and shine and her mouth seemed to wobble, as if she was having trouble keeping it closed.

'I'm sorry!' he said quickly, throwing his arms around her. This was another thing he had never done before, and he felt her body tense up against him. They stood awkwardly for a while, and he began to wish he had not hugged her even more than he wished he had not shouted, for he felt stupid and unwanted, tightly pressed against this rigidness. But it seemed that a hug could not be done in half measures and so he clung on until finally she pushed him away with a watery smile.

'I'll give you a lift on my way to the home,' she said in a clipped voice.

He sits in his car staring out through the windscreen at the various trucks and trailers. Some of them are moving now, getting into formation for the road. On the seat beside him his mobile winks with missed calls, and he thinks of his mother, waiting at home. Probably she has called everyone she knows by now. Probably she has been having quite a good time of it, he thinks. And probably someone or other who was at the circus last night has told her exactly where he's been and has voiced their suspicions as to what he has been doing. But he knows that when he gets in, though she will be angry and upset, she will not press him to tell her what he has been up to. She would much rather he keep it to himself.

He sighs and thinks of the future. How he will apologise to the head of administration and save his job, bow his head and listen contritely to his mother telling him how selfish he is, and how tomorrow morning he will wake up to the same room as always and once more his life will stretch out before him, uneventful as a long concrete road, each year bleeding into the next and nothing to distinguish between them. Suddenly he knows that he was wrong, that the memory of Vlad and last night is not and cannot be enough. He is desperate, it occurs to him, and this realisation makes him laugh, as if a bubble of hysteria had risen up his throat and popped. After he has laughed it is as if the tension inside has

31

evaporated. In its place is a curious euphoria and the knowledge that he has nothing left to lose. With this thought he twists the key and starts the engine.

He follows the last caravan to the junction at the edge of the park. Instead of turning right, onto the lane that leads back to town, he turns left, the same direction as the circus, onto the road that leads through the woods and down to the motorway.

At twelve o'clock, one after the other, the caravans and trucks all indicate left and pull into a large service station. Overhead the sun has developed into a blinding disc of yellow and the interior of the car is dusty and hot. He follows the circus, parking two rows back from them where he cannot be seen. He sits and watches people getting out of their vehicles, yawning and stretching limbs, heading for the cafeteria. Most of them are dressed in slack, loose-fitting jumpers and trousers with holes in them. Vlad is not among them. There are more people in the circus than he had realised, and he wonders for a second how many of them grew up on the road and what that must be like, to have no fixed place to call home.

A short while later the people from the circus return with baguettes and hamburgers. He is not hungry himself, and in any case he doesn't dare get out the car in case he should be recognised, but he knows he should probably eat. Instead, while the circus people have their lunches he switches on his phone and calls his mother. She answers after one ring.

'Hello?'

She sounds frightened and old and instantly he feels a surge of protectiveness towards her. He wants to assure her that everything is OK and that soon he will be home and there is no need to worry, so she does not have to sound that way. But he catches himself, because none of these things is true.

'I'm fine,' he says. His own voice comes out sounding flat and devoid of emotion. 'I just wanted you to know.'

'Oh God! Where are you? What's happened?'

He doesn't answer. She begins to tell him about the consequences of his absence – how she has been frantic and scared, how she has called everybody and reported his disappearance to the police, how he is selfish and cruel not to have called, how he has to come home because the heating has gone on inexplicably and she doesn't know how to turn it off and because she thinks she can smell gas and because there have been strange sounds coming from the roof which she doesn't dare investigate.

He waits. At first it seems as though she will continue forever, but surprisingly quickly her words cease to flow. Intermittent hesitations creep in, as she notices how he is not saying anything, not grunting in agreement or shame, until finally the fear overtakes, fear that something terrible is happening, or, even worse, that he is not listening at all.

'I'm going to be away for a while,' he says in the stretch of silence that opens up. He can almost see the panic in her eyes. The disbelief.

'If this is about yesterday . . .'

'It's not.'

'Then you're out of your right mind! Where can you go? You can't afford to take a holiday – you haven't even packed! And what about your job?'

'I've quit.'

She is shocked into silence once more, but this time it lasts only for a few seconds. When she speaks again, however, she has checked herself. There is a new note of caution to her voice, as though she is wary of being forced into saying something she will later regret.

'Look, I'm sorry about yesterday ... I didn't mean it if I said anything hurtful. I was angry and perhaps I should have listened. Come home and we'll talk. Where else is there for you to go?'

'I'll know when I get there.'

'Are you trying to hurt me? Is that what this is about?'

He says nothing. He knows that this is terribly cold of him, and it takes all of his willpower. But if he speaks, tries to explain and make her see, he is certain it will only be the beginning. His mother will wear him down with her questions and reproaches, using her frailty and his idiocy as weapons, until he can take it no longer and succumbs.

'Please ...'

Still he doesn't reply. Still he holds the mobile against his ear, listening to the wavering uncertainty in his mother's voice, the timbre of barely stifled terror at the realisation her son is not quite the person she believed him to be.

'I can't manage without you!'

This is her last card, her ace, and she lays it down desperately. A pang strikes his heart, not because he knows it is true, but because he knows it is not. The years have turned him into a fixture, like a sophisticated sort of domestic appliance, one that she has come to rely on to allay her little fears. His whole life he has only been useful, not essential, and it is this understanding that finally induces him to flip shut the mobile and switch it off. He has never ended an exchange this way, not with his mother. It seems to him he has effectively deleted her, and although he is racked with deadly guilt he also feels giddy and light-headed. His hands tremble as he places the mobile in the glove compartment and closes it, locking his mother away in a hidden dark pocket where he can forget that she even exists.

The first thing he will see when he opens the door will be the badge. Instinctively he will feel a rush of alarm, for he has never opened the door to a policeman before. But the feelings will quickly diminish, because it will only be Gordon, the local constable, standing there in his uniform with a patient smile creasing up his amiable old face.

'Some of your neighbours were a bit concerned,' Gordon will say. 'Asked if I'd stick my beak in and make sure everything was all right.'

'Everything's fine,' he will reply, too fast so that it sounds as if really everything isn't. 'I mean – thanks.'

Gordon will shift his weight from his right foot to his left as if trying to convey the message that he wants to believe him, but can't reasonably be expected to given the circumstances.

'I was very sorry to hear about your ma,' Gordon will say. 'A good lady. Can't be easy for you now, all shut up in this big house on your own.'

He will feel the muscles in his jaw tightening and he will struggle not to let his anger show. Who is this man? he will suddenly wonder, and since when did being a policeman give you the right to say such things? It is complacence, he will think to himself, the result of doing the same job for years and years, and being relied on by people who don't realise they don't need to rely on you. That will be what gives a person such self-certainty.

'Well, I'd better get on,' he will say coldly. 'Thanks again for stopping by.'

'Hold on just a second,' Gordon will say as he goes to close the door. 'Look, there've been some complaints of noise coming from your house. Hammering and that. You building something?'

'Yes, that's right,' he will reply. 'I've knocked down the ceiling in the kitchen in order to insert a truss so I can hang a trapeze from it.'

After a few seconds of digesting this information Gordon will sigh deeply as if he had hoped for much better. Then the policeman will wearily collect the lines of his face back into a smile, and he will have the sense it is the same expression he has used to deal with people like him – troublesome, emotional people – since he first embarked on his career in the force.

'Look,' Gordon will say, adopting an avuncular tone that contains the faintest hint of warning, 'you're going through a rough patch and everyone knows it. They all want to help. But what you're doing is shutting yourself away and making them worry about you. Pretty selfish, don't you think?'

The anger will flash like a stab wound, hot and violent. He will choke it back and grip the door, digging his nails into the paintwork.

'If people want to help me they'll leave me alone,' he will say, his voice shaking. 'And so will you.'

Gordon will let out another weary sigh, but this time he will cut him short before he can speak again.

'So unless you're planning to arrest me I'm going to get on,' he will say, and with this he will close the door, letting it slam and taking enormous satisfaction in the sound that it makes.

He will stand there for a long moment, his back against the door, tingling all over. In the past he would never have dared to slam a door on a police officer, especially not someone like Gordon, so well known and respected.

Slowly but surely a smile will creep across his lips.

It is late afternoon when the company turns off down a winding country lane so small they tear chunks of foliage from the over-hanging trees, sending clouds of fluttering ovals to dash against his windscreen as he follows behind. Every so often they encounter a car coming the other way, and there is a great burst of honking, as though the trailers were a herd of oversized cattle trying to intimi-date a smaller creature. Eventually the lane becomes so small move-ment slows to a trickle. But just as he is starting to worry they will have to turn round, the road opens out, and a short while later the caravans and trailers turn, one by one, into a large empty meadow. Cautiously he drives on past and pulls up on a muddy bank a little further up, under the shade of a large oak tree.

He sits for a long while, wondering what his next move should be. He is incredibly tired – so tired he can barely keep his eyes open. The sun is drifting towards the horizon, touching the tips of the tree above the car and gilding its leaves with a golden sheen. Without thinking he shuts his eyes, and a moment later he is asleep.

He wakes to the sound of a guitar and laughter. It is dark now and he can see nothing except the velvety sky above, pitted with stars. Stiffly he opens the door, creating a burst of harsh yellow as the inside light comes on, and thrusts his legs out one after the other so that he can stretch them. The music is coming from the field, and through gaps in the hedgerow he can now make out a flickering orange light. Groggily he staggers out and relieves himself noisily against the roots of the oak.

Moments later he is treading across the field towards the light and sound. Someone has started to sing – a woman with a soulful yet playful voice. She sings of being controlled by dark magic and cursed to spend her life tragically alone, and creates laughter with a refrain praising the wonder of online dating. As he gets closer he can make out the trailers, which have been parked in a circle to create space for a sort of enclosure, at the centre of which a bonfire crackles. The coloured lights of the big top have been strung between the trailers and illuminate the space around the bonfire, about which shapes sit, stand or sway to the music. The air is suffused with the smell of barbecued meat and thick with the heavy scent of marijuana. He feels a lurch in his stomach and realises he is almost faint with hunger.

But as he gets closer he starts to feel frightened and wonders if he should turn back. The image of his mother alone at the house flashes into his mind and suddenly he is paralysed by doubt, unable to take the necessary remaining steps that will announce his presence to the company. He leans against one of the trailers and puts his head in his hands, fighting the urge to start weeping.

'Excuse me, this is a private party,' says a voice coldly from the dark, making him jump and spin round with a gasp, so that he stumbles backwards over a rut in the ground and almost falls. He screws up his face as the beam of a torch strikes it.

'For invited guests only . . .' The voice takes on a note of surprise – 'What the fuck are you doing here?!'

Although he can't see him he knows it is the clown.

'I'm sorry!' he says quickly. 'I wanted to see Vlad. Do you know where he is?'

'You mean you followed us?' says the clown incredulously, keeping the torch trained on his face. 'What are you? Some kind of a psycho?'

'I just want to see him,' he says with a tremble. 'Could you possibly tell him I'm here?'

'Fuck off!' spits the clown.

'Please . . .'

There's a long pause, as if the clown is considering his next move. Abruptly he switches off the torch. There's the sound of a click and a tiny flame flares up, and for a couple of seconds he has a glimpse of the clown's angular face, smirking as he lights a cigarette. Then the image is gone, sucked into the night and replaced by the smell of smoke and the sound of a deep exhalation.

'What d'you want with him anyway?' says the clown in an unexpectedly conversational tone, as if toying with the idea of granting his request just for the hell of it. 'That good a lay, was he?'

'I . . .' He stumbles for the right words and realises there aren't any, or that if there are he doesn't know them. Besides, he has the feeling that no matter what he says to the clown it will come out sounding daft. 'I want to see him again. That's all.'

'Thought you'd continue your romantic little shagathon, did you?' muses the clown. 'Well, let me tell you something about our star aerialist before you go getting too lovey-dovey, my friend.

Round here we call him the universal unicycle – do you know why? Cos anyone who wants to have a go, gets to. And they all have too. Every town we've been. Should count yourself lucky if you haven't caught herpes. Or worse.'

The clown lets out a long stream of smoke that hits him full in the face and he knows he is still smirking at him. Then he watches as the glowing end of his cigarette moves past him to the side of the trailer where the clown's face is illuminated by orange as he yells out, 'Hey, Vladdy! Got an old friend of yours over here!'

There is a shout back, but only the word 'fuck', heavily accented, is distinguishable.

'Just you come have a little see!' the clown yells and turns back to face him.

'Thank you,' he says.

The clown does not reply, but in the glinting from the fire he can see that his eyes are aglow with malevolent enjoyment.

'What have you got?' says the aerialist, appearing a few seconds later. He sounds childish and petulant. He is carrying a lamp, and illuminates the whole space behind the trailer. He waits with bated breath for the aerialist to notice him, but Vlad simply stands beside him looking expectantly at the clown. 'I told you I'm not interested!'

Smirking, the clown points at him and the aerialist turns.

Vlad stares. At first he cannot meet his eyes but then he remembers that this is it, that he has nothing to lose and everything to gain, and that he does not need to be shy or afraid any more. He looks back at those two brown orbs with the full force of his own stare, waiting for the inevitable disgust and repulsion he knows is his due, preparing to be spat at, reviled, told to leave and never come back. And even though in a second it will all be over, and he will be trudging back to his car scarred from the rejection and failure, he feels alive again, a thousand minute shivers prickling across his skin.

'I don't understand,' says the aerialist. He does not sound horrified exactly, but rather astounded, as though he cannot believe his eyes.

'I followed your circus,' he says, hearing the words and feeling a wonderful sense of relief in their simple truth. 'I got in my car and drove after it. I'm parked on the edge of this field.'

'He's a stalker,' supplies the clown.

The aerialist continues to stare, his eyebrows dipping and one side of his mouth rising, as if two alternate reactions are competing for control of his face. Then, abruptly, the aerialist lets out a giggle. He glances back at the clown and says, 'My friend and I have some things to discuss, if you don't mind.' And then the aerialist's arm is around his shoulder and he is smelling that same smell as from last night, deodorant and the underlying scent of body odour. Both are overpowered by the aerialist's breath, which is hot and thick with the smell of whisky. The aerialist guides him away, across the grass and towards the bonfire and the singer. Behind them he hears the clown muttering, angry at Vlad's reaction. But he doesn't care because his spirits are soaring with triumph, so much so that he fails to notice how the aerialist is leaning on him, stumbling over the ground, hardly able to walk in a straight line.

'Attention, everybody!' the aerialist shouts over the singer, who stops mid-verse. In the partial light from the strung lamps and the glinting of the bonfire, he makes out the company all turning in their direction, the whites of numerous pairs of eyes twinkling against the dark.

'Everybody,' Vlad announces, slurring a little, 'I want you to meet my stalker. My stalker – this is everybody.'

Edward's house was large and old, with a big front garden that had a throng of short skeletal apple trees at the centre twisting up out of the grass like a giant spider. It lay on the other side of town, where the city folk tended to live, the ones who bought weekend houses, who the locals always sighed about because they disapproved of people owning two perfectly decent houses and then leaving one uninhabited for long stretches of time.

'Here we are,' said his mum. She drove the car up the driveway and stopped, keeping the engine running. She had been quiet since he had told her he could do what he liked, and he knew that in those few hot seconds he had disappointed her in a way that would take a very long time to repair. He had shown himself to be unpredictable, capable not only of lashing out but of far worse – of lashing out at his mother. She was suddenly afraid of him, and, irony of ironies, instead of being glad he was sorry. Only the prospect of spending the day with Edward prevented him from telling his mum he would rather go to the old people's home with her after all.

'I'll pick you up later,' she said. 'Give me a call at the home when you're ready.'

'It's OK,' he said. 'I can just walk back.'

He paused for a minute, not wanting to get out of the car without saying something more. But the silence was crushing him so he climbed out and with another glassy smile, just like she had given him the night before, his mum drove away.

He turned and made his way up to the front porch. The door opened before he could press the bell and Edward stood there, grinning from ear to ear, his head cocked to one side.

'Welcome to my humble abode,' he said and stood back, throwing open his arms with a grand gesture. He stepped past Edward and into the hall. It was three times the size of the hall in his own home and was painted a bright white. There was no furniture other than a little table and a coat stand, and on the walls hung three vast oil canvases, almost as large as he was, each a portrait of a naked woman holding some item of fruit and staring out at the observer with a feverish, angry expression. He was shocked. The only pictures they had in his house were of flowers or meadows, meticulously detailed and respectably proportioned.

'The womb does them,' Edward told him, sounding rueful. 'We've got hundreds. They're meant to be her — when she was younger.'

'They're really good,' he said uncertainly.

'They're fucking embarrassing, that's what they are,' snapped Edward. 'Just like she is.'

He jumped at the harshness in Edward's voice, his shock added to by Edward's use of the word 'fucking', so clean and casual. In his fantasies Edward had never sworn or spoken anything other than perfect English. Edward started up the stairs and gestured for him to follow. Before they had reached the landing one of the doors below opened and a woman with red-gold hair, in a long black dress decorated with seemingly random splodges of blue and green, poked her head out.

43

'Ah,' she called, 'you must be the friend.'

'Hi!' he said self-consciously, wondering if he should go down the stairs to shake her hand. It had not occurred to him until now that it might be awkward to meet the mother of the person he daydreamed about. But she did not take another step, merely bobbed her head up and down a few times.

'Good.'

With a final hearty nod she disappeared back through the door and it slammed behind her. He looked at Edward, unsure how to react. Edward merely rolled his eyes.

'The womb,' Edward said with a long-suffering sigh, and continued to lead the way up the stairs. He followed, thinking how glamorous it must be to have a mad artist for a mother. They passed an open door which Edward classified with the words 'My room – private', and continued up to the second-floor landing. It was lit only by a single circle-shaped window. A ladder stretched up to a dark square in the ceiling above.

'What's up there?' he said, suddenly wary.

Edward smiled secretively.

'You'll see. If you can keep up.'

They climbed through the hatch and into the dark space beyond. He peered about, able to see nothing but large, looming, block-like shapes. Then Edward flipped a switch on the wall and a pool of weak orange light spread out from a single bulb overhead, illuminating a city of abandoned furniture and cardboard boxes, packed in so tight he couldn't see the far wall.

'This is where I come to chill,' said Edward, leading him to the edge of a table and dropping to his knees. 'Come on!'

Without waiting Edward disappeared under the table. He crouched and peered after him, dimly making out Edward's shape as he squeezed his way through a small gap between a large bureau and a thick set of shelves. It looked dark, dusty and thrilling where Edward was going, and he knew his parents wouldn't approve. He didn't hesitate and crawled after Edward through a winding maze of chair and table legs, of displaced drawers precariously balanced atop rotting desks and of upturned bed frames with springs that jutted out, their coils tapering to sharp points like spearheads. Edward rocketed forward on his hands and knees, laughing his head off. It seemed to him he was supposed to catch him and so he reached out to grab his foot. But Edward was too fast and evidently knew the layout perfectly, for in a flash the foot was gone from his grasp, disappearing into the jungle of corners, angles and apertures. He did his best to follow, but the light source was now blotted out by towering sets of shelving, and when he paused to try and get his bearings Edward seemed to have vanished altogether. All he could hear now was his own heavy breathing as he made his way through the makeshift labyrinth. He caught his sleeve on a sharp edge and his left elbow jammed into the corner of an ornate box with metal ridges. Gasping at the pain, he tried to stand, and immediately banged his head against the surface of something hard and unforgiving. Without thinking he began to thrash. Suddenly he seemed to be struggling merely to breathe. He tried to call out Edward's name but his voice caught in his throat and instead all that came out was a gurgle of fright.

Then he felt something taking hold of his wrist and for a minute he didn't know what it was and fought against it with all his might.

But it did not loosen and a second later he felt himself being yanked. He slid across the floor and out through a square-shaped opening.

'Almost lost you there,' grinned Edward.

All at once there was light again and he found he was lying in a small clearing, presumably at the centre of the attic. On the floor beside him lay two packets of cigarettes, an ashtray stuffed with cigarette butts, a bottle of red wine half empty and a small pile of magazines. He sat up, dazed.

'This is my den,' said Edward proudly. 'All this junk was here when we moved in. I made this space all by myself.'

'What's wrong with your room?' he said ruefully, rubbing his arm. He instantly regretted it though when he saw the wounded look on Edward's face.

'I like it here.'

He nodded, though really he couldn't understand why a boy like Edward would want to go tunnelling around on his own in a dark attic. But the question was driven from his lips by the light pressure of Edward's knee against his own as Edward shuffled around looking for something and muttering under his breath, apparently unaware their legs were touching. Not sure if he liked the pressure or wanted to be rid of it, but not daring to move and call attention to it in either case, he looked at the magazines and received another shock. The cover of the closest one showed two burly men against the backdrop of a sunny cornfield, naked except for cowboy boots and Stetsons, their erect penises pointed directly at one another.

'Ah.'

Edward picked up something that looked like a crystal and clicked it, producing a small flame. He held a cigarette to his lips and offered another to him. He shook his head automatically, still staring at the magazines, deeply insecure and wondering all of a sudden what it was Edward wanted with him. Edward followed the direction of his gaze.

'You can borrow them if you want.'

'But they're for ...' He could hardly bring himself to say the word, it seemed so controversial. 'Men.'

'Of course,' said Edward simply. 'I'm gay. Aren't you?'

Inside Vlad's tiny room he curls himself up on the bed while the aerialist smiles drunkenly at him and starts to take off his clothes. Vlad gets stuck with his trousers, and half stumbles, half trips, knocking the little mirrorball above and hurtling into one of the shelves behind, bringing the contents raining down on himself together with a stream of curses. He watches the aerialist fumbling to pick up the pots and pans, still manacled by his trousers, and starts laughing. Vlad looks up and peers at him, his puzzled expression touchingly childlike under the spinning diamonds of light. He reaches down to him, suddenly confident and sure of himself, of what he wants and what he is doing. He clasps his hand around the back of Vlad's head and with all his strength jerks him up and towards him. Vlad lets out a little cry of pain at the violence of it, but does not resist. A second later he has Vlad on the bed with him, has straddled his lean body, and is running his tongue along the contours of his torso, tasting the salty surface of his skin, working his way down towards the penis which he knows will not work but wants to lick regardless. He reaches down to free his own penis, feeling it pulsate with longing. Only it is now his turn to struggle, as the zip refuses

47

to budge. In the end he wrenches the trousers down, hearing them rip as they pass below his thighs, so engulfed by the urgency of lust he doesn't care, is in fact glad and hopes they are torn to shreds. He resumes kissing the aerialist's stomach, marvelling at its firmness, at the sharp apex that lines his navel and points the way towards his groin. He weaves his fingers into the aerialist's underwear and gently probes the edges of his pubes before tugging the whole thing down, revealing Vlad's cock, short and stubby, very slightly swollen. He kisses it, shocking himself with his own boldness as he runs his tongue along the little crevice of the head. It is only as he takes the whole thing into his mouth that he realises it is not just Vlad's cock that is failing to respond, but that Vlad has not moved for a while now, and that instead of resuming stroking his head Vlad's hands are limp at the sides of his body.

He releases Vlad's penis and sits up. He cannot help but smile wryly at the sight that meets him. The aerialist's head is thrown back. His eyes are closed and his mouth is slightly parted, and he is snoring ever so faintly.

Letting out a gentle exhalation, partly out of amusement and partly out of disappointment, he studies the face before him. The shadows play a game there, elongating the aerialist's features, making dark hollows out of every groove while smoothing over the acne scars that pit his cheeks. He looks beautiful but strangely empty, devoid of character, like a discarded mannequin. Slowly, as he watches, the aerialist's features begin to take on the properties of another person, one he has thought of every day for years. He feels a fresh lurch of longing, not for the aerialist but for this other face, an urge so strong and so startling his breath catches. Softly he slides his body into the small gap between Vlad and the wall, and rests his arm over the aerialist's chest, feeling the gentle rise and fall of his breast and listening intently for the heartbeat within.

He will open the door to a burly man with a protruding belly that swells up out of him like a pregnancy. The man will be holding a piece of paper and looking up and down at the house with suspicion.

'Delivery of some scaff and truss?'

He will feel a little thrill as he takes in the large black van behind the man, with his co-worker who could also be the man's twin sitting behind the wheel, knowing what is contained in the back.

'That's right.'

'Truss is six metres, you know?'

'Yes.'

The man will glance back at his colleague, scratch his head then look down the road at the other houses, taking in the rose beds and flower borders, the neatly trimmed hedges, the meandering tendrils of clematis, the freshly mown lawns and the statuettes, gnomes and gazebos with which residents have attempted to characterise their little stretches of land. He will take in the black-and-white walls and thatched roofs of the cottages, and the mock-Edwardian red brick of the newer buildings. Then he will look back at him and shrug, still confused but nonetheless deciding he is just not all that interested in why someone might want to install a six-metre metal truss in this quaint country neighbourhood.

'Where d'you want it?'

He will meet the man's gaze steadily. He will know that all about the road there will be faces peeping nosily out of windows, waiting to see what will be removed from the van.

'In the kitchen.'

It was said offhand, the way people spoke on TV, as if it were just some charming incidental fact, not something momentously important that defined who or what you were. Not the way people spoke of it at school, where the word 'gay' was the worst insult you could apply and usually the cause of furious whispering and flurries of giggles.

'Yes,' he said after a long pause.

'I thought so,' said Edward.

'Why?'

He was suddenly paranoid, wondering what he had done to mark himself out in this way. Was his voice too high? His walk too girly? His wrists too floppy?

'Because you're different,' Edward replied mysteriously. 'Like me.'

Edward breathed out a long stream of smoke and then giggled at his face, apparently amused by his confusion.

'Look, don't worry about it, OK? It's cool.'

'OK,' he said, unconvinced.

He stared at the magazine and then reached for it. Inside a man with a ponytail was being taken from behind by a man with an eyepatch against a backdrop of a Spanish galleon. His heart thumped from fear. There was something repellent about the poses of the men, the grimaces of pleasure and pain on their faces, the unapologetic sight of their cocks pink and upright. Yet behind the fear he felt also a twinge of lust and something starting to swell in his crotch. Quickly he shut the magazine, trying to look unimpressed.

'Here,' said Edward.

He looked up guiltily to see Edward holding out the bottle of wine.

'It's good stuff. Vintage.'

He took it gingerly. At school some of the kids would boast about how much they could drink before they passed out. He had tasted alcohol only once before in his life, sneaking downstairs one Christmas after his parents were in bed to steal a gulp from the bottle of cognac his father had opened after dinner. It had been disgusting, he remembered, and had burned his throat. But he didn't want Edward to know this pathetic fact and so, preparing for a scorching, he took a decent-sized swig from the bottle. He was pleased to find that the wine did not burn like the cognac, and that it even had a pleasant aftertaste, like blackberries.

'So you want to know the story behind my parents?'

Edward eyed him craftily, as if he could tell he was dying to say, 'Yes!' This annoyed him, despite his awe of Edward, and he shrugged and made a show of studying the label on the bottle.

'Dad screwed another guy's wife,' Edward said. 'He was another author, this guy, who'd written some mean reviews of Dad's books in the Sunday paper. It's a big deal, this paper – guess he was pretty pissed off when he found out. Dad said we had to move because of all the reporters, but really it was because the womb wanted it. It was supposed to be just temporary, but now Dad says he likes it here and wants to stay.'

'Your mum . . .' he said. 'She must have been –'

'The womb hates him, but she also knows he's the only man in the world who'll put up with her. That's how fucked up my family is.'

Edward reached for the bottle and took a big gulp, then a big drag of his cigarette, which was followed by another big cloud of smoke. There was something abandoned about the process, as if Edward was only drinking and smoking out of disillusionment. Edward's mouth twisted into a smile, but it was a bitter smile, and he suddenly saw a new side to him, an unhappy vulnerable side that was ordinarily hidden by the smooth self-assurance that marked him out from everyone else. Once again, he didn't know how he was supposed to react. The truth was that if anything he was jealous – jealous of Edward for having these impossible parents who were mad and famous and had affairs. But he knew enough not to admit to this.

'I'm sorry,' he said.

'It's not your fault.'

'I mean . . . it must be hard, that's all.'

'Life is hard,' said Edward dismissively.

But suddenly he could see with crystal clarity that Edward's world-weary air was affected. It was like a piece of armour, to shield off hostility and loneliness. Edward was not effortlessly cool and collected: it took effort for the boy before him, a lot of effort.

Vlad is still sleeping when he opens his eyes and finds himself once more in the tiny compartment the aerialist calls home. His neck and back are sore, and he discovers it is because the aerialist's limbs are tightly wrapped around him as if clinging on for dear life. He is moved to find Vlad this way, but his bladder is full and throbbing. Gently he unravels himself from the aerialist's body, accidentally elbowing him in the process. Vlad lets out a groan, then says 'Shit' and mumbles out a sentence in what sounds like gibberish before turning over and huddling up into a ball, dragging the covering with him.

He sits up and manoeuvres himself over the aerialist. On the floor piled up are his clothes, and he puts them on, vaguely shocked to think this is the third morning running he has worn the same underwear and shirt. He casts another look at the sleeping bundle of Vlad's body. The aerialist's face is tightly screwed up, as if his dreams are making him concentrate very hard indeed. An irrational feeling of affection sweeps through him. He knows it is foolish, a fantasy, that he does not really know the sleeper before him and furthermore has no right to look to this man to save him from himself. Yet he cannot stop it. He has yearned for this – for someone, anyone – for so long that the desire has grown too strong for the feeble constraints of logic and too wild for the cold lessons of reality. Such is the nature of desperation.

Ever so softly he reaches down and traces the dark arch of an eyebrow with his thumb, lost in the beauty before him, a beauty that is half real and half projected onto the sleeper. Then a sharp ache reminds him why he is up and he turns quickly to the door.

The outside world is grey and uninspiring. The circle of trailers and caravans looks drab and mud-splattered, all the colour and fever of the circus locked away within, leaving only an uncomfortable and oppressive looking way of life to be seen from the outside.

At the centre of the circle, where the bonfire of last night crackled, now sits a blackened patch of land, an ugly unnatural blemish on the surface of the earth. The grass all around is strewn with cans of beer and the occasional glass bottle winking in the weak morning sun.

He peers around. The curtains to the windows of the trailers are all closed. Seeing no one he quickly unzips and lets out a stream of steaming piss that sizzles as it pitter-patters into the grass. As he finishes there is the sound of a door opening, and he quickly zips up again.

It is the clown. He stands in front of his caravan, the one furthest from the circle, and yawns. He weaves his way unsteadily across the site, coming to stand right beside him. Wordlessly the clown pulls down the front of his bottoms, flips out his penis and lets out his own arc of piss, producing a great moan of pleasure as it fountains into the air. He is embarrassed and doesn't know where to look. He ends up jamming his hands in his pockets and focusing on the clouds above, contemplating them as though it is a lovely spring morning.

'Get what you came for?' sniggers the clown.

He smiles warily, trying to seem amiable yet at the same time not wanting to show any sign of weakness. He understands the clown is not to be trusted.

'I suppose you'll be on your merry way then,' continues the clown. 'Nice day for a drive, isn't it? And you've got all that distance to cover, don't you? Back to the shithole you come from.'

The clown slaps his penis a few times to rid it of residual droplets.

'I'm not going back,' he says.

He surprises both the clown and himself with this — with the force in his voice and certainty of the statement. The clown makes a clucking sound and carefully stows his penis away. Then he turns to him. Close up, in unforgiving daylight, he can see how old the clown is. His face is deeply lined in places, as if he has suffered a great many hardships and each one etched a souvenir onto his skin. The clown's angular features rest naturally in a surly contemptuous look. Though he is not ugly, and even might pass for attractive under a street lamp or above a candle, the expression on his face is bitter and cold, and this creates an impression of ugliness.

'Well, best of luck anyway,' the clown says, bringing his lips into what he is already sure is a trademark smirk. He smiles back and the smirk instantly vanishes.

'If I were you I'd just piss off.'

He watches him amble away, whistling sharply as he goes, and wonders what would induce a person like this to become a clown of all things.

From then on they always sat together, in class and at lunch. People got used to seeing them as a unit and they were teased and threatened by Katy and the kids who sat at the back in their set. He didn't care what they said any more though because when he was with Edward he felt stronger, wittier, smarter. He could ignore the jokes and insults that previously would have cut him and made him retreat further into his shell. He could even laugh at them. When someone shouted out that the poofs had entered the room when they came in one morning, the remark bounced off him like a dud grenade: he even grinned at the person who had shouted it and blew him a mock kiss, just as Edward had done that first day with Katy. Edward was full of knowledge and insider information. He showed him how to inhale when he smoked and taught him how to roll his eyes upwards into his eyelids so that only the whites showed as if he was possessed. They watched films from Edward's father's collection that his own parents had forbidden him to see – *Straw Dogs*, *The Exorcist*, *If* and *Cannibal Holocaust*. Edward introduced him to the music of Patti Smith and the Who, to the films of Fassbinder and Douglas Sirk, to the writings of Gore Vidal and Oscar Wilde.

'The only thing worse than being talked about is not being talked about,' Edward would sigh as if overcome with ennui when they passed others in the queue for lunch and heard whispering break out behind them.

With Edward he felt as if he could be more than just a troublemaker or a nobody, and sometimes he would study Edward secretly when he thought he wasn't looking, idolising him, unable to believe this unusual boy was actually his friend. Now and then Edward would catch him doing it and would smile as if he knew just what was passing through his mind and tell him to stop 'acting like the womb'.

After school he would go back to Edward's house and they would ascend to his den to smoke cigarettes and page through porn magazines rating the bodies of the centrefolds. They would talk about kids at school and psychoanalyse them – Edward had a fresh perspective on everyone. Fred, a boy who was constantly in trouble for picking on younger kids, Edward said was obviously damaged because he was unable to live up to some ideal, probably set by parents or an older brother who bullied him relentlessly and got away with it, and that laying into smaller boys was his way of evening the score. Katy, Edward thought, was an especially interesting case: she was mean and loud and hung around with boys because she knew she was not very pretty and it was a way for her to get the attention she desperately craved, which she would never otherwise receive from the opposite sex. Edward had a theory about everyone, and sometimes, when he was on his own, he would find himself wondering what Edward's theory was about him.

Back in Vlad's room he finds the aerialist sitting up on the bed against the far wall with his arms wrapped around his knees and in one hand a glass of water at the bottom of which a white pill is fizzing and turning to cloud. He smiles at Vlad, but the smile is not returned. Instead the aerialist clutches his head and gasps, then takes a great swig of the water and screws up his face.

'How's your head?' he says, knowing that the answer is self-evident but feeling he ought to say something.

In reply Vlad emits a faint groan. He takes this as a good sign, for it seems to signal that the aerialist is not displeased by his presence, that the reason he did not smile back is his hangover rather than annoyance at the sight of him. He takes a step forward, meaning to sit on the bed beside Vlad, but at this point the aerialist's head snaps forward, his eyes narrowed and features contorted.

'What the fuck,' snarls Vlad abruptly, 'are you doing here?'

He stares at him, shocked.

'I just . . .' is all he can manage in reply.

'You're one of those very sad people, is that it?' Vlad spits. 'Who think that one stupid fuck means partners for life?'

'No!'

'Then what is it?'

'I wanted to see you again, that's all!'

'How old are you? What, forty? And you act like this!' Vlad gestures to him and snaps his fingers, producing a loud clicking noise. 'Like a teenager! Like a stupid fucking kid. What do you think this is going to be for you? Some sort of love nest?'

He is hit by a burst of anger.

'I don't fucking know, all right? I don't know what I thought!'

'Ah!' says Vlad, nodding his head up and down very fast, seeming to enjoy his flash of rage even more than he does. 'You don't know! So you are loopy as well as stupid?'

The anger dissipates, try as he might to hold on to it. All that is left is a great sense of shame. Vlad rolls his eyes as if despairing of the feeble creature before him. There seems nothing left to say, only the truth, and so tentatively he tries to say it.

'Watching you the other night . . . it made me feel something.'

'What?'

'That I . . . I don't want to leave.'

'Too bad!'

'I wouldn't get in your way. Maybe I could help –'

'Help? Help?! How could you help?' exclaims Vlad.

'I don't know.'

'Maybe I can show you some tricks,' suggests the aerialist, suddenly looking back at him and grinning. Disconcerted by the change, he nods. Vlad's grin deepens and he cautiously smiles back.

Then Vlad's grin vanishes and the aerialist takes a deep breath, as if filling his lungs with invective.

'You think it is so easy as you just run away and join the circus? One of those people who think that all it takes is for you to one day decide "Oh, I shall learn a few tricks today" and then hooray the next day – ha! – you can be a great aerialist, perhaps even the vampire Vlad?! Why not? Oh, I will tell you why not! Have I got news for you! Because it's not so fucking easy!'

'That's not what I –' he starts to say, but Vlad cuts him off.

'Where I come from you are made to do terrible things – terrible things! – awful, painful horrible exercises before you are allowed to even think about learning the tricks. You must sit for hours and hours with your legs in splits – until they are truly split! You must stand on your head until the blood is pouring out of your eyes and you must balance on one foot for a whole week and then on the other for another whole week, and you must smile while you are doing it also! And then the tricks! The tricks, they take years and years and years of practice. Years of dedication and courage. The timing and the strength, it comes not from nowhere, but from the training! The endless, endless training. And on top of this you need drive. You need spirit! You need what you can only get from years of living so poor it is not even living. From sleeping through icy freezing winters in the corner of some little tiny hut with nothing to keep you company but hungriness in your belly, the sound of the wind even hungrier outside, screaming because it wants to eat your soul! What you can only get from having to beg or steal in order to survive, let other people look at you and spit if they wish, do what they like with you, so long as they will give you a coin towards your supper. You need this and more, enough to make you want to go through any kind of pain and worse. To risk dying over and over. Break your limbs and carry on nevertheless. You must hurt and hurt and hurt and still you must keep on going because this is the only way you will escape. And this is what you think you got, eh? This is what you think you can just learn tomorrow? Stroll up and be in the circus? You think it is so fucking easy that just anyone can do these things?'

There is a long pause. Vlad now holds himself regally, his eyes flashing with proud fury. It is as if the aerialist is waiting for him to applaud.

'I meant maybe I could, you know ... help out,' he says falteringly. 'Not try and be an aerialist like you. Perhaps be ... your assistant or something. Help with the costumes, things like that.'

'Oh.'

The aerialist makes a sound like a snake hissing and whips his head away to stare sullenly, almost childishly, at the bedcover.

'I don't need no assistant,' he says gruffly.

'I'm sorry,' he says.

'You're fucking mad. Get out.'

He doesn't move.

'Get out!' Vlad screams.

But he is burning up, as if a volcano had erupted deep inside and spewed its lava into his bloodstream. His eyes sting and his breath catches. He sinks to his knees as the tears begin to slide down his cheeks, shuddering from the sobs that tear through his body. Vlad gapes at him, baffled by the transformation. A minute later the aerialist turns and starts to rummage among the bedclothes around him. He squeezes shut his eyes, trying to shut out the world, as if somehow this might also close off the source of his anguish. A moment later he feels fabric being draped around his shoulders and a voice whispering 'Shhh' in his ear as he is encircled by Vlad's arms and gently rocked back and forth.

After a long while with this gentle, almost motherly rocking he is able to get a hold of himself and he speaks. His voice is cracked and hoarse, strangely colourless too, all the blazing emotion having been burnt away, leaving behind only the weary ashen facts of his situation. Vlad listens in silence until he is finished talking.

'Oh fuck,' sighs the aerialist eventually.

He will listen to the silence of the house, a silence at once familiar and alien. He will not go outside any more, but will remain shut away, a hermit. He will not answer the phone or check his messages and emails. Instead he will spend hours and hours pushing his legs out to the side or in front of him, bending over them, tendons pulled taut and shrieking, reaching for an invisible middle distance and letting the pain spur him on till he is gasping and gaping. He will take hold of the banisters and do pull-ups, throw himself on his hands and do push-ups, lie back on the table and do bench presses, and jog on the spot or do star jumps until his sides are cramping up. As the days pass gradually the pain will start to recede and his body will begin to feel charged and alive, as if he is a dangerous animal confined to a pen, forced to circle its enclosure over and over, poised to break out. Then the need will overcome him, and he will break out – but not until long after dark, when he can be sure the sedate world of his neighbourhood has closed its watchful eyes for the night.

He will take the route at the end of the garden that leads through the woodland, ducking his head as he passes the hedge that borders the Goodlys' house and heading through a small gap in the under-growth, onto a wild path barely distinguishable from the thicket that surrounds it. He will head down this path for half an hour. If it is a cloudy night he will take a torch, but when possible he will prefer to let the moonlight show him the way. The brambles will tear at his sleeves and rake at his skin, and often he will emerge scratched and even bloody. But he will be glad of this, for it will add to the strange sense of achievement he will feel when he reaches the common.

He will feel that familiar old pounding of his heart as he recalls again the night he encountered the circus. He will allow himself to remember the hopelessness, the awe, and then the combination of terror and lust he felt at meeting the aerialist in the pools of shadow outside the big top. He will thrill at the memory, at the romance, and the syncopations of his heart will seem like a dizzy dance in which he has been lost and fumbling ever since. If only he could go back to that time, he will think. If only he could relive that world again. Just for one night, for one hour even.

Sometimes he will lie down in the field, right at the centre in the place he approximates the big top to have once been staked. He will stretch out with his arms wide and welcoming and stare up into the sky, imagining that he is at the circus again, only this time that he is performing in it, flying through the air, the stars above him the eyes of the audience twinkling with astonishment and admiration from the nether-space beyond the stage lights.

Later that morning the company is on the move again. He stays hidden in Vlad's caravan, like a stowaway. Every time they turn a corner the vehicle lurches and he feels as if an earthquake is taking place. But once they are on the motorway the journey becomes smooth and steady, and he grips the sides of the bed and lies there, staring at the ceiling and listening to the burr of the engine, strangely content.

After several hours they turn off the motorway and as he peeps out of the little window a sign tells him they are not far off Manchester. He thinks of his car and his phone, left behind at the side of a random field, and has his first real shiver of hesitation. But it is too late to hesitate. There is no going back now.

That night, after the company have parked their caravans and trailers in the new grounds, he waits as Vlad has told him he must until the aerialist returns from setting up and informs him the coast is clear. Then he follows Vlad out into the chilly darkness, through the camp and to the far side of the field, where Vlad takes him in his arms and kisses him.

'My dirty little secret,' says the aerialist proudly, as the kiss deepens. Later, after they have returned and lie with their limbs entwined on Vlad's little bed, the aerialist offers to tell him his life story. He is not really from Transylvania, he says, but from a village outside Craiova, in the south of Romania. He tells him that he came to Britain with his parents when he was twelve, and that they were illegal immigrants who crossed the Channel on a cargo ferry in a crate along with twelve others. His father had a contact in a circus who agreed to employ them, and eventually his father managed to get sponsorship from this circus to remain in the UK – but his mother and sister were sent back to Romania. The sponsorship deal turned out to be the equivalent of slave labour and they were forced to work like dogs, performing in the evenings and working through the days as if they belonged to the owner. 'These owners, they are all of them cunts,' Vlad spits. 'Every last one! Especially that Big Pete and his bitch of a wife!' After a few placatory gulps of beer the aerialist settles down and resumes his story: finally his father could take it no more and fled back to Romania – despite the fact that his mother had written to him that things were as bad as ever and they lived in abject poverty. But by this time Vlad had been there for six years and had only another year to go before he could apply for citizenship, and so he made the difficult decision not to return with his father. As soon as he got his passport he left the circus, making sure he smashed all the props and tore all the curtains before he went – 'That showed the bastards!' cackles Vlad gleefully. The only trouble was because of this stunt he had a bad name and for a long time could find no employment, since the owner had contacted all the other circuses he knew and told them under no circumstances to hire him. But circuses are suspicious of each other, especially the older ones, and sooner or later there is always work for good acrobats who will perform for low pay. Eventually Vlad found work with a small French-owned circus where he was given his own trailer compartment – a first. It was a difficult time though, because the other performers all hated him for being the most popular act, and no one would talk to him except to order him around or make fun of his accent. He stayed with the French circus for a couple of years until he'd saved up enough to buy a second-hand caravan of his own – 'A clapped-out old heap of junk that won't even fucking heat!' Vlad mutters. Then he left and a couple of circuses later joined Big Pete's show. It is his second season with the company.

He listens to Vlad in awe, trying to swallow his disbelief at this life he is describing, so impossibly alien to his own. Already he harbours a strong suspicion that Vlad exaggerates for dramatic effect, but he considers he has no right not to take him at his word, and he makes the requisite gasps of astonishment and sympathy as his narrative unfolds. The truth is he wants to believe him, for though the story is harrowing and nightmarish at times, there is something hauntingly romantic about it, and to be there, listening, in his caravan in a field under the midnight moon, he feels himself to be taking part in that romance, making an appearance in another chapter in the ongoing fairy-tale adventure of the aerialist's life.

Vlad does not ask him much about himself. He does not seem to want to know any more than what he has already told him. Instead Vlad appears to have accepted him for what he is, like a wounded baby bird found at the side of the road which the aerialist has taken it upon himself to nurse back to health until the time comes, once it is older and its wings mended, for the bird to be lobbed out the window. And he is glad Vlad does not ask questions, for he does not wish to talk about his own life.

'We stay here for a couple of days,' says Vlad the next day when he returns to the trailer with ploughman's sandwiches from the nearby supermarket for lunch. 'Have to wait for a fucking part for the winches. The stupid wanker should have got it last week. But it's fun, no? This sneaking around.'

He likes it too, though sometimes during the day the little room gets so hot and stuffy it feels as though he is trapped in an oven, slow-baking. But he feels protected too, cushioned and closeted away from the outside world and all its problems, incubated and safe. He knows soon he must venture out, if he is not to go crazy, but for now he is glad to be where he is. It is the closest to non-existence he has ever come.

The following afternoon he puts the caravan in order while Vlad is out training, getting ready for his performance at the end of the week. The aerialist warms up just outside the trailer, so that he can watch him from the little window as he arches his back impossibly high and flips over his head and onto his legs, seemingly defying gravity in the process.

'What have you done?' Vlad cries when he comes in, sweaty, for a towel so he can use the shower in the camping grounds. For a second he is worried the aerialist is genuinely angry, but then his face breaks into a smile of pleasure as he surveys the tidy space. 'Now I will never find a thing!'

Vlad kisses him on the cheek and a shiver of pleasure runs up his spine. He is afraid to admit to himself how happy he feels. That night he listens to the music and the screams coming from the big top twenty yards away and sneaks out of the trailer, moving not inside the big top but just nearer to it, so that he might be closer to the aerialist and the performers, and the magic inside.

★   ★   ★

Edward never came to his house except for once, early on, when he took him because Edward insisted that he was dying to meet the people who had exerted the most influence over his life. They showed up unannounced after school, and his mum, who had just come in from the old people's home herself, started when she saw he had Edward with him, inspecting the drab furniture and the watercolours on the walls with wide-eyed amazement as if he had never beheld such quaintness.

'It's a pleasure to meet you,' Edward said warmly, shaking her hand.

'Thank you,' she murmured, eyeing him as if he were an alien, which he thought Edward might as well have been. Then his mum panicked, as if a thought had just occurred to her. 'Are you staying for dinner?'

For a moment he was panicked too, dreading lest Edward should answer yes. He didn't want Edward to sit through one of their deathly boring dinners, in which his parents made observations about the weather and about their jobs, as if competing to deliver the greatest platitude. He knew Edward would find such conversation unbelievable for its sheer inanity.

'Oh no,' Edward assured her, 'but thank you.'

He breathed a sigh of relief and his mother visibly relaxed herself and suggested a cup of tea, which Edward thought was a wonderful idea. Edward began to tell her about himself and she listened carefully, looking increasingly charmed. Edward told her about his impressions of the town and the school. She smiled and nodded when he called the local church beautiful and said how peaceful life was in the country. Finally Edward said, 'Of course Mum and Dad don't think much of it here, but then that's the point.'

'The point?' asked his mum, smiling.

'Yes – we came here so Dad can't fuck around any more. And there's no one else's bed within half a mile's radius, so it's physically impossible for him!'

Edward laughed gaily but his mother blanched and a few minutes later she developed a headache and remembered something she had to do in the other room. He looked at Edward and saw he was mystified that she had not laughed too. He was sure he must be horrified by their immaculate little home with its pictures of meadows and vases of flowers, its uncluttered shelves, perfectly plumped cushions and spotlessly hoovered floors. But he was wrong about this.

'I like her,' said Edward quietly. 'She's normal. You're lucky.'

He had never thought of himself as lucky before. He wanted to deny it, to explain how often he felt like he was being smothered by the cooped-up politeness of his parents' little lives. But he saw then that Edward would not understand this, he would only tell him he didn't know a good thing when he had it. He resolved then and there not to bring Edward home with him again.

From time to time his mother would ask about Edward and fuss about how much time he was spending over at his house, saying she was sure his parents must be tired of him. But he knew really it was because she'd been frightened by Edward, and was worried he might be picking up bad habits and grand ideas – which he secretly knew he was.

That night he will survey the other items the men delivered: twelve metres of shipping rope, two rope thimbles and a steel bar for the trapeze, three foot long and welded to thimbles at both ends.

He will measure out three metres of the rope then will take some shears and cut it. He will lay the shorter piece on the floor, take up the frayed end and pick at it until the weave of the rope has come loose and flows in three thick curling locks through his fingers. He will wrap these locks around one of the thimbles and will then work loose a single lock of the rope further down. He will then begin to weave the rope back into itself, working free more locks and plaiting the loose ends around them, creating an eyelet. He will tighten this eyelet until it is firm and secure around the thimble. The process is painstakingly slow, but gradually he will succeed at splicing the rope to the trapeze. Then he will measure out another three metres, cut the rope, wrap it around the other thimble of the bar and repeat the process.

He will spend several hours binding the spliced ropes to the thimbles by looping a spool of tough thread through the metal eye of each thimble and around the rope, pulling them tightly together. After this is done he will cut out strips of foam which he will use to cover the hard edges of the metal thimbles and the knots of rope above, securing them there with hockey tape, until the join between the rope and trapeze is completely obscured from view.

Next he will cut out strips of velvet, wrap them around the padding and fix them with pins while he sews them into place. This endeavour will be long and frustrating, for the velvet will keep slipping and will need to be checked with every stitch. But bit by bit he will cover the padded thimbles and the spliced ends of the rope. When it is done he will wind the tape in diagonal stripes around the bar itself, folding the tape back over itself at each end.

Once the fixings are complete and the bar covered, he will move onto the loose ends of the ropes, which he will splice into eyelets around the remaining thimbles, tightening the rope around them until the ducts are snug inside the rope.

The trapeze will take him three days to make and he will work constantly, breaking only to eat, drink and urinate, and to rest his eyes and fingers from the effort of so much concentrated fine work. When he is finished he will lay the trapeze flat on the floor and inspect it carefully for flaws. But he will know that the only true test of it will be when it is hung, and he will look up at the ceiling to consider this next step.

The following morning they wake to a violent pounding on the door of the caravan. 'Open up, fuckhead!' a deep voice is shouting. 'I know you've got some cunt in there!'

Vlad leaps up, but before he can reach the door the latch splits and it veritably explodes open, a huge fat red-faced man standing there with veins popping out on his neck and forehead and eyes blazing with fury. It is a few seconds before he recognises him as the ringmaster from a few nights ago.

'And what the fuck is going on here?' bellows the man, charging into the compartment like a crazed bull. 'What do you think this is? A travelling brothel?'

'Get out!'

Vlad hurls himself at the ringmaster but merely seems to bounce off the man's vast bulk and go slamming into the wall. Undeterred, Vlad picks himself right back up and throws himself at the man once again.

'Get fucking out!' he screams. 'You can't come into my private space! Get out! Fucking get out!'

The aerialist rains down punches on the ringmaster's back, but the man ignores Vlad as if he is no more than a gnat, and stares at him. His gaze is quite terrifying and he crams himself into the corner of the room, drawing up his knees protectively in front of his chest.

'You!'

The ringmaster appears so astonished at placing him that his anger momentarily seems to evaporate. 'Get out!' Vlad is still screaming – almost weeping now. 'Just get out!'

'What are you doing here?' demands the ringmaster, sounding almost reasonable in his surprise.

'I . . .' he says, the words caught in his throat. 'I followed . . .'

Just then Vlad aims a punch at the ringmaster's neck and finally targets a vulnerable area, for the man lets out a fresh bellow, turns to the aerialist and catches him neatly by the throat.

'There's no live-in guests allowed in my circus. You know the rules!' he hisses. 'Now I don't give a shit about your one-night fucks, but this I won't tolerate. Get rid of it.'

'He's not a guest – he's my assistant!'

'Get rid of it!'

The aerialist responds by kicking the ringmaster in the shin hard, producing nothing more than a snarl. The ringmaster tightens his grip, draws back his arms and then sends Vlad hurtling backwards out the door of the caravan. There is a great cheer from outside. The ringmaster follows in the direction he threw Vlad, leaving him alone.

He crawls from the bed and creeps over to the window. Outside he can see what looks like the entire company assembled. Among them are the two silks girls, one of them holding a basket of washing, and the clown with his mean smirk. They are watching the ringmaster and the aerialist, who he cannot see from the cramped little window but who he can hear because they are both shouting at each other at the top of their lungs. The ringmaster is bellowing that Vlad is under contract, that it is his circus and that he is cheapening it and costing him money. Vlad meanwhile has switched to Romanian and is unleashing a steady stream of what sound like gypsy curses.

He suddenly has the distinct sense it is all for show, that both of them are deliberately putting on a performance – perhaps because it is all they know how to do. Nonetheless he is frightened, for he is at the centre of the argument, and all the people standing around are witnessing a fight over him. Most of all he is frightened of the outcome – that the ringmaster will insist on him leaving, and that Vlad will back down and agree to it.

Just then he hears a woman's voice, loud and authoritative, join in: 'Oi, what's this ruckus? You two pansies got something to fight about then do it elsewhere, eh?'

At her command the fight grows more distant, and there is the sound of a door shutting and then quiet. The assembled company, apparently satisfied they have witnessed all the major pyrotechnics, begin to disperse. Only the clown remains, still smirking, casually toking on his cigarette. Suddenly the clown flicks his gaze towards him and for a second their eyes lock. He stumbles quickly away from the window and back to the bed.

Vlad returns twenty minutes later, panting, his mouth twisted into a triumphant grin and his head held high, as if he were a hero just returning from war.

'What happened?' he asks tentatively.

'You can stay,' announces Vlad. 'But you will have to work.'

'I'll do anything he wants!'

'I tell that arsehole, I been putting up with your shit for too long. You say no to me and I quit! Then let's see how you and your fucking crap circus get on then, eh?!'

'My God –' he says. 'But what if he'd fired you?'

'He can't fire me, I'm the best act he's got,' says the aerialist smugly. 'Without me this circus stinks and he knows it. He makes this big show for them out there but there's not a fucking thing he can do – ha!'

He is overwhelmed with gratitude, for he is sure no one has ever done something so kind and wonderful for him before. Vlad seems to notice his expression and proudly sits down beside him on the bed, patting his knee gently, as if he is an invalid who needs to be taken care of.

'You stay as long as you like,' says the aerialist. 'Fuck all the rest of them.'

He saw Edward's mother frequently, as whenever he was over she would always poke her head out of her studio to say hello and give him one of her long disturbing looks as if doing her level best to penetrate the depths of his soul. Yet he only caught occasional glimpses of Edward's father – usually in the kitchen when he wandered through unshaven and still in his pyjamas while they

73

were drinking juice after school, pale as a ghost, his face set in a frown and his eyes tunnel-visioned as he made his way to the fridge. Whenever he appeared Edward would usher him quickly out of the room.

'He'll be like this for months,' Edward confided in him once. 'The womb calls them his benders, while he's working on a new novel. Then he'll finish whatever it is he's writing and suddenly he'll be everybody's best friend. The prick!'

But he knew by now from what his parents said that this prick was important, considered by magazines and critics to be a writer at the forefront of modern literature. Despite Edward's disparaging remarks he was in awe of this phantom father who broke all the rules, and he had the sense Edward could not really think as little of his father as he claimed either. Even from his few sightings of the man he thought it was obvious he had a magnetic personality – that he was someone you couldn't fail to notice, the sort of person who'd never blend into the background, who people either loved or hated, one or the other and nothing in between.

It wasn't until three months after he started going round to Edward's house that he met Edward's father properly, while waiting on the porch before school for Edward to fetch his coat.

'Ah,' said a deep voice to his side, making him jump. He turned and Edward's father seemed to materialise beside him. 'You must be the friend who's been making my son feel less alienated at his new school. I apologise if I haven't introduced myself up until now.'

He looked into a pair of brown eyes that were so dark they were almost black. Edward's father looked nothing like Edward. Close up he was rather unspectacular, short and squat, and he looked as if he had dressed in the dark. His shirt was about four sizes too big and hung off him like a draped sheet and his socks were mismatched, his feet stuffed into sandals, something Edward had long ago explained to be a cardinal fashion sin. But his eyes contained that exact same penetrating quality as Edward's mother's, and, at times he had noticed, Edward's too.

'Well, put it there, partner!'

Edward's father thrust his hand at him. He took it gingerly.

'Jeez, you're a shy one, huh?'

He smiled awkwardly and received a dazzling smile in return.

'I guess.'

'Hmm. What are they teaching you at school these days? Anyone interesting? Bakhtin? Any Derrida? Foucault?'

He shook his head, not knowing what any of these things were.

'But surely some Freud at least?!'

'No . . .' he said, recognising the name but not being able to place it and feeling like he was being made fun of.

'Well, I'll be damned. What is the educational system in this country coming to if no one's even teaching the upcoming generation some of the basic psychoanalytic concepts about death and sex? In that case, it's my duty to impart some wisdom to you boys. After school, what do you say? A private seminar on the death instinct?'

It did not sound like something he particularly wanted to do, but he nodded lest those fiercely intelligent eyes should take offence. He could suddenly tell this man was dangerous, and quite capable of switching, abruptly and without warning, into someone vicious and fearsome.

'Excellent! The death instinct it is!'

At this moment Edward appeared at the door behind his father, who turned and put his arm around him. Edward shook it off with a shrug of annoyance.

'We're going to do a little home schooling later on!' Edward's father said jovially. 'Your young friend was just agreeing to it. He says they don't teach you anything at all at school about death or sex.'

'Dad,' sighed Edward, 'fuck off.'

Edward's father grinned back at him as if he'd been caught in the middle of a naughty caper.

'Well, perhaps another afternoon then,' he conceded. 'But really they are the two most important subjects on the planet. It's what everything comes down to in the end, you know. Run along then, children, before I get any more ideas and start trying to force-feed you Kristeva.'

He gave them a mock salute.

'Fight proud, youth of today. Remember, you're the front line of your generation! And, Edward, please don't be late home. I've a mild surprise in store.'

With these words Edward's father turned and bumbled off around the side of the house, whistling to himself. When he turned to look at Edward he was almost glowing with pleasure. Edward saw him looking and shook himself, as if trying to throw off the smile that was plastered over his face.

'He seems cool, your dad,' he said carefully.

'He finished his new book and he's full of himself,' said Edward with a deliberately bored sigh. 'He'll be father of the year now, maybe for a month or so, and then something else'll come along. Let's go.'

But all that day Edward was distracted and kept looking at his watch. And for once Edward wasn't keen for him to come back home with him either. Edward claimed he was tired and had too much homework to do, but he knew that Edward was never tired and never did homework, and the real reason was obviously his father.

He will fix four strops to the furthest bar at either end of the truss. These he will attach with karabiners to two loops of climbing sash, leading all the way up through the demolished first floor to poles of scaffolding on the side of the wall in what used to be his mother's room. These poles will be fixed to the wall with seven eight-inch nails, drilled into the brickwork. The sash, a good twenty metres in length, will attach to the tops of the poles where they meet the ceiling and will lead all the way back down to two blocks of wood nailed into the floor, around which the cord will be looped.

Taking the end of one of the sash cords and setting his foot against the block of wood, he will take a great mouthful of air, and pull as hard as he can. The loop around the truss will tighten until taut and then, quivering as if with effort, the truss will rise on one side a foot into the air. He will tie off the sash in a figure-of-eight knot and grip the other cord. Then he will pull hard again, using the friction of the loop around the block of wood to prevent the cord from slipping. Again the truss will rise, this time on the opposite side. He will continue to pull until he has achieved the height of two feet on this side from the floor. Then he will tie off the sash and return to the first side. In this way he will gradually winch the truss all the way up to the ceiling, so that it is suspended at equidistance between the two poles of scaffolding.

He will climb the stairs to the next level and then carefully side-step around the residual border of floor until he reaches the furthest scaff-pole. He will climb to the second rung of the pole and detach one of the karabiners, then clip it onto the hole at the top of the pole. He will repeat this with the other karabiners, allowing the cord to fall away to the kitchen floor below. The truss will now be held in position by the strops between the poles. As a security measure, he will take two more strops and attach them to the upper bars of the truss on either side. These he will then wind around the thin wooden beam that stretches from one side of the ceiling to the other. He will fix them in place with four steel shackles.

He will return to the ground floor to examine his handiwork. The truss will be fixed – a mesh of intersecting metal bars attached to the ceiling six metres above. Everything will be ready.

That night, after he has thrown together a meagre supper for them from the pitiful contents of Vlad's little fridge and they have had a couple of beers, the aerialist suggests it is a good time for him to go and see Marie, Big Pete's wife – for it is she who will give him work.

'Aren't you coming too?' he asks, suddenly panicked.

'Oh, silly,' says Vlad, reaching across and pinching his cheek. 'You must face her sooner or later, my little bird. Don't let her scare you. The bark of that bitch is worse than her bite.'

He has seen Big Pete's temper and heard his wife shouting, and is not sure what evidence there is to support this statement. But he steels himself, takes another gulp of beer and sets off for Big Pete's trailer. After all, he reasons, he must meet the woman eventually if he is to stay.

'And don't let her take the piss,' calls Vlad after him as he closes the door.

Big Pete and Marie's trailer is the largest and the newest of the vehicles, painted cornflower blue with a bright red door, garlands of fairy lights bunched around each window. According to Vlad, Marie is very house-proud and hoses it down every time they settle at a new site. He approaches with his heart thumping and pauses at the door. Behind some orange blinds he can see the silhouettes of a man and a woman moving across the room, and he can hear Marie screeching at her husband for some undefined act of stupidity. He swallows, thinking he cannot do it alone after all and that he will return and get Vlad to come back with him, but just as he is about to leave the door opens and Marie stands there. She is small and squat, almost comically disproportionate to her husband; even standing a foot higher on the ledge of the trailer, she is still an inch shorter than him. But her red cheeks, wide chin and narrow eyes bespeak a personality that takes no shit from anyone.

'Where'd you come from? Who are you? What d'you want?' she demands in quick succession. She is holding a basin of dirty water and he has the impression that at any second she might choose to dump it over him.

'Vlad sent me,' he says in a rush. 'To see what work you've got for me.'

For a second she looks blank, then her eyes gleam.

'Ah, you're the one 'e's shacked up with!'

She inspects him, her gaze travelling slowly from his feet to his head. A small smirk not unlike the clown's plays on her lips, quickly replaced by a grimace of distaste. She sniffs loudly, as if she has just smelt something putrid.

'I mean, what can you do? Don't look like you ever done a day's labour in your life!'

'I've worked all my life,' he protests.

'Oh yeah? Doing what?'

'As . . .' He suddenly does not want to say what he does and trails off, looking down at his feet. 'At an office.'

'Well, take a look around you,' suggests Marie. She sets down the basin on the floor beside her and points over his shoulder, peering carefully herself as if to demonstrate what she wants him to do. He follows her eyes. 'Now you tell me something. You see any offices round 'ere?'

She grins as if she has just been extremely witty and folds her arms across her little body.

'I see the box office,' he says carefully.

Marie loses her grin.

'You tryin' to be smart with me?' she snaps.

'No, ma'am.'

'Oi, Marie! Who you talking to?' booms an unmistakable deep voice from inside the trailer. 'Something you need me to come and sort out?'

He quakes lest Marie should tell Big Pete to come.

'Like you've ever sorted out a fucking thing in your worthless piece of shit existence!' yells Marie in the general direction of behind her. 'And I'd sure as hell be sorry if I ever had to rely on your flabby arse!'

She turns back to face him.

'You be here at seven tomorrow and I'll give you something to do. And mind you're not late cos I'm a busy woman, ain't I?'

With these words she picks up the basin. He jumps to the side as she flings the water into the air, where for an instant it glistens under the stars in a spangled splash before falling to the grass and being lost to the earth forever. He turns to say goodnight to Marie and is just in time to have the door shut in his face.

That week Edward did not act like his usual self. It was as if he'd slipped into an exclusive universe of his own making, one that could not be tarnished by anything said or seen in reality. He smiled a lot at the teachers, even at other kids at school, and once or twice he heard him humming snatches of the very sort of pop music he professed to hate. When Katy passed by at lunchtime, her tray loaded with food, Edward did not whisper to him his usual comment about a hippo feeding, and when Fred yelled at them from the back of the assembly room that they were bum chums he did not so much as bother to give him the finger. Edward even put his hand up once or twice in class when no one else knew the answer and offered it to the teacher in a voice devoid of sarcasm.

After school Edward's father picked him up. He was always doing something with him – taking him to an arts cinema in the next town to watch a documentary on Slovakian immigrants, or to a local gallery to see rare imported Aboriginal art. One morning Edward didn't even show up at school and the next day he said he'd played truant in order to go shopping with his father in London. 'There's this really cool thing we do,' he said. 'We walk into a designer shop and Dad pretends he's deaf so I have to do all the talking. I can say anything I want and so I tell the assistant he nearly drowned trying to save my mother after their luxury cruise liner capsized, and they were never able to get the water out of his ear holes – shit like that. But it's a fucking hoot! They always look like they don't believe you, but of course they can't say so because they want to make a sale!'

He couldn't help himself: he was deeply jealous of Edward's relationship with his father, and hurt that Edward never asked if he wanted to tag along. He thought he could hear Edward's father in Edward's voice too – a put-on optimism with which he greeted the world, as if optimism itself were an ironic joke which everybody else was too dumb to understand. Moreover he was maddened by the hypocrisy of it. Had Edward just forgotten all the things he had said about how useless and pathetic his dad was? Now all Edward could do was talk about his father as if he were the most brilliant giver of life on the planet, about the games they played to see who could come up with the best one-liner or who could make the most cutting riposte, and the trips to museums, theatres and cinemas. He wanted to shake Edward and tell him to snap out of it, but he didn't dare, and so he kept silent while Edward chatted away about the trip to Cornwall that his father was taking him on that weekend to meet some old writer friends, knowing that while Edward and his father sipped cocktails with intellectuals and played at who could think up the catchiest aphorism, he would be at the old people's home with his mother, sitting beside absent-minded octogenarians being told what a fine and good-hearted young man he was.

The next morning he is outside Big Pete and Marie's trailer at seven. Inside it is dark and the curtains are drawn, and he waits twenty minutes before getting up the courage to knock. From within he hears a man's voice swearing and then some stomping coming towards the door. Marie throws it open and stands there glaring at him. Her hair is a mesh of frizz around her head and she is wearing a beautiful pink silk kimono with silver birds embroidered on it, inelegantly draped over her stumpy frame.

'You told me to be here at seven,' he says quickly.

Marie looks him up and down.

'I said eight,' she replies in a voice that dares him to contradict her.

'You said . . .' He thinks the better of this. 'Shall I come back?'

Marie considers for a minute.

'No,' she says. 'Since you've woken me and my 'usband up you can get started now. Round the back is a bucket and sponge. Get cleaning.'

She starts to close the door.

'Sorry . . . but what do you want me to clean exactly?' he asks.

She gives him a withering look as if it is the most moronic question she has ever heard. He is suddenly reminded of Katy from school, and how she would sometimes jeer at the other kids when they put up their hands to ask questions, as if the fact that they didn't know the answer and wanted to was a shameful thing.

'The trailers,' Marie says very slowly, as if talking to an idiot. 'Them things with the wheels, all around us. See?'

With this she slams the door.

With the trapeze in place he will gently swing it back and forth, testing for space. On the back swing it will be a good three metres from the wall, but on the front swing he will hit the side of the room, just beneath the lip of the torn-out floor. He will go to the garage and retrieve the hammer, as well as a chisel and a saw.

It will take him another three days to beat his way through the wall, during which he will sleep and eat sporadically, paying no attention to the clock or the movements of day and night outside the house. Time will become irrelevant, a system with no basis in his world. He will knock out great chunks of brickwork, which he will ferry to the garage every hour and pile up beside the empty space where he used to park the car. When he takes breaks he will do chin-ups and sit-ups on the trapeze bar, and sit on the ground with his legs splayed out either side of him, reaching for an invisible middle distance, trying to will his chest towards the floor.

At the end of three days he will be covered head to toe in dust and paint flecks, the skin of his arms and hands hidden beneath a thick layer of grime. He will go to the bathroom and run a bath as hot as he can bear into which he will lower himself, centimetre by centimetre, until he is submerged to his neck. He will wonder as he lies there if he feels guilty or sad, but the searing heat will seem to deny things like guilt and sadness, as if purging him clean of any unnecessary state of emotion. He will lie there until the water has turned ash grey and lukewarm.

Clean, flushed and wrinkled, he will towel himself dry, put on a bathrobe and slippers and make his way downstairs to inspect the space he has created. A huge chunk of the house will have disappeared, as if an explosion had ripped through it. His mother's room and the wall that separated it from the landing, as well as some of the landing itself, will be missing. When he climbs back up to the trapeze, lifts his legs and swings back and forth, space will no longer be an issue.

Marie gives him the worst jobs and he knows she is doing it deliberately. It is a sort of game, to see if she can break him, get him to give up and leave. She makes him clean the toilets and empty the sewage out of the buckets. She has him scrub the wheels of the trucks to dislodge stones and clumps of mud, polish the windows and hose down the paintwork. When this is done she makes him iron costumes and fold them, all the while berating him for not doing it carefully or fast enough. Whenever he is finished with a task she inspects his work rolling her eyes and muttering to herself, as if to say what is the point of bothering? Nothing he does is good enough. Nothing he does is right. But what Marie doesn't know is that he doesn't mind. She thinks she can break him but he knows she can't, no matter what she tells him to do or how much she swears and tells him off for failing to do it properly. He is happier than he can remember having been in a very long while, and sometimes he smiles to himself to think that he can enjoy life while mopping up piss or scouring mud from the step of a trailer. After all, he's been doing jobs not unlike these for years, and been snapped at by people no less rude than Marie for never getting it right.

Vlad is always busy during the day, either rehearsing on his trapeze inside the big top, stretching out his limbs in the sun on the roof of his caravan, or else taking long naps inside it. Sometimes he crosses paths with the aerialist, on the way back to Marie's trailer carrying buckets of bleach or baskets of wet costumes.

'That woman,' tuts Vlad. 'She takes advantage. You should tell her where to stick it.'

But Vlad does not tell her this himself, and after a while he realises that Vlad is afraid of Marie too – that everyone is afraid of her, and that whatever she yells at Big Pete to do, after a few token fireworks, he does.

'Wishing you hadn't left a perfectly decent job for this crap, eh?' she says one morning while they are scrubbing down the bleachers with scours and soapy water. 'Had a fella once who followed us from place to place pestering us till we agreed to give the stupid wanker a job just to shut 'im up. Lasted a whole three days, 'e did. You weirdos always think it's going to be like something out of a picture book or a film. All romantic and shit. Bet you don't think that any more though, do ya?'

With this she laughs to herself, a short burst of dry air. He waits to see if she will say more but afterwards she closes up and does not speak to him again all day. She is a hard woman who evidently enjoys giving the impression of having been through a lot. He does not doubt she has the scars to prove it though, and thinks it is little wonder everyone in the company tiptoes around her.

Although he does not contradict Marie, the hard work has by no means rid the circus of its romance. While he works all about him he gets to see it come to life. When it is sunny the couple who do the acrobatics come out to train on the grass outside the big top – a man who balances his tiny wife in impossible positions, culminating in a single-armed handstand off the centre of his head. A woman with a snake tattoo contorts on a foam mat, and the two silks performers do sun salutations and sit with legs akimbo to one another, stretching out each other's limbs. Even the clown can occasionally be seen practising his steps, falling backwards so that his feet rotate up into the air and coughing up mouthfuls of glitter. Sometimes when Marie is not there to shout at him he pauses to watch the company, wondering if they are aware of their glamour – though indeed part of that glamour seems to be their lack of awareness, as if the mad world of impossible feats they are part of is simply the norm. As if each day is just another day at the circus.

He is not of this world though and nobody lets him forget it. The hardest thing is not the work, it is the fact that people do not acknowledge him. 'They will come around,' Vlad assures him when he mentions this, 'once they get used to you.' But he sees no sign in support of this promise. When he passes by in the morning no one greets him, not even a smile or a nod, let alone any other indication of acceptance. He understands that they do not want him here and resent the fact that he has been granted permission to stay. They think he deserves to do hard labour and are amused that Marie has turned him into her slave. They are waiting for him to be broken too, for him to throw in the towel and leave.

On Monday Edward met him outside his house, flushed with excitement. He would not say what was on his mind though, and he was quiet all the way to school, smiling secretively to himself. But halfway through class he couldn't keep it in any longer.

'Dad's taking us to France!' he burst out in a whisper.

'What?'

'I'm going to live with Frogs in a bona fide chateau!'

'France!'

'*Oui! C'est formidable, non?!*'

They were the cruellest words he had ever heard. He couldn't even smile, never mind laugh as though he thought it was wonderful. As Edward chattered on about how he would have to learn to speak French properly and drink lots of red wine in preparation, he felt his features freezing up and he tried to turn his head so Edward wouldn't notice. But Edward did notice and his flow of happiness faltered.

'Of course you'll come and visit me lots,' Edward said quickly after a short pause. 'And we'll write and phone each other. You'll still be my friend, you know. It won't change anything.'

But this wasn't true and he wasn't sure if Edward understood this and was just being kind, or if he really believed what he said. Edward would be in a new school, in a new society, with new things to see and do and talk about. Edward would have no need of him and within a few months the short time they had been friends would fade from memory along with their friendship, until it was forgotten altogether. He knew it, as certain as the bones beneath his skin. Meanwhile he would be here alone, struggling to maintain the image that he didn't care when the other kids ribbed him and called him a queer, struggling to be someone, struggling for a reason to struggle.

'Yeah,' he said. It came out as a choke, a cross between a grunt and a sob, and he quickly stood up. The teacher peered over at him.

'Something the matter?'

'May I use the toilet?'

'May I use the toilet, sir,' corrected the teacher. 'Go on.'

He hurried out of the classroom and down the corridor, feeling as though his insides were being churned – a rising sensation of dread was filling his stomach and he wanted to vomit it out before it became too much to bear. But when he reached the toilet bowl all he produced was a small lump of phlegm that splatted against the yellowy water below and floated there like an egg white. He knew he should return to class but could not raise himself up from his knees. The idea of spending the rest of his school years without Edward at his side was dizzying and the feeling in his stomach would not go away.

The bell rang and he was still there. He heard voices and doors and feet and laughter. Soon the toilets would be full of other kids, he knew, the slackers who went there to smoke cigarettes and Tipp-Ex their slogans on the cubicle walls. Knowing that he would not want to be found by them finally gave him the energy to force himself up.

Outside Edward was waiting.

'Hey,' said Edward, 'are you all right?'

'Yes,' he lied. 'Fine. Why wouldn't I be?'

But he could see that Edward got it, for he acted nicely towards him for the rest of the day and even suggested that on Sunday when he got back from Cornwall perhaps he would like to come over. Though it was exactly what he really wanted to do, he shook his head and said he couldn't. For some reason he knew he must not go. He was ashamed of the way he had acted and was sorry that Edward had noticed. Already it felt as if Edward had started to become a stranger.

He watches as they set up the big top. He has asked Marie if he should help but she curtly informs him they do not need him and he will only get in the way, and instead sets him to hand-washing curtain material in a large basin of cold soapy water outside the costume trailer. 'Mind you get all the grease spots out,' she tells him, 'or else you'll have to do it all again right away. It's gotta be dry for tomorrow night.'

Big Pete and three other men are in charge of setting up the tent, though everyone seems to be expected to assist at certain times – at which point Big Pete will bellow, 'Oi, every cunt out here now!' and everyone will emerge from their caravans or stop what they are doing to help carry the vast expanse of canvas and lay it out flat across the grass so that it resembles a navy lake of painted planets and stars. He notices that Vlad does not come to help, though he knows he is in his caravan because he left him sleeping there that morning, and he realises he is making himself scarce on purpose.

Setting up the big top takes them just three hours, from start to finish. First they erect two twelve-metre poles, feeding them into eyelets at either side of the central section of the giant pool of canvas. These poles have a piece of truss to link them, and are held upright by two of the men while Big Pete and the other man drive them through the canvas and into holes they have tunnelled into the ground with great groans of effort, until the poles stand firm. The truss between the top of the poles is then used as a winch, and four metal cords feed through pulleys and are attached to a large piece of circular scaffolding that forms the central turret of the big top. Once this is all in place the men begin to drive metre-long stakes into the ground all around the circumference of the tent, using a great mallet to beat the stakes into the earth until they stand a foot high out of the grass. These are then attached to ropes that feed through loops on triangular flaps of the canvas. Everyone is called back again to assist with carrying a seemingly endless number of two-metre poles out of one of the trailers, which are then laid out beside the stakes. The men insert the poles through the fabric and pull them erect all the way around the tent. Now it is time to raise the turret, which is done with large rotating contraptions at each end of the big top. The metal cords feed into these machines and the men turn two large handles on either side in order to draw the turret up into the air, a few centimetres at a time, until it dangles precariously just beneath the truss, a good ten metres from the ground. It is amazing to behold, for it seems as if out of nowhere a palace has been constructed, something towering and three-dimensional out of what was previously flat. Once the cords are secure the company are yelled for yet again, this time to assist with slotting together six more poles, which are then ferried inside the tent in order to buttress the canvas around the turret. There are plenty of shouts and sounds of swearing from inside, and he suspects this is the most arduous part of the labour, though he cannot see what is going on, only the outside, where the canvas rises as each pole is put in. He would like to go and assist, or at least sneak a look, but Marie's ever-watchful eye keeps him scrubbing like Cinderella at the bucket of never-ending washing.

He woke to the sound of pebbles spattering against the window. Switching on the lamp, he crawled out of bed and went over to the glass. At first he couldn't see anything in the gloom below, but gradually he made out a figure, standing by the hibiscus bush. He opened the window, letting in a rush of cold night.

'What the hell are you doing?' he hissed.

'Let's go for a walk!' called Edward, making no effort to keep his voice down. He sounded merry and he held up a bottle of something that glinted half empty in the moonlight.

'My parents –'

'Ah, screw 'em! Come on, you're only young once!'

He paused, pretending to be in two minds as to whether or not he wanted to. But there was something deeply exciting about seeing Edward here at his house in the middle of the night, and really there was nothing to debate.

'Stay there.'

'Ain't going nowhere without you, kiddo!'

'And be quiet!'

He threw on some clothes and shoes and poked his head out of his room. The lights in the house were all off, which he assumed meant his parents had not woken. He gave silent thanks and hurried downstairs to let himself out the back door.

'You took your time,' complained Edward, from somewhere in the soupy darkness of the garden. He appeared before him, grinning from ear to ear, his teeth illuminated and the rest of him no more than an outline, like the Cheshire cat.

'But I'm here now,' he said, grabbing the bottle. He unscrewed the cap and took a swig, almost coughing it back up again as the liquid burned down his throat.

'What is that? Paint stripper?'

'Vodka. Russia's finest.'

'Yuck.'

He gulped and handed the bottle back. He could tell Edward was smiling at him. Suddenly the world seemed bursting with new-found life and unexplored possibility.

'So where do you want to go?' he said.

'This way.'

Edward pointed towards the woods that lay at the side of the house.

'Are you crazy? We'll get torn to shreds!'

'So what? Afraid?'

He sighed and allowed Edward to lead him down to the bottom of the garden. They passed the hedge where Edward had thrown his bicycle, which lay in a mangled twist of metal and leaves, and ducked into the trees.

'I can't see a damn thing!'

'Hold on to me then.'

He reached out and groped for Edward's hand. As soon as he caught it Edward let out a little whoop and began to rocket through the woods, forcing him to run after him. He hadn't a clue if Edward was keeping to the path or not. The world was silent except for the sound of their panting and every so often swearing as they caught a foot on a root or a leg or hand on a bramble.

'This is insane,' he breathed in Edward's ear, but he did not pull back or try to make Edward stop. Instead he held on tightly and followed like someone with no choice. He thought of all the times he had come down here when he was very small on the short cut to the park, his mum holding onto his hand and refusing to let go while he tugged at her, trying to break free so he could run off and play away from her watchful eye. It seemed ironic and hilarious that this time he was the one who was holding on as if for dear life.

Finally, just as it seemed the path would never end, they broke through the other side and onto the common. Edward sank down to his knees on the wet grass, giggling and spluttering.

'Oh God,' Edward cried. 'That was great!'

'You're a psycho,' he told him, gingerly touching a graze on his forearm.

'Maybe I am,' Edward agreed. 'But look at the stars. It's gorgeous! How come nobody ever comes here at night? It's by far the most beautiful time for a visit.'

'Probably because they're all asleep.'

'Well, in that case I think we should propose a moratorium on sleep,' declared Edward in a mock-pompous voice. He reached out and took his hand to pull himself up.

They walked along the side of the field. For a long while neither of them spoke. As his blood began to slow down and his heart rate returned to normal, he felt a foreign sensation settle over him, something like contentment. He thought he could happily walk around in the dark with Edward by his side forever.

'Dad's gone to Antibes,' Edward said abruptly. 'The womb decided they needed a break from each other. He left yesterday while I was at school, so he wouldn't have to say goodbye. Didn't want to deal with any fuss. I found this letter from him on my bed when I got home.'

He withdrew a folded piece of white paper from his jacket and held it up where it caught the moonlight. In a sudden motion he crumpled it up, wrapping his fist around it as tightly as he could, then swung his arm back and out, lobbing the ball of paper high into the air.

'Arsehole,' said Edward, as if putting paid to the matter.

'Hey,' he said.

It came out sounding gruff and adult and Edward glanced at him. Without thinking he pulled Edward into a tight hug. At first Edward resisted but then he seemed to melt in his arms and he felt Edward sobbing against him, which had the effect of making both of their bodies shudder. They stood like that for some time, until Edward's sobs finally subsided. They did not separate though. The wind rustled through the nearby branches and from far away came the mournful hooting of an owl.

'You've got an erection,' observed Edward.

He felt his cheeks grow hot with blood.

'So have you.'

Edward kissed him. He was so stunned that he did not think to close his eyes, and suddenly saw Edward's face up close in the moonlight. He felt lips pressing against his own and then Edward's tongue probing inside his mouth for the briefest of seconds before he drew back and detached their bodies from one another. Tentatively he ran his tongue along his lower lip, and thought he saw Edward doing the same.

'How was that?' Edward said nonchalantly.

'OK,' he said, swallowing.

'I've never kissed anyone before. Have you?'

'Uh. No.'

'I think we should practise on each other, so we can get more skilled at it.'

'OK.'

They pressed together once more. Edward's kissing was hungrier this time, almost as if he was trying to eat him. He felt his body responding with shivers and his penis growing harder until it seemed as if he was about to burst. Wordlessly Edward let go of him, undid the button of his jeans, pulled down the flies and dug his hand into the underwear. He copied Edward's movements, pushing his hand down into his own pants and touching his erection. They pressed themselves against one another again and began to rub their bodies. He felt Edward's breath hot on his face and the smell of his skin and the wet grass and cool night air pervaded his nostrils. He did not know then how this would become an evocative smell, so that years into the future whenever he scented the dew late at night this moment would come rushing back to him, dizzying him with an impossible yearning. As he came, a few seconds before Edward, he clutched at the boy before him and let out a high moan that was then immediately echoed by Edward. Then they were laughing, simultaneously trying to do up their jeans as they fell about giggling on the dew-soaked common.

While the big top fills up he helps Vlad to stretch backstage, a section separated from the auditorium area by a long black-and-red screen. He holds onto Vlad's wrists while he arches his back up towards the painted stars on the ceiling like a cat and then flattens it dramatically before sinking into a curve. The space is awash with activity. The two silks girls, who Vlad has told him with a pitying voice are from a German circus school and whose names are Franka and Griselda, are each balancing on one foot and extending the other away from them in a shape Vlad calls the arabesque. Beside them the contortionist is rocking back and forth on her elbows with her feet around her neck, complaining of stiffness. Meanwhile Marie is trotting from person to person, fussing with costumes and examining make-up with a studious eye, issuing orders for more lipstick or white paint or eyeshadow to be applied. Today she has not bothered to inspect his work, and when he went to her earlier on, for his next task after cleaning the doors to the box-office trailer, she told him to get lost and to stay out of her way.

The big top is packed out for the first time in the season and a sense of deep excitement charges every molecule in the space. People are laughing more than usual, cracking jokes in high-pitched voices about costume malfunctions and then getting into sudden fevers of panic over an undone corset or a wonkily drawn eyeline, little storm clouds that dissipate almost as soon as they arise. He too feels the excitement infiltrating his blood, making him nervous and twitchy so that Vlad, now doing a handstand and holding onto his ankles while he sits, cries out, 'Please stop shaking so I do not break my neck before we even start!'

Someone laughs. It is Pierce, the male acrobat, who is his forties with an ordinarily grey bread that has been brushed with silver face paint for tonight's show. Pierce catches his eye and grins at him and his heart soars. It is the first time he has been acknowledged by someone in the company.

'Got your fluffer to hand, I see,' says the clown sourly from the corner by the props table where he is fitting his feet into the long spangled comedy shoes he wears for the show, which are three times the length of an ordinary foot. Without his wig the clown looks freakish, even evil, like a character from a horror film. Instantly his good spirits are laid flat.

'Ignore that talentless fuck,' Vlad instructs him loud enough for the clown to hear. He comes down out of his handstand and gives the clown the finger, apparently loath to take his own advice. 'He is just old, ugly and nervous.'

The clown's lips twist into his trademark sneer, which he recognises even beneath the black stripe of mouth painted across the clown's face.

'That's right, concubine,' the clown says. 'Just ignore me.'

'What do you call him?' snaps Vlad. 'What is this "concubine"?'

'Learn to speak English, immigrant fuck.'

Just as Vlad is about to lose it completely Big Pete appears in full costume and make-up. The ringmaster's outfit has been dramatically upgraded since he saw the circus a week ago. Marie has sewn silver tasselled pads to either shoulder and white stars on his waistcoat to echo the stars on the canvas of the big top. He now has a top hat with a huge silver feather fastened with a glass emerald to a black ribbon around the brim. As before he wears a collar of black feathers which rise out around his neck as if he were a showgirl. The result is magnificent and unsettling, and the whip that he brandishes as if ready to start lashing completes the effect, making him look like an intergalactic super-villain.

'What's this poof doing here?' demands Big Pete, looking directly at him and ignoring the whistles he receives from the rest of the company. 'This area is for performers only.'

'I said he could help me,' says Vlad, crossing his arms defiantly. 'He promises not to get in the way.'

Big Pete's eyes burn into his.

'I don't give a shit. You do what you want in your private time but don't you be bringing your laundry into my tent. This area's off limits, so he can fuck right off!'

'He's been 'elping me, so you can quit running your A-hole,' screeches a voice from behind. Big Pete turns to Marie, who looks him up and down and cocks her head to the side, her nostrils flaring.

'Nothing's straight!' she snaps. 'You dress with your eyes shut or something?'

Big Pete subsides into a chair while Marie fusses over his costume, shaking her head in an ostentatious display of impatience. It is amazing to see this bear-like man cowed by such a little woman. As Marie goes around behind her husband to tighten his collar, she looks over at him and winks. He is so surprised by the wink that he starts, and by the time he has realised that a wink is indeed what it was, Marie has finished with Big Pete and is berating Imogen, the female acrobat, for tearing the frill on her sleeve.

'Time!' comes a gruff shout from the main space.

Everyone falls silent as a deep gong sounds. He recognises the gong and a cold thrill runs through him. Vlad takes his hand and gives it a quick squeeze before skipping away to the corner to dust his hands with rosin – a sticky chalk-like substance to prevent his fingers from slipping on the bar. All about the performers stand stock-still, waiting for their cues. At the last second Marie notices a stray lock of hair that has escaped from under her husband's hat and fixes it down with a hairpin from her own head. The ringmaster takes a deep breath and walks proudly towards the ring entrance, chest puffed out and shoulders pushed back. The circus is starting.

He will open the door and find not only Mrs Goodly but four other women from the neighbourhood. They will each have their arms folded and their foreheads will be dramatically creased. He will almost laugh at the sight of them, for they will put him in mind of an elderly female mafia.

'We need to talk,' will say Mrs Goodly firmly.

With these words she will thrust her body towards him and, not wishing to touch her, he will instinctively flatten himself against the wall. This will be all she needs, and she will push her way into the house, followed immediately by the other women – Mrs Spencer, Mrs Collins, Mrs Lenard from the bottom of the road, and old Mrs Hancock with her two walking sticks.

'Oh my God, look at the place!' Mrs Spencer will shriek at what is left of the kitchen, surveying the hillock of wood, bricks, paint and nails collected at the side of the room which he has yet to ferry to the garage.

'Like the Blitz!' Mrs Hancock will murmur, resting her elbows on her sticks.

Then, simultaneously, as if they have rehearsed it, their heads will all drop back as they look up to see the trapeze dangling from its rig. There will be a collective gasp, followed by a long pause.

'What can I do for you ladies?' he will say, as five pairs of eyes drift slowly down to fix upon him. 'As you can see, I'm quite busy.'

'Busy? Busy?!' Mrs Lenard will screech. 'Busy with demolishing this beautiful old house? Why, your mother'd have a fit if she could see it! He needs help!'

'Shhh, Anne,' Mrs Goodly will say quickly, resting a soothing hand on Mrs Lenard's shoulder and patting her as if to stop her from charging at him. She will clear her throat. 'We wanted to come and say to you that enough is enough. You need to stop this . . . unusual behaviour . . . before it gets out of hand.'

He will not respond, merely fold his own arms.

'I think you have to admit,' Mrs Goodly will continue falteringly, 'that what you're doing here are hardly the actions of what you'd call a . . . a reasonable-minded person.'

'We can hear you. Every night and every day – endless banging!' Mrs Spencer will exclaim. 'Sounds like a war zone going on.'

'We're worried!' Mrs Collins will supply.

'Extremely worried,' Mrs Goodly will pick up the thread, raising her hand to quieten the others – there is no doubting who is leader here. 'You've not been yourself of course, and that's understandable, I'm sure. You've a lot to deal with. But after all . . .'

She will trail off again, uncomfortable under his stare. But then she will thrust her chin out determinedly and turn to Mrs Spencer.

'Margaret?'

Mrs Spencer will nod and take a card out of her purse. Quivering, she will hold it out to him in the manner of one forced to feed a wild animal. It is his turn to be astonished. He will take the card from her and she will snatch back her hand as if worried about infection. On the card will be embossed the name of a doctor from the next town, above the word 'Psychotherapist'.

'My daughter recommends him,' Mrs Spencer will say timidly.

'It's all the rage now, you shouldn't be ashamed,' Mrs Goodly will add quickly. 'Tilly's been ever so much happier since she started going, hasn't she, Margaret? Can't go often enough from what I hear.'

Mrs Spencer will nod her head up and down very fast.

'Thank you,' he will reply, wondering if politeness will get them out of the house more swiftly than anger.

'You're very welcome,' Mrs Goodly will say, pleased with his reaction.

'They really can do wonderful things these days,' Mrs Spencer will say.

'And what happened with your mother is ever so sad,' Mrs Lenard will contribute, evidently encouraged enough now to try and be civil. 'We all know how much she loved you. A shame about that whole ... you know, situation, of course, but that's all in the –'

'Anne!'

'Yes?' Mrs Lenard will appeal with both hands. 'He ran off to God-knows-where and left her all by herself! Helpless! Not so much a word or a phone call. It's hardly surprising if he feels guilty, is it?'

'That's enough!' will declare Mrs Goodly, gritting her teeth in a show of good-natured annoyance. She will turn back to him. 'We'll be getting out of your way then, and let you finish up with your'

– she seizes inspiration – 'refurbishments. But you will contact that doctor, won't you?'

Without waiting for his reply she will begin to usher the other women out of the kitchen. They will all crane their heads around until they are outside, drinking in every last detail, and he will know that he is soon going to be the subject on everyone's lips within a five-mile radius.

'I had an aunt who was a tightrope walker,' he will hear old Mrs Hancock say conversationally as she negotiates the front step.

He will wait thirty seconds and then hold up the card once more. Twisting his lips into a wry smile, he will tear it in two and toss the pieces on top of the pile of rubble.

That night after the circus Vlad is tense and surly and eats the meal he prepares without so much as a thank-you, chewing ravioli without relish and staring sullenly into space. He is deeply uncomfortable with the aerialist's silence, worried that it means he no longer wants him around.

'What's wrong?' he asks finally.

Vlad says nothing and hunches his shoulders as if annoyed by the question.

'Did something happen tonight?'

Still no answer.

'They loved you,' he says nervously. 'I loved you too. What you do – it's extraordinary! I mean, it's so dangerous and yet you also make it look so effortless and easy!'

'Well, it's not easy!' snarls Vlad. 'It's not so fucking easy as it looks and if you think it is then why don't you give it a try?'

'But I don't think it! I mean . . . that's not what I meant –'

'Oh, really? Then why say I make it look easy?'

He realises that Vlad is working himself up into a fury. He has seen him do this a number of times now – bursts of temper catalysed by the smallest of things, such as a stubbed toe or a broken mug, once even a missing article of clothing.

'I'm sorry. It was meant as a compliment.'

'Some compliment!'

'There's no need to get cross.'

'I'm not getting cross! Now you're telling me what is going on inside my head as well? Who the fuck are you?!'

It is like trying to escape a wild horse that is determined to trample him down. He hangs his head and takes a forkful of ravioli. There is more uncomfortable silence except for the sound of them both chewing.

'You know what you are?' hisses the aerialist then. 'You're nothing but a loser. You can't do anything! Just some cock from some nowhere-place with nobody who gives a rat's arse about him. I let you stay because I pity you. That's the only reason! So you better not tell me how to do my own fucking job!'

Vlad stands, lifts his plate and send it crashing down onto the table, where it collides with his own meal, erupting in a volcanic explosion of tomato juice that splatters across the already stained T-shirt he has been borrowing from the aerialist. Vlad turns on his heel, wrenches the door open and storms out of the caravan.

An hour later, after he has cleaned up and is waiting in bed swaddled in blankets because he does not want to switch on the electric blanket without Vlad and be berated for wasting precious electricity, the aerialist returns, gliding in and plonking himself down beside him. He turns away from Vlad towards the wall and curls his body up into a shell-like position. He is still hurt by what Vlad said and he wants the aerialist to know it.

'I'm sorry,' says Vlad. 'I was a jerk.'

He waits. Vlad's fingers probe the blankets and start to peel them away, layer by later.

'Last night I almost missed a catch with my feet,' Vlad says. 'It is very upsetting as it has never happened to me before. I felt the rope slide and I thought it might be a miss and I was going to end up dead meat on the ground. Now I need to practise and work out why this happened.'

He is somewhat chilled by Vlad's expression 'dead meat on the ground'. The aerialist is down to the last blanket, which he tugs out from under his arms and pulls away from his body. Vlad slides his arms around his torso, digging his hands in under the red-spotted T-shirt so he can rest his thumbs lightly against his nipples.

'Are you still furious with me?'

He feels the aerialist's lips against his ear and his tongue tracing its outline. He thinks for some reason of his mother, wondering how she is doing. She will never have been by herself in that house for so long before, and he wishes there was some way he could make sure she was OK. But he knows she will never understand this, what he is doing, and will only demand he return home. To her his leaving is nothing but a betrayal, because she has never allowed herself to see the silent hatred he has always had for that little town, and for that clean and lethally tidy house. He wonders if she doesn't have this hatred too, only buried deep down where she doesn't know about it, and he shivers, feeling a chill that has nothing to do with the cold. The aerialist tightens his arms, countering that chill with his own warmth.

'I'm not furious,' he says.

'You do realise we're not virgins any more,' Edward said. It was a week after his father had left for France and they were lying on their backs in the den, smoking cigarettes and listening to the dim sound of Blondie, which Edward's mother was playing at full volume in her studio, something she had been doing, Edward claimed, ever since his father's departure.

'Don't be daft,' he said. 'We didn't . . . you know.'

'It's still sex if you come,' said Edward knowledgeably. 'We popped each other's cherry. Look at you – you're blushing.'

'Shut up. I'm not.'

'Yes, you are. You're positively crimson.'

There was something new between them now. It was not what they had done so much as the fact that they had a shared secret. When he looked at Edward and Edward looked back at him it felt as if there were an invisible thread between them, linking them in a way they were not linked to the rest of the world. They had not repeated what had happened on the common, but had discussed it at length, what it meant and how it had changed them, and the possibility of its happening again lay undefined yet potential in every look they exchanged.

'Well,' he said, and left it that.

Just then a shaft of sunlight fell across the minefield of junk like a column of translucent gold, and he stretched out so he could insert his hand into the light and compare the warmth of it to the cool dark of the unlit attic. He couldn't remember having ever been so happy before, and lazily considered whether it was bad to feel this way, since he was dimly aware that his happiness had come about through Edward's misfortune with his father. He wondered if it wasn't slightly false, his euphoria, and if Edward wouldn't still rather be in Antibes settling into a new life with his parents still together. But selfishly he realised he didn't much care – happiness was happiness, he thought, however it came about. But in spite of his complacency he was aware that it was a dangerous feeling, that happiness was rare and fragile and easily lost.

He watches as Vlad holds onto the trapeze bar and beats his body back and forward beneath it, over and over as if he is a human pendulum, his legs rising high in the air above him only to plummet and then rotate suddenly backwards and up into the air again behind. Every five beats his legs will carry on up over the bar followed by the rest of him and he will land with the trapeze in his midsection, a position he will hold for half a second while his legs continue to revolve before dropping backwards and resuming the beats. This is one of various exercises the aerialist calls 'conditioning'.

'OK,' pants Vlad when he returns to the ground patting his arms, which are red and swollen into cartoonish conglomerates almost the size of tree trunks, with a latticework of veins popping out across them. 'Your turn.'

'You must be joking!'

'It's easy,' says the aerialist. 'Go on. Up!'

Vlad leans in and kisses him hard. The aerialist's breath is bad in the morning, but he does not pull away or say anything. He smells the sweat on the body before him and is aroused and wants to go back to bed, but Vlad draws back and points at the trapeze. They have got up early in order to train with no one else around, and Vlad has dressed him in an old tracksuit that makes him feel like a thug.

'OK,' he says uneasily, taking hold of the rope and wrapping it around one foot. He starts to climb in the way Vlad has showed him, stepping on the foot that is wrapped and straightening his legs, then holding himself with the elbows bent and unwrapping and rewrapping so he can repeat the motion. After three such manoeuvres he is exhausted, there is a painful throbbing in his forearms, and his hands are begging to be unclenched and relaxed. He looks down to see he is only a couple of metres off the ground.

'Jesus,' he breathes.

'Carry on,' instructs the aerialist, folding his arms.

Clenching his teeth he manages the remaining distance to the bar and then reaches out and clutches it for dear life. He struggles to take the bar with his other hand and clumsily pulls himself up to a sitting position, looking down at Vlad who seems terrifyingly small and far below. They have dragged a moth-eaten king-size mattress to sit underneath the trapeze, but it is of scant comfort.

'Vlad,' he says timorously, 'I think I want to come down.'

'Don't be a silly fool,' says the aerialist. 'You want to be part of the circus, don't you? So do some beats. It's fun.'

Not wishing to argue, he takes a sizeable gulp of air and lowers himself backwards so that he is dangling from his knees. This position is much more comfortable and he rests for a few seconds until Vlad barks at him to continue. He reaches up and takes hold of the bar with both hands, releasing his knees and falling to an upright position underneath. Vlad has coated his palms in a layer of sticky rosin, and they feel almost as if they have been welded to the bar.

'Now beat!'

He tries to copy Vlad's motions, thrusting his legs up into the air. He feels gravity resist the movement and then overcome him, propelling him backwards. Down below the aerialist is watching his futile efforts with a grin. His legs go hurtling up behind him and then something screams in his back. As it does the force of his body rips his fingers loose of the trapeze and suddenly he is falling. 'Shit!' yells the aerialist from somewhere in the whirling periphery. He just has time to realise he is surrounded by nothing but air before there is an almighty slamming sound as he connects face first with the mattress. He lies there immobile for a few seconds, not daring to move in case he has broken his neck. Then, very slowly, he raises his head.

'What happened?' demands Vlad, sounding cross.

Ever so gently, lest he be haemorrhaging internally, he starts to pull himself up. Amazingly, despite falling at least a storey, he seems to be wholly intact. It is only when he tries to stand that his left knee buckles, causing him to shriek.

'Fuck,' he shouts, falling and clutching wildly at his knee.

'Let me see,' orders the aerialist, pushing his flailing arms away so he can inspect the leg. He lies back on the mattress while Vlad pokes and prods.

'Fuck!' he shouts again.

'Fuck,' agrees Vlad. 'However did you manage this?'

'You made me! It was your fault!'

But Vlad only shrugs.

'Well, that's what you get,' the aerialist says philosophically, as if he was some sort of overenthusiastic child who had insisted on going up when he should have remained on the ground where it was safe. 'No more trapeze for you!'

He will grip the bar firmly, ignoring the soreness that spreads through his hands as the skin on his palms is compressed into pleats and folds. He will raise his legs in front of him and then thrust them backwards hard. As he swings out his shoulders will lift and his back lengthen. He will keep his legs straight and his entire body taut, though the instinct is to relax and go floppy, to allow the forces of nature to have their way. But this is how to injure yourself. He will remember the golden rule of the circus and will repeat it to himself like a mantra – that the more difficult it feels, the more correct it must be.

At the top of the swing he will feel a second of weightlessness. Every time, even with the strain in his arms and shoulders, this feeling is a delight – almost as if he is floating in mid-air. As the momentum fades he will beat his body forward, his legs whipping straight towards the other side of the trapeze. Then he will lift himself, feel the pull in his biceps as he uses strength to resist gravity and propel himself up over the bar. He will fold to land on top, his hips against the bar, and will curl his torso upwards, rotating his shoulders back and pushing his legs out. Here his movement will slow for a second, as his toes continue to push into the space beneath. It will be the most unnatural part of the routine, but before he loses his form or has second thoughts he will thrust himself away, pushing out in a dish shape as he drops backwards. As the momentum in his legs recedes he will catch himself and swing, returning to the original beating movement.

He will repeat this exercise until his shoulders are hot and throbbing and pleading for respite. Then he will lift himself to the bar one last time and pause with it bisecting his body, torso from legs. He will take his hands off the bar and balance there precariously for as long as he is able, his arms outstretched as if embracing the air. All of a sudden he will flop forward only to immediately raise himself up, straining the muscles in his stomach as he forces the trunk of his body back to the balance once more.

When he has done as many of these raises as he can he will grasp hold of the ropes on either side of the trapeze and rotate his body to a sitting position. He will point his legs until they are at right angles from his upper body, then re-grip the ropes above his head. Pushing outwards with his arms he will lift his entire body up as high as he can and hold it for half a second, before lowering it back down. After eight such lifts his arms are quivering from the effort, and he will let himself gently backwards, bending his legs around the bar and hanging from it by his knees. Pushing his left toe down towards the ground and tightening his thigh over the trapeze with all his might, he will take his right leg off the bar for as long as he can and then replace it and do the same with his left. The backs of his knees will shriek at the weight of him, the skin bunching up agonisingly against the bar. But he will grit his teeth and straighten each leg out, then rotate it to behind his body and then back up again, refusing to obey the pain that insists he hurry, that he give up, that he cut the exercise short and be happy with what he has achieved so far.

After he has completed this exercise he will reach up and take the bar with both hands once more. Hanging underneath it he will ignore the urge to drop and instead will raise his legs up towards the ceiling, keeping them as straight as he can with the feet arched and pointing, trying to bring them all the way to his face, making his stomach contract with spasms. He will only be able to manage three of these movements before his body is unable to cope any more. As the sweat streams down his face and clams up his hands so that he can hardly keep his grip he will reach out for the rope with his foot. Hooking it and pulling it towards himself, he will summon up his last reserve of strength to climb on and slide down to the floor.

Marie takes in the sight of him limping to her trailer without comment, merely compresses her lips and trails her eyes down to his leg, where over his jeans Vlad has wound a strip of stretchy support elastic. But there is a glint in her eye that suggests she finds the sight of it funny.

'Here,' she says, handing him the key to the box-office trailer, where the cleaning supplies are kept. 'Don't strain yourself.'

He reaches for the key. He wants to say thank you, for standing up to Big Pete the previous night, telling him that he was helping her so he could stay in the big top. But whatever split second of solidarity existed between them is gone. It is almost impossible to reconcile that sly wink with the hard, closed features of the angry little face before him.

'Oi!' says Big Pete, suddenly looming behind Marie. 'He's helping me today. Got to pick up the scaffs, remember?'

Marie turns.

'And why can't you get one of those lazy-arsed cronies to help you? Or do they need their beauty sleep this morning?'

'Midge's testing the motor and Benny's patching the tent. Like me to do it alone, would ya?'

Marie looks like she's about to agree that yes, she would. But then she shrugs and retracts the hand with the key.

'All right, you heard that stupid pig,' she says to him and goes back inside, leaving him facing Big Pete, who gives him a long hard glare before striding past him.

'Come on then,' the ringmaster snaps over his shoulder.

In the truck Big Pete is silent, toking now and then on a cigarette and blowing the smoke sideways out of his mouth in jets that seem to be aimed deliberately at his eyes. He coughs, turns away and studies the road. Each house they pass reminds him of his home town. In two front gardens stand a pair of old ladies chatting over the fence. He pictures his mother, seeing her surrounded by excited and righteously outraged neighbours as she repeatedly tells the story of how her son abandoned her until it becomes local folklore. He wonders if he will ever return, and receives an unexpected nightmarish flash of reality about what he has become – an unwanted hanger-on at a travelling circus show, voluntary slave to obnoxious scary carnival folk, living in a shoebox with a crazy acrobat. But in his heart he knows it doesn't matter, for the prospect of returning is inconceivable.

He comes out of his thoughts to find they are no longer passing through residential streets, but are turning into the grounds of a dilapidated factory with a windowless grey tower block that juts up into the sky like an obelisk. The place is obviously abandoned, and he has a sudden spooky premonition that Big Pete has brought him here to do something awful. He scrutinises the ringmaster, who rolls down his window and spits his cigarette out, sharply turning the wheel so that they career past the side of a building, almost shaving it with the wing mirror, before coming to a dramatic halt round the corner, in front of a run-down trailer.

'Where are we?' he says.

Big Pete ignores him and sounds the horn. After waiting a few seconds he does it again and from the trailer emerges an old man with a greatly wrinkled face and a mane of steel-coloured hair that rests on his shoulders like wire wool. Big Pete chuckles and sounds the horn again and the man gives him the finger and staggers up to the window.

'All right there, Matt?'

'Damned bastard. Whatcha have to wake me for?'

'Wouldn't be decent not to say hello, would it?'

The old man grins, showing a maw of toothless pink gum.

'So how's the show going?'

'Oh, y'know. Hand to mouth.'

'And the wife?'

'Still a nagging bitch.'

'You give her my love. Spare an old codge a fag?'

Big Pete hands his pouch of Drum to the old man, who takes from it a paper and a pinch of tobacco and transforms it instantaneously into a cigarette with remarkably nimble fingers. Raising it to his lips as Big Pete hands him his lighter, the old man squints past the ringmaster as if he had only just noticed him sitting there. 'This your daughter?'

Big Pete emits a chuckle which sounds more like a growl.

'Where is it then?' the ringmaster says, suddenly sharp.

The old man breathes in with a groan of pleasure, as if all his life has been leading up to this one short blessed smoke. He jerks his thumb over his shoulder.

'Mind you don't take more 'n we agreed,' mutters the old man, and without another word he staggers back towards the trailer.

'He actually lives there?' he says in amazement.

'Matt's old school,' replies Big Pete, guiding the truck over to the corner of the pile of junk and killing the engine. The ringmaster gets out and he follows curiously. Rolling a new cigarette, Big Pete inspects the junk suspiciously, then glances at him.

'Right. I want them scaffs in the back of the truck. Get to it.'

It is his turn to survey the mountain. Now they are up close he can see that it is composed of thick metal poles, all about ten feet in length and layered up on top of each other to almost the exact same height as Big Pete. He suppresses a giggle at the sheer ridiculousness of the order.

'You can't be serious!'

Big Pete's eyes narrow. Tendrils of smoke snake their way out of the ringmaster's nostrils and he smiles, his cigarette dangling precariously on the edge of his lip. It is a dangerous smile.

'Yep,' he says flatly.

Gingerly he approaches the pile and looks for a pole to try to lift first. They are all buried under one another and the only loose ones are at the top of the stack, unreachable. He glances back at Big Pete who is watching impassively. Gritting his teeth, suddenly angry with both the ringmaster and himself, he takes hold of the nearest pole and gives it a mighty wrench. There is a sound like a peal of thunder and he jumps back just in time to avoid being buried alive under the scaff-poles as they come rolling and clattering down in a great avalanche. He lands painfully on his bad leg and gasps.

'Ain't got all day, you know,' says Big Pete.

He begins to heft the scaff-poles one by one into the back of the truck. They are heavy and must be lifted from the centre, then slotted into the truck and pushed until they are up against the seating compartment. It is a lengthy process and hard work. To make matters worse the scaff-poles are slippery and several times he drops them, narrowly missing his feet. The whole while Big Pete watches, not lifting a finger. He can almost feel the ringmaster's eyes boring into the back of his head while he works, and he knows he is still wearing that dangerous smile. As with Marie, he is being tested to see how far he can be pushed before he cracks.

When he is done, he sits gasping on the ground while Big Pete saunters over to the back of the truck. He wants to hurt the ringmaster, to run at him and push his face into one of the pole ends jutting out from the back, to hear the satisfying sound of his skull clanging against the metal and to see red gore gush out from his nose. He waits while Big Pete counts the poles he has stacked and inspects them again for signs of rust.

'All right,' says Big Pete, flicking his cigarette away and shutting up the doors. 'Let's go.'

He pulls himself up and clambers into the passenger seat. Big Pete toots the horn and the old man re-emerges from his trailer and gives Big Pete a wave which the ringmaster returns. They turn off out of the factory grounds and onto the road, where they pull up at a red light. Here the ringmaster turns to him. For a second he thinks he is going to congratulate him on a job well done.

'I don't like your sort,' Big Pete says quietly. 'And I'm not talking about being queer either. That I couldn't give a shit about. I'm talking about being soft. Seen 'em like you a hundred times. Come in, watch the show, clap and shout and don't think nothing of the work. Reckon it's easy, like just anybody can do it.'

The ringmaster's eyes burn into his. For once he stares right back. The work of lifting and stacking the poles has given him a new-found sense of power and defiance.

'I'm trying my best!' he snaps. 'What more do you want from me?'

Big Pete's face briefly registers surprise, either at what he has said or at the mere fact that he has dared to answer back. Then the light turns to green and the ringmaster transfers his attention back to the road.

'You're only here cos of that fuckwit you've shacked up with,' he says as they take off once more. 'Soon as he gets tired of you, you're out. Don't you forget it.'

Three or four times a week he went to the old people's home. His mother had got him a summer job there, a role she called 'general assistant' and said would be character-building. He was expected to move chairs, lamps, mattresses and sometimes even people, to clear up spilt tea and any other sort of mess, to mop corridors and to be at the beck and call of all the carers should they require anyone to carry things or hold old men upright when the nurse came round to administer her various demeaning health checks.

'General assistant, my arse,' he complained to Edward. 'Unpaid slave labour is more like it.'

'My poor little lamb,' replied Edward in a sugary voice, but then to his surprise offered to come and help too.

When he half-heartedly suggested this to his mum she told him the home could not handle too many helpers and he was lucky to be getting the work experience. He knew it was really because she was nervous of Edward, but truthfully he didn't mind because he didn't want Edward to come to the home either. He didn't ever want to have to associate Edward with that place, to have Edward tainted by the smell of old people, of rose toilet soap and musk, which pervaded every room of the home and could not be got rid of no matter how many windows were opened or how much air-freshener was pumped into the atmosphere.

The town seemed different to him that summer, as if he were seeing it anew, because he was with Edward and it was Edward's first summer there. They followed the canal all the way through the marshland that sat behind the rougher estates and right down into the woods that were privately owned, which Edward said was ridiculous because nature didn't belong to anyone. They vaulted the fence and wandered through the calm pristine undisturbed carpets of green and yellow and the whole time he was worried they would be caught and shouted at. But no one else came or bothered them, not even once, and soon the pretty woods became a favourite place for them to go in the day when it was too hot to remain inside.

They almost never went to the arcade, a shopping mall that had opened a couple of years ago in the town centre, only to go to the cinema that had been built into its lower floor. There they saw the older boys and girls from school out together, and sometimes encountered boys and girls from their own year chastely parodying these dates. Sometimes they saw Fred and the rougher kids, and when they were seen by these kids they were shouted at and had popcorn and chocolate wrappers thrown at them. They saw Katy once or twice, but she no longer seemed a threat outside of school. She was ignored by the boys she hung out with, and it almost made him sad to see her trying to impress them with her loud talk and insults to other girls who were prettier and more attractive than she was. He thought that all along Edward had been right in his assessment of her. The boys would wolf-whistle and suggest rude possibilities in the back row of the auditorium to girls in their year, and the girls would duly hold their heads high and tell them to fuck off. But there was often something flirtatious in their responses, and sometimes they entered into playful banter with the boys and even laughed at their jokes.

'Behold the mating rituals of our generation,' Edward proclaimed, an eyebrow raised, when they came out of the cinema one day and almost ran head-first into a boy and girl from their set kissing beside a propped-up cardboard cut-out of the Terminator.

It seemed like a whole other universe and he was intensely glad of the private space he and Edward inhabited, insulated from the crassness he saw around him. What they had was special, he thought − not without smugness − and he allowed himself to believe that the rest of the world looked at them and was jealous, and that this was the real cause of its scorn.

On the ground he will feel an almost overpowering urge to collapse and lie still for a very long time. But again he will refuse to listen to his body's pleas. Instead he will take several long cool breaths then start to stretch. He will begin with his shoulders, pressing them back against the walls and pushing his chest out, raising them over his head so he can push down on his elbows, flattening them against the floor and sitting back on his haunches, trying to reach the ground with his armpits. When he is done with his arms he will move onto his back, lying on his front and arching up towards the ceiling, holding the position for as long as he can, focusing on a point in the broken tiles and concentrating on it with all his might. He will straighten his legs and push up, creating an L-shape, trying to curl his back towards the floor as he pushes his heels backwards one after the other, then both at the same time. Last of all he will move to his legs. He will lunge on each side for a good minute, then lie back on the ground and lift each leg in turn, straightening it towards the ceiling and gripping it by the ankle, trying to draw it towards his head while at the same time keeping his hips against the floor.

When he has finished his muscles will feel alive and elastic, and he will be breathless and shot through with pounding energy. What he will feel will be like a mania, but a glorious one. Only now will he allow himself to lie down and close his eyes, meditating on the delicious feeling of blood galloping up and down his body.

The new ground is on the edge of a small town on the seafront, and the second he sets foot outside the caravan he is hit by an icy blast that causes his teeth to start chattering.

'Too cold,' groans Vlad from the bed, where he has holed himself up under a mountain of blankets and jackets. 'You people and your ridiculous country with its stupid weather!'

He shuts the door and continues towards the toilets, and almost runs face first into Big Pete. The ringmaster's cheeks are bright red but his sleeves are rolled up in flagrant refusal to acknowledge the freezing wind.

'Come on, arseholes!' he is shouting at the dark windows of a trailer, where Benny and Midge, the roustabouts, reside. 'Let's get this tent set up before the fucking Second Coming, OK?'

There is no response from the trailer, and Big Pete raises his fist and slams it down on the door, making the whole structure shake as he screams that he is not paying them to sleep. Leaving Big Pete, he heads over to the toilets, which are situated at the very edge of the grounds. They are always the first thing to be set up – according to Franka it is written in her contract that toilets be provided, though he could not tell if she was being serious or not. The toilets have no heating or lights, and they are almost as cold inside as out. He pulls down his trousers and sits to shit as quickly as possible, the sound of his stools hitting water deafening in the silence of the cubicle. He is hurrying back to Vlad's trailer when a voice calls out.

'Oi, you!'

He turns and is alarmed to find himself face to face with three men in hooded tops. Two of the men are huge and seem to tower above him in twin walls of muscle and flesh. The other is short and wiry with a rat-like face, twisted up as if from a lifetime of bitterness at being the smallest of the three. All of them have shaved heads and narrowed eyes. The two furthest away have their arms folded: they are all staring at him, exuding menace. He glances back at the caravans and trailers, which are a good thirty yards away, and wonders if he could make it to them were he to bolt.

'We don't want no fucking circus around here,' says one of the bigger men, a diamond stud winking in his left ear. 'You and your carnie freaks can fuck off where you came from.'

'I'm not in charge,' he says quickly. 'I just work here.'

'Carnie cunt!' growls the other big man, spitting with such force it makes an audible splattering noise as it hits the ground.

'Didn't you hear what I said?' says the one with the diamond stud. 'Said, we don't want you here. Said fuck off where you came from. Got that?'

He nods because it seems like the only smart thing to do.

'I'll tell the boss,' he says.

'Yeah,' says the man. 'You do that.'

'We don't like your sort,' adds the smallest man, somewhat unnecessarily.

He turns and walks quickly towards the camp, his heart hammering, wondering if at any second he is going to feel a fist in the back of his head. But nothing comes.

Big Pete is still yelling at the roustabouts, who are now hefting the two large poles that form the base of the truss. He debates briefly whether or not to tell him about the local men, but one look at Big Pete's large angry face decides him against it. Big Pete will not listen, he knows, and anyway if the men are really going to cause problems, they will make the fact known soon enough.

When he next opens the door there will be a young woman in jeans and a black polo neck standing there holding a Dictaphone. Behind her, fiddling with a large camera, will be a man in his forties with several days' worth of stubble and eyes ringed with tiredness, clad in a leather jacket.

'Hi there,' the woman will say brightly. 'My name's Susan – I'm from the local rag. How's it going?'

He will nod to her warily.

'So listen . . .' she will say, launching straight in, 'I caught wind that you're building a trapeze rig in your house, which I thought is something that'd make an absolutely fantastic article.'

She will beam at him expectantly.

'I hope you don't mind me just showing up like this. I did try to call only there wasn't any answer . . . you're a tough person to get in touch with!'

'Listen,' he will say. 'Thank you. It's very kind. But no thank you.'

Susan will take a deep breath.

'If we could just ask a few questions and have a look around, it won't take up much of your time, and as I say, it would make a great story. Perhaps we could even get a few pictures of you on your trapeze? I bet the readers would love that!'

She will peer past him and he will pull the door against his body to restrict the view as much as possible.

'It's such a far-out idea. What made you decide to do it?'

'Actually, I'm very busy,' he will say, trying to keep the panic out of his voice. 'I'd really prefer it if there was no article.'

He will smile back at her and close the door. He will wait a few minutes and then creep upstairs, sidestepping his way around the remaining ledge of floor and then peeping out of the front window. The woman and the photographer will still be there by the gate, and she will be saying something to him and making big gestures with her hands. Then the photographer will take a few steps backwards and carefully inspect the house. Then he will retreat a little further. Fitting a very long lens over the eye of his camera, the man will raise it up and start to take pictures.

It is the hour before the show is due to start and he is waiting for Vlad. He has just finished wiping down the windows of the insect-splattered box-office trailer, and he feels tired, cold and hungry. He enters the backstage area of the tent and looks around for the aerialist. Just as he is about to ask someone if they have seen Vlad, and if not hurry down to the caravan and bang on the door to rouse him because in that case he is probably still asleep from his afternoon nap, Griselda bursts in panting.

'Some yobbos are beating up on Vlad!'

He does not wait to hear more. He tears from the tent into the freezing cold outside. Instantly the night envelops him like a blanket, and for a second he can see nothing but blackness. He totters, uncertain if the grass is even there under his feet, for an instant suspended in space, as if he has been transported right back to the beginning of time when all was quiet and still and nothing but potential. Then in the distance he makes out some pinpricks of light, the houses of the local town, and above him even fainter pinpricks of the stars. He stumbles forward, not knowing which way to go. Then the lights of the big top are suddenly switched on, strings of coloured bulbs flooding the ground with streaks of yellow, blue and pink. At the same second he becomes aware of screaming and yelling off to his right and he hurls himself in that direction.

It takes him twenty seconds to reach them and in this time he realises how foolish it is what he is doing, rushing alone head first into danger as if he himself possessed a strength to repel an attack that the aerialist might not. But there is a fire in him such as he has never felt before, bloodthirst and fury. There is something joyous about it too, almost religious, and he hears a cry issuing forth from his own mouth, loud and primal, determined to protect the person who belongs to him whatever the cost to himself.

The three men are now four. Two of them are holding Vlad while the others take it in turns to deliver punches to his face. The aerialist's body has already gone limp and he is letting out faint begging whimpers. The two men beating him turn as he arrives, one of them throwing up his fists and advancing immediately towards him. He does not stop running, but throws himself at this man, sending his weight hurtling at him like a missile. The man's fist lashes out and catches him on the side of the face, but it is no match for the full force of his body as it flies through the air. He takes the man with him onto the grass where they land with a hard thud that makes the man groan in pain and sends a shock wave through his own skull.

'Faggot!' growls the man, grappling and trying to get a grip on his neck. But he thrashes, refusing to be caught, punching and kicking and even biting.

'Jesus fucking –!' the man curses.

His mouth clamps onto something soft and he clenches his teeth into it and hears a scream. He barely has time to register his delight at the sound when something hits him on the side of the head hard, dazing him and knocking him off the man completely.

One evening his parents said they wanted to have a talk. It was after dinner and he had just stood up to put the cutlery and plates away. As he did his mum darted his dad an expectant look. Right away he knew something was up, for they had both sat quietly throughout the meal, neither one of them saying a word.

'Leave that for a minute, son,' said his dad with a frown. 'Sit back down again please.'

He sat. It was the word 'son' that let him know it was serious. They were both smiling, and he had the distinct sense they were about to tell him something awful. His heart began to pound. For a while they remained silent, his mum casting meaningful looks at his dad, until finally, apparently losing patience, she cleared her throat.

'It's about your father and me,' she said gently. She glanced again at his dad before continuing. 'We've decided to separate.'

'What do you mean?' he said, stupefied.

His dad reddened and studied his place mat.

'We're going to get a divorce,' said his dad, not raising his eyes.

He knew plenty of kids at school with divorced parents. Some even had just one parent and some didn't even know who the other one was. But the fact that his own parents might also one day decide to divorce had never before crossed his mind. Somehow it hadn't seemed possible, and still didn't, even as they sat before him, smiling anxiously, awaiting his reaction.

'Why?' he managed finally.

They both looked uncomfortable.

'Because your mum and I haven't been in love for a while now,' said his dad. His mum looked down and nodded. 'We've been waiting for the right time, and we've decided . . . it's now or never. I'm sorry, son.'

'Don't get upset, love,' added his mum.

She hadn't called him 'love' since he was a little boy.

He tried his very best to feel upset, because the situation seemed to call for it, but found he could not muster the slightest feeling of unhappiness. If anything he felt amused, amused because something life-changing was finally happening to him and it didn't seem to matter. It was typical that his parents would manage to tell him of their divorce in this way, he thought, without the slightest shred of drama. Instead of the scene he was sure it ought to be, with screaming and shouting and pleading and threatening, the whole thing was as hushed and unemotional as if they were informing him of a simple domestic decision, such as to repaint the house or trade in the second car.

'What's going to happen now?' he said finally.

His mum looked relieved – apparently the moment for any big reaction had passed and they were on to practicalities.

'Well, for the time being nothing at all. Your father's not moving out right away or anything. He's got a new job in Swindon, which he's going to be starting in the new year.'

'In Swindon?'

'You'll visit him all the time,' she added quickly. 'You don't have to worry. Nothing's going to change.'

'Right,' he said.

He tried to think of something else to say, but could find nothing. He stood up and his parents glanced at each other, exchanging a rapid silent communication. Then his dad sighed and nodded.

'There's something else we wanted to discuss,' his dad said.

'What?'

'It's about that boy –'

'His name's Edward,' supplied his mum hurriedly.

'Yes, about Edward ...' said his dad.

'What about him?'

'We're a little concerned.'

He waited, but his dad did not seem to know how to put what he wanted to say into words. Seconds ticked past, until once again his mum gave up waiting and took over.

'What your father is trying to say is that we're not happy for you to be over at his house all the time. Everybody knows what's been going on with his family – his mother's made no secret of it – and it's natural you'd want to be sympathetic of course. But ...' She trailed off.

'What with everything, we think it'd be best if you cooled things a little,' his dad said. He looked rather pleased with himself for having had the inspiration to put it this way.

He stared at them blankly and once more they glanced at each other in silent exchange. Suddenly he saw something he had never seen before, which was how well suited they were. They both wanted exactly the same thing out of life, which was for as little difficulty as possible. It seemed terrible and ironic that he should only be noticing this now, minutes after they had announced their separation. He tried to imagine how it had come about – what discussions, even arguments they must have had to reach the decision they no longer wanted to be part of one another's lives. But it was impossible, just as it was impossible to imagine them meeting, courting and getting married in the first place. How did people like his parents, so prim and resistant to every form of risk, ever manage to find each other? For they must have taken a risk, even if it was only the barest minimum, in order to have got together. To have made that initial appointment. To have leaned across and invaded personal space in order to instigate that very first kiss.

'I know it's difficult,' said his mum.

'We're thinking of you,' said his dad.

'I don't get what you're saying,' he told them, though he thought he was starting to get it perfectly well. But he wanted to make them spell it out. He wanted to see if he could get them to give up.

'We had a call from the school,' said his mum. 'They've been keeping an eye on you and Edward ...' She paused. Then, ever so quietly, she said, 'They're not sure it's a healthy relationship.'

He felt himself colour. Out of nowhere the anger and hurt he had been unable to feel at the news of their divorce came flooding into him. He felt furious – with the school, with other people, with his parents, but most of all with himself and with Edward, for feeling so superior, as if they could get away with whatever they liked.

'Why?!' he demanded hotly. 'What are you trying to say?!'

'You're just boys,' said his father, trying to be calming. 'No one's passing judgement. No one's saying it's against nature or anything like that. But you're both too young. That's all.'

'You shouldn't go over there any more,' said his mother in a frightened voice. 'We'd both prefer it if you came home after school now.'

He rounded on her. He was suddenly certain that she was the one who was to blame for all this.

'You've always hated him! You've no right to – you don't even know him!'

He pushed back his chair. It made a loud sound as it scraped against the floor, causing both of his parents to flinch.

'You can't tell me not to see him!' he shouted. 'You can't tell me not to do anything! You don't have the right –' he stuttered and then, without caring if it was logical, spat out, 'you're getting divorced!'

'No one's telling you anything,' said his father. 'We're simply asking you –'

'No!' he all but screamed, his hands clapping to his ears, refusing to hear any more. Then his body was carrying him out of the kitchen and up the stairs to his room and before he knew what he was doing he had slammed his door and was face down and shaking on his bed. It was the most dramatic exchange he had ever had with his parents and his skin itched and throbbed from the excitement.

It was some time before his heart slowed to its regular beat – long after he heard the footfall of his parents on the landing outside and his mum calling his name and the low murmur of his dad telling her to let him be and that he'd be more reasonable in the morning. He wondered where they were both sleeping now – if they were still sharing the same bed – and if not, for how long they had been sleeping separately. He wondered why they had ever got married in the first place and if it was possible they had once been recklessly in love. But most of all he wondered if things would be different now, and if he still had to worry about what they thought, or care if he disappointed them. Though he felt no regret, he knew that by their own standards they had let him down in some fundamental way.

But most of all he couldn't wait to see Edward and tell him what had happened.

The others arrive ten seconds later. Still dazed from the blow, he is dimly able to make out the ongoing fight in the darkness. He hears shouts, swearing and groans, and then Griselda yelling that the police are on the way followed by Big Pete roaring at the locals that they'd better keep away from his circus or he'll hunt each one of them down and fuck them up. There are catcalls from the locals, and one of them even laughs. He drags himself up and crawls through the dark towards the spot where he thinks Vlad is. A foot comes stamping down out of nowhere, narrowly missing his hand, and he rolls to the side just in time to avoid being crushed by a body, flailing under the force of somebody's fist. As he rolls he hits something large and soft which emits a light moan.

'Vlad?'

The only answer is another moan, and, not knowing what else to do, he throws his arms around the aerialist's body and holds him tightly to shield him from any further blows or falling bodies that might be coming their way.

But the fight is over. With the entire company more or less assembled, the local men are dramatically outnumbered. 'You fucking plebs!' Marie is screaming as they depart, her voice loud and high-pitched as a siren. 'Come on then if you reckon you're so tough! I'll kick your arses in so bad you won't shit right for the rest of your miserable inbred lives!' The locals flee across the field, shouting back insults about the carnies and how they'll get what's coming to them. 'Cunts!' snarls Big Pete, off to his left. He huddles into the limp body beside him, running his hand gently up the arm and to the face, where he touches something warm and sticky that he knows can only be blood.

'Vlad's here,' he croaks, his voice hoarse. 'He's hurt!'

A vague shape looms and he cringes. But the shape turns into Midge, the roustabout, who kneels over Vlad and starts to examine him with the light from his phone. Behind him Benny appears.

'You OK?' says Benny, gripping his shoulder. It occurs to him that it is the first occasion the roustabout has so much as spoken to him. But it is no time to be pleased.

'Fuck,' breathes Midge as he inspects the aerialist. 'This is serious. Help me carry him.'

Midge gets Vlad under the shoulders and Benny takes his feet. With a grunt of effort they stretcher him across the field to the big top. Off in the distance Marie can still be heard shouting insults at the locals, demanding that they come back so that she can single-handedly take them on and teach them the sort of lesson their mother didn't have it in her to teach. In the backstage area Benny and Midge lay Vlad down gently on the mat. The damage is horrific. Vlad's face has been beaten almost to a pulp, his forehead and mouth are leaking blood, and one of his eyes has swollen completely shut. There is blood on his jersey and more on his jeans. There are awed mutters of 'Fuck' and 'Jesus' from the people as they gather around.

'Vlad?' says Midge. 'Vlad, can you hear me?'

Vlad moans, and a shiver runs through his body. He feels tears of sheer fright welling up, and in a timorous voice he asks if anyone has called an ambulance. No one answers. Then someone pushes his way roughly through the company until he is standing over them. It is Big Pete, red-faced and breathing heavily. He stares at the battered body of the aerialist for a few seconds, the rage gathering visibly in the swollen veins at his temples.

'If they've ruined him, so help me God I'll track every one of 'em down and break their fucking legs,' he solemnly promises.

It was at the school's Christmas party that Paul first entered his life. Paul had started at the same time as Edward, but their paths had never crossed because unlike Edward he had gone straight into the top set and stayed there. Paul did a lot of extra-curricular activities, such as the Duke of Edinburgh Award, chess and orchestra, and he was a prefect of the English and music departments. As far as the rest of the school was concerned, Paul's defining attribute was that no one could touch him, since he was every teacher's star pupil, and any excessive picking on him would be akin to taking on the establishment. Outside of the school he would have been fair game, except that he never went out. As a result he had become all but invisible.

The party for their year was set up in the sports hall on a weekday afternoon near the end of term and attendance was mandatory. He and Edward stood to the side of the hall watching groups of boys who were eyeing up and jeering at groups of girls, who were in turn studiously ignoring the boys and throwing their limbs around to pop music. Some of the braver boys were tentatively mimicking the dance steps of the girls, and a few well-known couples had dispensed with the ritual altogether and were disappearing down one another's throats in the darker pockets of the hall, where teachers stalked them between songs and split them up again.

'Doesn't it make your eyes hurt?' said Edward with cultivated disdain as they watched one boy suddenly break into a dance like a chicken, wiggling his elbows back and forth and throwing himself into the middle of a group of dancing girls, producing a flurry of squeals. 'It makes me want to poke sharp objects through them!'

The boy slipped over and landed on his back, but he continued to dance, kicking his feet in the air. The girls all shrieked with laughter, and over by the door the two teachers who were standing sentry rolled their eyes and gave each other mutually despairing smiles.

'I've got pencils,' he offered.

'No,' Edward sighed dramatically. 'I don't want to risk vegetabli-sation. I'm going to the toilet to drown myself instead.'

He watched Edward make his way through the swaying girls and boys to the teachers, one of whom listened to his request with a dubious expression, as if he suspected him of some far shadier purpose, before jerking his head at the door.

'Hi,' said a voice to his side.

He turned to find Paul smiling up at him and clutching a plastic cup of Coke.

'Having fun?'

Paul had the look of someone who was in pain. His smile was so forced it was like a parody of a smile, and his shoulders were hunched as if he wanted to shrink into himself and hide. He was smaller than most of the other boys in the year, had straight mouse-coloured hair and wore glasses to boot, which made his appearance almost ridiculously nerdish, as if he had styled himself that way for a fancy-dress party.

'Not exactly,' he replied. 'It's like a fucking death camp.'

Paul's eyes widened as if he had said something shocking and hilarious, and he let out a short, near-hysterical laugh.

'Yes!' Paul cried. 'It's so awful, isn't it?'

He nodded and turned away. It was nasty of him, he knew, but there was something instantly dislikeable about Paul, a light of desperation in his eyes that repelled you. He knew that behind him Paul must be freezing up, could imagine his intake of breath, could feel the twin flashes of hurt and anger. He rested his eyes on the pull-out climbing frame latched to the opposite wall, which had been threaded through with streamers of tinsel, and told himself it was mean, that he should turn back round and be nice to Paul. But when he looked behind him again Paul was nowhere to be seen.

★   ★   ★

He will not see the paper until late afternoon, having been busy with his exercises. He will be crossing the kitchen to make some food when his eye will fall across it poking through the letter box. He will have not cancelled his mother's subscription, and a strange, sick sense of apprehension will propel him to pluck out the paper and open it. On the third page there will be the headline THE MAN WHO BUILT HIS VERY OWN CIRCUS, above a picture of his trapeze taken with a telephoto lens through the window of the living room. It will be followed by an article about him. The article will begin with the line, 'Concerned neighbours reported strange noises from next door. But never in their wildest dreams did they have any notion of what was taking place . . .' There will be interviews with the neighbours, Mrs Goodly and Mrs Lenard, who respectively say what a shame and a shock it is. His eyes will haze at this point and he will be able to read no more. His pulse will increase with fury beyond reason, and before even giving a thought to what he is doing he will have stormed out the front door and onto the lawn and will be glaring about in all directions of the neighbourhood. Then he will catch sight of movement on one of the lawns further down the road. He will need no more incitement.

'Are you happy now?' he will screech.

In the end it is Big Pete who drives Vlad to the hospital, himself and Benny in the back with Vlad propped up between them and swaddled in coats and scarves like a mummy. Big Pete is quiet and broods the entire thirty minutes of the drive, producing only the occasional snort while Benny fills the cold air of the unheated truck with cigarette smoke. He cradles Vlad in his arms and whispers to him that he isn't to worry, he is going to be just fine. Now and then Big Pete glances round at the aerialist, and he feels his eyes passing over him and inspecting him also. He thinks Big Pete is probably sickened by the way he is behaving, by this further evidence of his softness, but he does not care – he cares only about the trembling body beside him.

They wait for almost an hour to be seen in the accident and emergency clinic, and are eventually shown into a large room full of beds where a young doctor who cannot be more than thirty sits Vlad down, examines him, and then to everyone's disbelief pronounces him to be bruised but otherwise uninjured. Vlad groans every time the doctor touches him, and lets out a faint string of curses in Romanian at the diagnosis. His face by now is almost uniform damson purple.

'But look at him,' he cries. 'Shouldn't you at least X-ray him?'

'He's taken some knocks, that's all,' says the doctor wearily, who despite being young has a look in his eyes as if he has lived a hundred years and is weary of other people thinking they know better than he does. 'Take him home and let him get a good night's rest. And put an ice pack on that eye. We'll give you something for the swelling.'

'But don't you even want to keep him here for observation?'

'In a word, no.'

He opens his mouth to protest, but realises there is nothing he can say to this man, who has the absolute authority to declare what should and shouldn't be done. Big Pete lays a hand gently on his shoulder. In ordinary circumstances this might make him jump, it being the first physical contact they've ever had, but in this instance he doesn't even notice.

'You heard the kid,' says Big Pete, eliciting a resentful look from the doctor. His voice is kind and compassionate, a tone he wouldn't have believed the ringmaster capable of were he not hearing it with his own ears. 'Old Vlad here's just being a drama queen, trying to get out of next week's shows. What he needs is a good night's kip.'

He peers into Big Pete's face in amazement, at the small permanently angry eyes above the huge fleshy red cheeks and the broad bulbous nose. The amazement recedes and he wonders vaguely who this man really is beneath his tough exterior.

'C'mon, let's go,' says Big Pete.

That night he watches over Vlad like a fretful mother over a sickly child, listening for the slightest murmur of discontent. Vlad meanwhile sleeps like a log, so still and sound as to be almost dead. The following morning he does not wake up until late, and so they lie there with the white sunlight streaking through the little window, listening to the sounds of the others striking the big top.

He puts his ear to Vlad's chest and hears the steady thump of life from within, and he whispers experimentally, in a voice so soft the words feel like nothing more than a strand of gossamer on his lips, 'I love you.' Vlad says nothing, though whether it is because he is asleep, has not heard or is choosing not to reply he does not know.

After the party he would have forgotten all about Paul, except that Paul had no intention of being forgotten about, and the following week Edward told him at the beginning of class there was someone he wanted him to meet.

'Who is it?'

'You'll see.'

He rolled his eyes but Edward smiled mysteriously and refused to say anything more. When the bell rang Edward took him by the sleeve and he followed him outside to the shed where the school's games equipment was kept. Edward looked dramatically from side to side as if to check they were not being followed and then, his finger on his lips, led him round the back.

Paul was standing there staring at the wall, hands clasped in front of him, his straight back and mousy hair unmistakable even from behind. He turned as they arrived. He had a serious expression, as if they had official business to conduct.

'What's going on?' he said, looking from Paul to Edward.

'Paul's gay,' said Edward, in the blunt, plain-speaking style he sometimes liked to adopt. 'He has no friends and wants to hang out with us.'

Paul smiled at him and he thought how complacent he looked. He knew instantly he didn't want Paul to be their friend. He didn't want him to join them on their wanderings, or sit with them at lunchtime or listen in on their conversations and contribute his own opinions. But most of all he didn't want Paul to be gay. He had the feeling it was part of some sort of conspiracy of Paul's to pull them apart.

'Prove it,' he said.

Paul lost his smile and gaped. He much preferred this expression on Paul's face.

'How can he do that?' said Edward, sounding intrigued.

'I don't know,' he admitted. 'But if he's the same as us then he should have to prove it, don't you think? Why should we take a risk?'

'I can't prove it!' cried Paul, shocked. 'That's not the sort of thing you can prove!'

'I know,' he said, ignoring him. 'He has to kiss another boy.'

At this Paul turned pale with fright. Edward looked thoughtful.

'That's an interesting idea, but the only boys who'd let him kiss them are you and me.'

He hadn't thought of this. In fact he'd hoped Edward would have a better idea – or at least another suggestion – but Edward was looking at him expectantly and he suddenly realised he had just dug himself a hole, one he could not shovel his way out of. He glanced back at Paul, who was looking between them, aghast.

'Fine then,' he said. 'We'll both kiss him and see what happens.'

Paul looked rooted to the spot in horror, and he wanted to laugh at the sight. Edward seemed to be giving the matter serious consideration.

'Look,' said Paul, sounding desperate and staring solely at him, 'I don't need to prove anything and I'm not kissing you. Just because I'm gay doesn't mean I fancy you!'

But it was Paul's prim reaction that enabled him to boldly reply, 'If you can't kiss me then you're not gay, you're a homophobe, and there's no way that I'm hanging out with a homophobe.'

He smiled maliciously. Paul looked like a fawn that was about to be slaughtered and roasted, his eyes wide open, the size of two penny coins.

'Fine!' Paul said suddenly. 'Come here then!'

Without another second of hesitation Paul stepped towards him, screwed up his face, and then leaned in. Since there was no backing down he closed his eyes and a second later he felt Paul's lips touch against his own. It was the lightest of touches, no more present than a breeze, for instantly Paul jumped back as if he had been scorched. He opened his eyes to see Paul blushing furiously and Edward sniggering.

'Brilliant!' Edward proclaimed, stepping forward and wrapping a congratulatory arm around Paul's shoulders. 'After that display of passion there can be no doubt you're a fag of the highest calibre!'

Paul shook him off violently. His skin was now scarlet and his eyes flashed daggers.

'You're both so bloody juvenile!' he screeched. 'I hate you!'

With these words Paul fled.

He looked over at Edward and gave a shrug as if to say that was that. But in reality he was quivering slightly. He had been a little scared of the kiss too, and he was glad Paul had bottled it.

'Oh well,' he said, trying to sound nonchalant.

Edward raised an eyebrow at him. He had the feeling Edward knew perfectly well that he disliked Paul and didn't want him to be their friend. Yet he also had the sense that Edward was not exactly cross about it, but even rather pleased.

For the following week Vlad complains to everyone who will listen of agonising pains in his chest every time he moves and insists he cannot possibly perform. Grudgingly Big Pete agrees to a couple of days' recovery, but he visits each morning to see how the aerialist is doing and when he opens the door the ringmaster always greets him with a big smile. He is somewhat unnerved by the smile, which looks so difficult for Big Pete to sustain, and only nods in reply and stands back so he can make his way inside the little compartment.

'How's the invalid today?' jokes Big Pete, peering hopefully at the lump under the blankets. 'Any better?'

In answer Vlad only groans and pushes back the cover so Big Pete can see how bad his face looks. It does look impressively bad still – his left eye has become a black mound, the skin at the corners yellow as if with jaundice. Big Pete grimaces.

'Well, no hurry, no hurry at all. You just concentrate on getting better. Won't have no one say it of Big Pete he doesn't take care of his own, eh?'

At the door Big Pete turns to him.

'You make sure he gets well, you hear?' the ringmaster says to him in what might be meant as an avuncular tone. He nods again to the ringmaster, afraid that if he answers Big Pete will somehow morph into his usual volcanic self and add a string of expletives. At Big Pete's instruction Marie has let him off most of his duties while he is looking after Vlad, although she makes it clear she thinks Vlad is wasting everybody's time.

'That layabout was born to take the piss,' she sighs when he comes to collect the mop for the toilets, a chore she insists he continue to do because she claims nobody else does it properly. 'You ask me, what 'e needs is a good kick up the backside. Has my dumb 'usband even thought to ask 'im why those inbreds started on 'im in the first place?'

Secretly he knows Marie is right about Vlad. After the second day the swelling around his eye does not look nearly so bad, and so Vlad takes out his stage paint and dabs it with violet and rouge and yellow to make it appear awful again. The pain in the aerialist's chest was always a fabrication, he suspects, since although there is a smattering of bruises he has no problem writhing around in bed when they have sex. But Marie's last comment is what disturbs him. He knows she has a point.

By the fourth day of Vlad's recuperation Big Pete begins to lose patience. His 'Good morning' is gruffer than before and he peers at Vlad's injury critically, muttering about how they should go and get him checked out again, it being suddenly obvious that the 'spotty teenager' who saw him knew 'fuck all about medicine'. Vlad only groans in response and in a weak voice promises he'll be all right in a day or so.

'Do you think it's a good idea to lie about this?' he asks Vlad once Big Pete has gone. In response the aerialist throws his head back and lets out a hoot of laughter, then tosses away the sheet and yanks him towards him. 'Fuck me hard,' Vlad orders him, pushing his legs wide around his crotch.

Sex with Vlad has not changed since he joined the company. Vlad is perfectly capable of having an orgasm, but his penis still swells only a little and then quivers before he ejaculates. 'An accident on the trapeze bar . . .' Vlad has whispered to him, but will not say more, merely putting his finger to his lips and shaking his head as if to say it does not bear thinking about. He wonders if the aerialist has seen a doctor, and supposes he must have heard of Viagra, but really he does not mind. The aerialist's favourite activity in bed is to lock his lips around his penis and suck, something Vlad never tires of doing and he does not tire of either. When he penetrates Vlad, the aerialist becomes almost wild – but his bouts of thrashing are always tempered with moments of extreme tenderness, when Vlad will pull himself up and hold onto him tightly, staring into his eyes with such intensity it is as if he is searching desperately for something vital yet indefinable, even to himself. These moments are what he loves most about being with the aerialist.

'Can I ask you something?' he says when they are finished and are lying across one another, a mesh of limbs and panting.

'Ask me anything, my love.'

'How come those men were fighting you?'

'Eh? What are you saying?'

Vlad is instantly on the alert.

'I mean ... how come you were – talking to them in the first place?'

'They were being friendly. Said they wanted to know more about the circus. I was trying to be a nice guy. Shows what you get!'

Vlad leans over him and reaches for a packet of cigarettes. It seems to him that the aerialist is avoiding looking at him in the face. He waits until Vlad has lit one and puffed out a cloud of smoke before asking, 'What sort of things did they want to know more about?'

Vlad coughs and turns to him. His eyes flash and he recognises the danger signs of the aerialist's quick temper.

'What is this? An inquisition?'

'No, I –'

'You think that I must have asked for them to beat me up?'

'Of course not!'

'Then how about you shut your fucking hole?'

He swallows down his questions, leans back into the pillow and closes his eyes. A minute later Vlad lies back too, his whole body softening as he wraps his free arm around his shoulders.

He asks the aerialist nothing more, but there is something about it that continues to bother him, long after Vlad has put out his cigarette and started to snore peacefully away beside him. He stares up at the nicotine-stained ceiling of the caravan and although he will not admit it to himself, in his bones he knows perfectly well what Vlad thought he was doing out in the dark field with those men.

There will be a pounding at the door, as if an elephant is trying to break in. He will come running down the stairs, expecting another reporter, ready to use his fists to repel them if necessary this time. But when he flings open the door he will see a familiar face, the same age but without his smattering of crow's feet or worry lines, tanned almost orange from hours dedicated to the sunbed.

'Hi,' Paul will say. He will be panting slightly and rubbing his knuckles. 'I've been banging on your door for ten minutes.'

'Hi,' he will say. Then, 'Sorry.'

For a few seconds neither of them will say anything more. They will simply stand opposite one another, as if each is waiting for the other to make the first move. Then, without warning, Paul will launch himself at him and wrap his arms around him in a great bear hug, squeezing him as tight as his gym-built muscles will allow.

'It's good to see you!' Paul will exclaim. 'I called about a billion times but you never answer. Then I sent about a thousand emails and still nothing! I thought maybe you'd died until I saw that article – did you know you were on the BBC website? Of course I didn't believe any of it –'

At this point Paul will look past his shoulder and into the house, where he will have a full view of the missing floor and the trapeze rig. Paul will push him away and stare, his jaw plummeting two inches.

'Oh my sweet Lord!' Paul will breathe, shaking his head dramatically from side to side. 'It is true . . . you've really gone and flipped out, haven't you?'

By the end of the week Big Pete's good humour is all used up. Instead of greeting him in the morning the ringmaster merely pushes him roughly aside as if he were no more than a curtain in the way and strides purposefully into the caravan. Without speaking Big Pete raises his hand and brings it down hard on the hillock of blankets, causing Vlad to let out a roar and throw the covers back in fury.

'You get out of bed and start training, you useless lying lump of shit!' Big Pete bellows. 'You're going on tonight and that's all there is to it! And tell your fairy chum here' – Big Pete jerks his thumb in his direction – 'this ain't no charity I'm running and if he wants to stick around he'd better start pulling his fucking weight!'

After he has stormed off Vlad pulls himself out of the bed with a groan. The bruises on his chest have completely disappeared now and when he washes the make-up off his face there is only a slight shading left around his eye, as if a permanent shadow had been cast across it. He smiles at the aerialist.

'Suppose I'd better get to work.'

'Poor us,' says Vlad mournfully before pulling him close for a kiss. 'The holiday is over already.'

He promises to help Vlad stretch later on and pulls on his shoes and a T-shirt. On his way to visit Marie to find out what chores need doing he passes by the clown's caravan, which sits several feet further out of the company's circle than any of the others, as if he were trying to distance himself from them as much as possible. He has not seen the clown for a while and is startled by the sight of his ravaged face and Mohican, and the demonic smirk that instantly appears as he sets down his juggling balls and nods at him as if to say good morning. He nods back warily. He understands enough now to know that nobody from the company much likes the clown.

'And how's the star of our little circus coming along?'

The words do not seem to come from his mouth, but rather from a space beyond his smirk, which seems thinner and more like a battle-worn mask than ever. There is so much bitterness in the clown's dark eyes that he decides not even to acknowledge him, recovers his composure and passes by without a word.

'Off to see the boss?' calls the clown after him. 'Do give him my very best and tell him what a fine old time I've been having, waiting around doing nothing while you screw the unicycle!'

As he gets closer to Big Pete and Marie's trailer he becomes aware of a group gathered outside, listening to raised voices coming from within; screams of fury, followed by the unmistakable sounds of household items shattering.

'What's going on?' he asks.

At first it seems as if everyone is just going to ignore him as per usual, and he feels himself flush. There is another crash from inside and the sound of Marie screeching 'Bastard!' over and over. Then someone in the crowd turns – it is Midge, a smouldering roll-up attached by spittle to his lower lip – and says in a deep conspiratorial voice, 'Ain't never seen 'em go at it like this. Gonna bring down the whole show.' He breathes a small sigh of relief at being noticed, and peers with the others at the shapes passing behind the blinds of the trailer windows.

Suddenly Big Pete throws open the door. Some of the people try to look away, as if there might be some other reason why they are all gathered there outside like a convention of nosy neighbours, but most simply applaud as if they were an ecstatically pleased audience. He watches as Big Pete's face turns from red to purple and his cheeks swell to even greater proportions than usual.

'Get out of here, you bunch of talentless fucks!' shrieks Big Pete, shaking his fist at them. 'Get out of here before I fire the whole fucking lot of you!'

The crowd instantly disperses, hurrying off to their respective caravans while Big Pete continues swearing and threatening about how he will leave them stranded at the next town. But beyond Big Pete's yells and threats can be heard the curiously heart-rending sound of Marie sobbing.

'Well, I have to say I like your improvements very much,' Paul will say, accepting the mug he offers him. 'I always thought this place was rather too drab.'

He will smile.

'Thank you for coming all this way out to see me.'

'Right then,' Paul will say, assuming a militant tone. 'As simply as you can, I want you to tell me what the hell is going on.'

He will admire the easy familiarity of Paul's manner of speaking. It will feel like a long time since he has seen a friend. But friend or not, he will see no way to explain himself that Paul, with his hedonistic London life of clubs and gyms and casual sex, will be able to comprehend.

'There's nothing going on,' he will reply. 'I'm just doing what I want to do. That's all there is to it.'

'Sweetheart,' Paul will say patiently, 'there is no "all there is to it" about what's been happening in there —' He will jerk his thumb in the direction of the kitchen. 'It's like an assault course. You're not in training for the Foreign Legion by any chance, are you?'

'I like your hair,' he will say to change the subject. Since he last saw Paul it has been cut into a spiky plant-like shape and bleached blond at the ends, giving Paul's head the look of an exotic breed of mushroom.

'Thanks!'

Paul will raise his hand to his head as if to check it is still there.

'I'm still getting used to it. Of course everyone else thinks it looks gay. And by gay they mean crap.'

'No, it's great,' he will say, though privately he will think everyone else is quite right. 'Don't listen to them.'

'I never do, but all the same … one does get paranoid. But enough about my do. You've become quite a sensation. At least all over the Internet anyway!'

He will let out a 'humph' and look at the floor.

'Come come,' Paul will coax. 'Tell Paul everything.'

'It's really nobody's business but mine,' he will say finally. 'I didn't ask them to write that article. I wish they hadn't.'

Paul will give him a long-suffering smile, as if he is being a delightfully dense child.

'Sweetheart, you're subverting the very essence of suburbia. How do you expect people to react? You're rubbing their own boring trapezeless kitchens in their faces. You can't be surprised if they're a little – what's the word? – resistant.'

To this he will laugh. It will surprise him, his own laugh, at how natural and simple it feels, and he will feel a rush of affection for Paul, who will grin lopsidedly. Then the grin will fade, and so will his laugh, because they will both know that at the heart of the matter lies something deadly serious.

'Darling,' Paul will say softly, 'have you really gone crazy? Are you in need of professional care? Should I be staging an intervention or something?' Paul will pause before adding, 'It's not because of me, is it?'

This, he will know, is Paul's real question. The reason he has come all the way from London to see him. Quickly he will let out an exaggerated groan and shake his head.

'Not everything in this world is about you.'

Paul will immediately pretend to look shocked.

'Really?'

'Really.'

Paul will relax, slumping into his chair.

'Thank fuck!'

Then Paul will surprise him by leaning forward and appraising him slowly from the feet up. He will feel his eyes passing over him as if taking in every inch and when Paul's eyes finally come to rest on his face and meet his own gaze, he will be startled. It will be as if Paul knows it cannot be as simple as this – as if he will be trying to say that he understands and is sorry. But then Paul will roll his eyes up towards the ceiling and sigh loudly.

'Well, it's your life,' Paul will say reflectively. 'I just hope that contraption in there has some safety features.'

Without further ado Paul will start to tell him about the young man he is seeing, who he will say has been acting like such a diva he is already considering dumping him. It will be incredible to him, this ease with which Paul will talk of his life – of the clothes he will be considering investing in, of the complete and utter bitch a certain friend will have morphed into since beginning a trial for a new cancer drug, of the stranger he will have sucked off last Friday night who tried to hit him up for money afterwards. He will listen and smile and laugh and pretend to look outraged. But for once he will not feel envious or sorry for himself. Such feelings will have no basis in his world – not any more.

He was expecting Christmas to be strange and awkward without his father but it did not feel particularly different in the end, except that fewer distant relatives dropped by on their way to visit other distant relatives, stopping in for annual reports over a cup of tea and a mince pie. His mother still spent every day of the holiday cleaning, scrubbing and cooking, and when he grudgingly offered to help she smiled distractedly and said she'd prefer it if he got out from under her toes. The house had been transferred into her name now, and his dad had finally moved out of the bedsit in Swindon he'd been living in since September and had taken a lease on a small chilly flat, which he reluctantly visited on Boxing Day.

'It's not much,' said his dad with a shrug after giving him a tour of the three rooms that constituted the flat, then showing him the pull-out sofa bed where he would be sleeping that night. 'But then

I'm not here much either. Didn't make any sense to get somewhere bigger.'

He looked over at the plastic Christmas tree his dad had put in the corner, decorated with a few gaudy pink and red baubles, and at the token strand of silver tinsel he had Blu-tacked above the front door. Apart from the bed and a couple of stools at the sidebar, the flat was otherwise unfurnished. It seemed so pathetically spartan that he giggled – a thin trill. His dad peered at him but did not ask what was so funny, and he understood from this that his father was no more pleased about his visit than he was.

'I thought everything would be different when he moved out, but nothing's changed at all really,' he told Edward when they met at Edward's house the following day. 'Funny, but I just don't seem to care. I guess that makes me a bastard or something?'

Edward didn't reply at once, and he looked over in case he was laughing at him. But he wasn't. Rather he was staring into the dark recesses of the den with a solemn look on his face, as if lost in thought. Eventually Edward heaved a long sigh.

'You're just like me,' Edward said with authority. 'We don't really have homes. We never did. That's how we were born.'

He did not think Edward's statement overblown – rather he was thrilled at being lumped into the same category of person as Edward. Secretly he felt at times like an impostor, running around with this boy who had seen, done and experienced everything already, pretending he was the same when in reality he knew himself to be a product of ordinariness at its most bland and inoffensive. He sometimes scared himself by imagining that the intense feelings he had for Edward were unrequited, that the day would come when Edward would get bored of him and dismiss him with a flick of his hand, revealing that he had only ever been tolerating his presence while waiting for something better to come along. To be told he was the same as Edward by Edward himself, and to be looked at with such sincerity it made his cheeks flush boiling hot with embarrassment – it was so wonderful he wanted to cry. Instead he confined himself to a subtle nod, as if all along it was what he had been thinking too.

He waits for an hour, until Big Pete has driven off into the local town for supplies, then returns to the trailer to see Marie. Biting his lip, he knocks on the door. There is no answer, but without the keys to the box office, he can get none of the cleaning materials, and the risk of being yelled at later outweighs his fear, so he turns the handle and timidly pokes his head inside.

'Hello?'

The inside of the trailer is dark and quiet. He takes another step, thinking to turn on the lights and see if there is somewhere obvious the keys might be kept, but just then there is a rustling sound and a shadowy figure emerges. As she passes the window the light from outside reveals that Marie's silk dressing gown is dramatically torn across one shoulder, and that her heavily made-up eyes have streamed lines of mascara down her cheeks, so that it looks as if she has been crying tears of ink.

'Sorry,' he says. 'I came for the keys.'

She stares at him and for a few seconds he braces himself to be screamed at. But Marie only nods.

'Yeah,' she says. 'I'll get them.'

She begins to cry and, not knowing what else to do, he steps forward and pats her shoulder. Marie tenses for a second, then reaches out and pulls him to her in a tight embrace. He is so surprised he does not hug her back at first, merely stands there with Big Pete's wife weeping and clinging on to him as if for dear life.

'Fuck,' she mutters after a while, pulling him back into the darkness, then hurrying around him and closing the door. 'Everyone'll see!'

She switches on the light. He blinks. It is the first time he has been inside the trailer and he is amazed at how large it is – far more spacious than its outside appearance indicates, like the Tardis. He is impressed by how much it resembles the inside of a real house. The trailer has been divided into three areas – before him is a living-room area with a long L-shaped sofa, a Persian rug and a little table with a portable TV on it. Behind the sofa is a kitchenette, complete with a sideboard and mini bar, containing a sink, an oven, a hob, a fridge and a microwave. Across from the kitchenette, at the other side of the space, is a long dining table with five chairs around it. Some shelves by the window hold books, folders and an array of little glass figurines. There are three small oil paintings on the walls, one depicting a vase of flowers, one depicting a sunny meadow, and one featuring a beautiful gypsy girl with jet-black hair, a small smile on her pouty red lips as she stares excitedly out into the space before her. There is a divide with a door in it at the far end, which he guesses must lead to Big Pete and Marie's bedroom, and another small door opens to one side which he thinks must be the bathroom – Vlad has told him Big Pete and Marie's trailer is the only one with its own shower facility. Everything in the space is immaculately clean and tidy, as if the owners lived in the constant expectation of important visitors.

'What a nice place!'

Marie ignores him and goes to the table where she throws herself into one of the chairs and blows her nose loudly. He stands uncomfortably by the entrance, unsure of what to do.

'Sit down,' says Marie.

There is no question of disobeying, though he is petrified that at any minute will come the sound of Big Pete's truck as he returns from town, and he does not want to be found here or be caught between them during another blow-up. He sits, waiting for Marie to say something, looking at the portrait of the gypsy girl.

'That's me, you know,' says Marie eventually. 'Not that you'd think it now, eh?'

The girl in the picture looks nothing like Marie.

'Sixteen years old. Pretty, ain't I? Those are the days when you think the world's your bloody oyster, know what I mean? You must have had 'em too. Everyone does at some point in their lives.'

He nods.

'Me's proper circus. Born and raised. Not like that jerk of an 'usband of mine. Oh, 'e wishes he was, that's for sure, but 'e's just another stupid josser, like all the rest of you on this half-arsed show. My family never liked 'im. When 'e said he wanted to run 'is own show they thought 'e was trying to do 'em out of business — that's a joke! But of course I supported 'im. Thought it would be magical, our very own circus . . .

'Everyone thinks it's all very thrilling, this moving back and forth all the time, the life on wheels, the make-up and the stupid shiny costumes. Admit it, even with all the work, you still reckon there's something to it, don't ya? I've seen 'ow you look at 'em. Like they's fairy folk or something.'

He opens his mouth to deny it, but Marie isn't interested.

'I bought into that exact same crap meself, and no one should know better than I does just what crap it is. Now look what's 'appened. Five years on and we're still struggling, still got fuck all, still on the brink of going bankrupt. That idiot with 'is stupid temper and 'is daft ideas about what the people want. 'E don't know 'ow to work our laundry machine, let alone run this bloody operation.'

There is another pause. He does not know what to do with this information she is giving him and so he sits and waits with an awkward smile. Marie seems to be lost in her own world anyway. She heaves a long deep sigh.

'I been on circuses all me life, since I was born, and sometimes what I'd really like to do is just stay put. Put me feet up and not 'ave to worry no more about fucking costumes blowing away, or the tent caving in, or flat tyres at three o'clock in the morning, or the aerialist falling on top of a punter ... any of that bollocks. Sometimes I reckon what I'd really like to do is quit!'

She announces this with fury, then flicks her eyes towards him as if she has suddenly become aware of who exactly it is she's been addressing. Abruptly her expression goes cold, as if a mask were descending over her face. She stands up, sending her chair ricocheting off the wall behind her.

'I'll get you the keys,' she mutters.

★   ★   ★

One afternoon a few days before school recommenced, he came home and his mum told him that a friend of his was waiting for him in his room. He knew instantly, even before she clarified it, that it was Paul. His mum looked pleased.

'He seems like a really nice boy,' she said.

Contained within her statement was the unsaid opinion that Edward was not such a nice boy, but he did not pause to glare at her for it. She had been cleaning the kitchen again, he noticed, and he knew this was not normal behaviour because she had spent all the previous day cleaning it too.

He took the steps two at a time and threw open the door to his room. Paul was sitting on his bed reading one of the porn magazines he had borrowed from Edward, which he no longer bothered to conceal under his mattress because his mum had at long last agreed that his room was his private space and promised never to enter without his permission.

'What the hell do you think you're doing?'

Paul looked up at him. A split second of guilt showed on his face, but it vanished almost immediately as he straightened his neck and pursed his lips. He put down the porn magazine and stood up.

'I've come because I want –'

'Get out!' he shouted. 'Get the hell out!'

In response Paul shut his eyes and clenched his fists. A bead of perspiration appeared above his left eyebrow and slid suddenly in a dramatic arc down to his cheek. Paul looked so ridiculous that his fury vanished and he burst out laughing.

'Oh God,' he said. 'Look – I don't want you here, OK?'

Paul opened his eyes and stared at him.

'Why do you hate me so much?' Paul said. 'What did I do?'

He was stumped by the question. He could not explain that it was greed essentially – that he prized Edward above all other things and did not want to share him. That the last thing he wanted to do was invite a stranger into the exclusive world he had built with Edward. Yet somehow he suspected Paul already knew this.

'It isn't anything you've done,' he said finally. 'It's just that you and I are very different people and I don't think we can get along.'

There was a certain perverse pleasure in being able to say this to someone – especially someone he did not like. Paul turned silently away and faced the wall, his fists clenching up again and his body trembling. He felt a stab of pity for Paul then, and for a second he even wondered if he wasn't being ridiculous, treating this feeble and insignificant creature as if he was some sort of threat.

'Look, I'm sorry,' he heard himself say with more authority than he felt. 'It's not your fault. But that's just the way it is.'

'Only because you've decided so!' responded Paul bitterly. 'You could just change your mind – it wouldn't cost you anything, you know!'

From downstairs came the noise of suctioning air – his mum was vacuuming again.

'Why do you want to go round with us anyway?' he said, wishing Paul would just leave. 'Why is it so important?'

'Because I'm gay like you are and there's no one else!'

Paul turned back to face him passionately.

'All I'm asking is that you give me a chance. A chance! If you still don't like me after that then I'll leave you alone and it'll be like I never bothered you in the first place!'

Paul's eyes bulged slightly. He seemed to be trying to use will-power to force him to say yes. He debated. Each passing second seemed to gather momentum until it was as if his answer would be of such consequence it would go down in history.

'All right,' he sighed. 'But no promises.'

Paul's face positively radiated happiness and he thought that perhaps he'd done the right thing after all. Paul stepped across the room and held out his hand. It was a clichéd gesture, he thought, and combined with Paul's smile it made him suddenly regret being persuaded. But it was too late to change his mind. Feeling stupid, he raised his hand and let Paul shake it.

At the door Paul will pause and peer around at the neighbourhood, at the surrounding gardens with their tasteful pine gazebos, freshly mown lawns and little stone sculptures of fauns and dwarves that peep tentatively out from beds of poppies and roses.

'God,' Paul will say. 'It's been so long, I'd almost forgotten what this place was like. It really does feel like something out of a horror film, doesn't it? You can just see a serial killer hiding out behind that hibiscus.'

He will smile, but by now he will just want Paul to go, to get back in his car and drive off back to his big fast life in the city and leave him to concentrate on his own tiny world.

'You know,' Paul will say, oblivious to his impatience, 'there's nothing to say you have to stay on here.'

He will deliberately look down at the front step and not respond. But Paul will not read his body language and will cheer-ily continue.

'You could sell up and move to London. Find a nice little pad, maybe somewhere near me. Even with your – ah – let's say alterations, I'm sure this place must have some value. And you don't have to stick around, do you? I mean, your mum doesn't exactly need you any more –'

'I don't want to move to London,' he will say sharply.

Paul will be startled and will look at him closely.

'You're really OK, aren't you?'

'Yes.'

Paul will exhale, making a sound that is half a sigh and half a raspberry. Then he will lean towards him and envelop him in another bear hug, shaking him from side to side as he squeezes, then letting go and air-kissing him on both cheeks.

'You let me know if you need anything? And don't turn all Norma Desmond or anything, holed up here on your lonesome, OK?'

'I won't.'

'Bye-ee then.'

'Bye.'

He will watch Paul amble down the road to his car. As he does Mrs Lenard from the bottom of the road will come out of her house with a shopping basket and squint over the hedge at them. Paul will give her a big wave as he gets into his car. Confused and obviously trying to work out if she knows him, she will half wave back. Then, just before Paul's hand disappears inside, it will turn upside down and give her the finger. Mrs Lenard's face will register outrage as Paul revs the engine and drives off up the road honking his horn.

★　　★　　★

Audiences have begun to dwindle. In the previous two sites the crowds filled less than thirty per cent of the big top, and Big Pete has snarled at the company that if they do not start putting their backs into promoting the show, they can expect it to fold. Whether or not the threat is real seems to make little difference, as people make no more effort than before, and when Big Pete yells at the bleary-eyed and hung-over performers each morning to come with him into town and hand out flyers, they excuse themselves on the grounds that they have to practise, leaving Big Pete to drive in and do it himself. The performers rarely do much practise though, and it is obvious none of them don't have the time. They just do not want to do it, and the aerialist is no exception.

'Let him promote his own fucking circus,' Vlad yawns. 'What am I supposed to be? A street entertainer?'

Sometimes Big Pete takes him along in lieu of anyone else, and waits in the truck smoking furiously while he jumps out and Blu-tacks posters onto the doors of shops and the porches of village halls and onto bus shelters. If he takes longer than a minute Big Pete loses patience, and yells at him to get his arse back in the truck, so that the serene village street is suddenly filled with ugly noise and people poking their heads out of their windows to see what the commotion is about.

'Not one of those lazy bastards gives a shit,' Big Pete hisses under his breath as they drive back to the circus. 'No loyalty. You put your back in, you work day in day out all year, and this is what you get.'

Big Pete often complains to him, criticising the company. The ringmaster assumes that because he does not answer back his silence denotes agreement, and although he dislikes Big Pete, he cannot help feeling slightly sorry for him now too, with his puffed-up temper tantrums and sudden attempted transitions into being everyone's best friend.

It is obvious to people that the ringmaster's marriage is on the rocks. Marie never comes out of the trailer except at show times, in order to run her expert eye over the costumes and touch up make-up. The second it is time for the curtain call she hurries off and is not seen again until the following day's matinée. He has heard from various sources, including Vlad, Griselda and the roustabouts, that she has not stopped arguing with Big Pete since the season began. Rumour has it she is threatening to leave and he has responded by shouting at the top of his lungs that nothing would please him more.

'Fair play to Big Pete, he has tried to do something different with this,' says Franka one afternoon, gesturing to the surrounding trailers and the half-erected big top, which sits before them like a giant navy mushroom cloud. She and Griselda are showing him their routine for stretching, a series of static positions that incorporate yoga, Pilates and Alexander technique, showcasing their impressive flexibility. 'Trouble is it doesn't work. People – especially the kids – they don't want to see contemporary performers like us, they want to see people do tricks – ta da! – the end.'

'Big Pete wants to be an artist,' asserts Griselda. 'He thinks he's being classy and pushing the boundaries. But he's losing money. We're not trad enough. These little towns, they're not interested in art. They want funny clowns and girls with big tits being sawed in half. Not aerial dance on the tissu and corde lisse . . . now push your back leg out – like so.'

He tries to copy her and a pain like he has never known before shoots down his thigh. He rolls off the mat and onto the grass with a yelp and Griselda and Franka smile knowingly at one another. Over at the showers the contortionist waves to them and they wave back. He feels included in the wave and waves too, and nobody looks at him as if he is crazy. People have accepted him as a piece of the ongoing madness around them in his own right – and he allows himself to imagine that to them he is the guy who ran away with the circus, no longer just some plaything picked up by the slutty lead act, who everyone laughs at because they are waiting for him to get fed up and leave.

It has been two months now since he left his home town, got in his car and chased after the aerialist. When Vlad is asleep he some-times gets up and goes to the little window and peers out at the big top and the surrounding circle of caravans and trailers, and allows himself to indulge in the thrill of merely being here, of belonging. He sometimes even thinks he could be happy to call this sort of world his home.

The day after Paul's visit, he went and met him in town and together they walked to Edward's house. He was wary about taking Paul there, but he did not know what else to do with him.

On the way over Paul would not shut up. He chattered on excit-edly about what a lame place the town was for teenagers, how it had nothing to offer them, and how it was no wonder they all took to drinking and graffiti. He went on about how much he hated the other boys at school and his two older brothers who bullied him. He described how he couldn't wait until he was at university because that was when life would really begin. On and on Paul went, until finally he looked over his shoulder at him and said, 'You know, you might get less out of breath if you didn't talk so bloody much.'

Paul looked aghast for a second, then red and angry. He seemed to be about to say something, but then, as if remembering he was on probation, he sucked his lower lip into his mouth, dropped his head, and didn't say another word for the rest of the way.

When Edward answered the door he looked horrified for a split second at the sight of Paul, but he quickly hid it with a smile.

'So, we have a virgin to sacrifice – excellent!'

Edward stepped back and threw out his arm in an exaggerated welcome. Paul giggled, unable to hide his pleasure, and he resisted an urge to make another cutting remark. It was painfully obvious that Paul was besotted with Edward, and he didn't know why he hadn't seen it before.

'Let's show him our private boudoir, shall we?' said Edward.

Paul could scarcely contain his excitement, and as they went up the stairs he started chattering again about his own house, and how vastly inferior it was to Edward's in every way. Edward glanced back at him and gave him a quizzical look. He shrugged in response.

'Exactly what I want – men!' cooed an excited voice from behind them, just as they were embarking on the stairs to the second floor. 'How would you big strapping boys like to give me a hand?'

Edward's mother stood at the door to her studio, smiling pleasantly. She was wearing an azure kimono with a motley collection of silk scarves wound round her neck. He had caught only intermittent glimpses of her since Edward's father had left for France, as she flitted in and out of her studio on the first floor in paint-splat-tered smocks and kaftans, and it was the first time in a long while she had actually addressed a whole sentence to them. Edward spoke of her scathingly, saying she was pouring her fury at his father into her pictures and drinking herself to death at the same time. But Edward had stopped calling her the womb, he noticed, and he thought that secretly Edward must feel sorry for her, because in the end she had been abandoned just like him.

'We're busy,' Edward said curtly.

'Well, I'm sure you're not too busy to give me five minutes. I need you to help me move my work into the downstairs hall. I've some exciting news – I'm holding an exhibition!'

He knew about the exhibition already. Edward had told him, and said it was only because she was an old friend of the gallery owner, who was humouring her, as everybody knew her work was crap.

She led them across the landing and into her studio. Edward rolled his eyes and he did likewise, but secretly he was fascinated, for he had never been inside – though Edward assured him it was nothing amazing. He was disappointed to find Edward was right: it was a bright spacious room with white walls, and apart from some shelves and a table piled with art materials, there was hardly anything in it.

'If you boys wouldn't mind,' said Edward's mum, pointing at a pile of canvases covered with brown paper and stacked behind the door. 'One at a time, please.'

Edward sighed and nodded at him. They took a corner each of one of the paintings, which was heavy and smelt faintly of rising damp. He was curious to know what the picture looked like, but Edward didn't seem remotely interested.

'And who's this handsome young squire?'

His mother was looking at Paul, having only just noticed him. Paul blushed furiously.

'His name's Freddy Krueger,' replied Edward.

'Well, Freddy,' said his mum without a trace of irony, 'it's very nice to meet you.'

Paul giggled and took her hand and shook it. Edward gave him a knowing glance and they lifted the canvas and started out of the studio, leaving Paul and his mother struggling with the next one. On the stairs Edward said, 'So what's the story?'

'He begged me on his hands and knees. I felt sorry for him.'

'You old softie, you.'

'I know.'

There were thirteen pictures and it took half an hour to get them all the way down to the hall. Edward's mother thanked them vaguely as if they had merely held open a door for her, her mind already focusing on where the taxi might be that was coming to take her to the gallery. But as they were leaving she stopped him by touching his shoulder. He turned, surprised.

'Why don't you bring your mum along?' she said, handing him a card that featured a painting of a naked girl with a terrified expression on her face, her name handwritten in elegant curly letters in a blank space above. 'I've never met her and Edward tells me she's in a similar situation. Tell her we'll get drunk, track down the bastards and make 'em pay!'

She laughed as if this concept was quite hilarious, but there was an edge to it that seemed to imply it was not far from what she would like to do in reality. It had not occurred to him to compare his own mum's situation to that of hers. He doubted his mum would want to make the comparison herself.

'But seriously, do tell her to come. I'd love to meet her.'

He smelt alcohol on her breath and thought to himself there was little chance of his mum ever attending an exhibition by this mad woman with her dramatic face and wild gestures and crazy dress sense. But he took the card and politely put it in his pocket.

One night Marie does not turn up for the show. Her absence could not be more conspicuous, though nobody dares to mention it. Big Pete paces back and forth in the performers' area, barking at anyone who gets too close to him, his eyes flaming as if challenging people to point out she is missing. 'Make sure you fucking smile!' he snarls at Franka and Griselda, quietly warming up in the corner. 'This show ain't just about pretty beaver, it's about teeth! And you' – he turns to Pierce and Imogen – 'no embarrassing gaffs like last night. If I wanted to see amateurs I'd go watch kids fucking around in the playground!'

He wants to make himself scarce, but Vlad requires him to be a human buttress for him to stretch off, so he keeps his head bowed in the hope that Big Pete will not notice him. It is almost time to begin and there is someone else besides Marie who is missing – there has been no sign of the clown all day. As twenty minutes to the show turns into fifteen the ringmaster's face begins to redden excitedly as it occurs to him he may have a real reason to get angry.

'Where is that motherfucker?' he bellows, obviously past caring if members of the audience might hear him over the music. 'If he's not here in the next ten seconds I'm gonna skin his miserable scrawny hide!'

The ringmaster glares proudly around at the company, but despite the oath the clown does not magically appear. Big Pete snorts and charges from side to side like an enraged bull trapped in a pen, and the performers back away to the sides of the space.

'You –' Big Pete snarls finally, extending a finger in his direction, 'go and fetch that cuntface!'

Without need of further instruction he scurries from the performers' area and out of the big top.

It does not take him long to locate the clown. He is in his caravan, slumped over the table snoring. Asleep, the clown's expression looks curiously innocent and free of the cynicism that usually keeps his face lined and cruel. It is almost like looking at a different person altogether. He thinks he can even see the little boy the clown must once have been, a mischievous and naughty child perhaps, but not yet twisted and cold like his adult persona. It is almost touching, this new version, and he thinks it is a shame to wake him. But there is no time and so he puts his hand on the clown's shoulder and tugs hard.

The clown jerks upright and raises his arm as if to ward off an attack, his eyes wide and saucer-like. When the clown sees who it is his eyes narrow to their usual slants and he emits a snake-like hiss.

'Get out of my space, shithead!'

'Show's starting in ten minutes,' he says. 'Big Pete's pretty mad.'

The clown glares at him for a few more seconds, poised to retort. Then his words sink in and the clown's face morphs. He lets out a long groan and puts his hands on his head.

'I'm fucked!'

'Where's your make-up?'

The clown doesn't reply, but he spies the make-up case on the table by the clown's elbow, a bottle of Scotch resting precariously on its rim. He seizes the case and puts the bottle down at the far end of the table, out of the clown's reach.

'Hold still.'

'What?' The clown looks confused. Then it dawns on him what he is going to do. 'Gonna paint my face, are you? That's a good one!'

But the clown does not resist as he slaps a layer of the greasy white foundation over his features. It goes on surprisingly easily, like slime. He picks up a small cube of sponge, dips it into the black and wedges it over the clown's left eye.

'Aw, you fuck!' screams the clown. His tone falls to a soft, insidious pitch. 'Let me ask you something I've been wondering about, OK? What are you even doing here? Even a moron like you's gotta be able to see this is the shittest circus ever. Everyone else I can understand. We all joined this shit detail cos we couldn't get better. But you – you're not even getting fucking paid!'

The clown laughs to himself, a guttural grunting noise. He swallows. He feels like he should get angry, but he isn't angry especially. There is something too pathetic about the clown, and besides, anger seems to be what the clown is hoping for and he doesn't feel like indulging him. Instead he rubs the sponge across the other eye.

'You know,' continues the clown conversationally, 'you must be some special kind of needy bastard to follow that unicycle and shack up with him. A world-class loser.'

'Yeah,' he replies. 'I guess so.'

'Ha!' snarls the clown, looking like he might have more to say. But his mouth is stopped by the sponge dousing his lips in black. He sits back. The effect is not at all bad, he thinks. It is nothing like as good as Marie's flawless artistry, but the white face, the big black eyes and the line of dark mouth are all in place, and he has got the eyebrows exactly right – big curling question marks over each eye, as well as the sad laughter lines that are painted in on either cheek.

'You better go,' he says.

The clown rises as if to leave, then pauses. For a second he thinks he is trying to cough out some sort of a thank-you, but then he realises he is searching for something. The clown dives back to the table and seizes the bottle of Scotch. As they hurry across to the big top he unscrews the cap and takes a sizeable gulp. The clown shoves the bottle at him just before entering the big top, and he waits outside, hearing Big Pete release a burst of swear words from within, only to be drowned by the sound of the gong that signifies the start of the show.

He will follow the man through the pound and down a path lined with the bodies of crumpled cars, the track strewn with entrails of engines and rusty amputated wheels. The man will turn back to give him a withered old smile as they walk, as if drawing pleasure from their eerie surroundings.

'All sorts of models here,' the man will say. 'Cos all sorts abandon their cars. Got it all planned out.'

'Oh, really?' he will reply, feigning interest.

The man will pause and extend a hand to the towers of trashed automobiles and sweep it grandly outwards, in the manner of a tour guide presenting a remarkable vista.

'Suicide alley, I call this bit.'

He will start at the name.

'Excuse me?'

'Call it that cos those are all the ones what their owners killed 'emselves in. Most of these 'uns had 'em still inside when they was found. 'Cept for a couple of 'em, where the drivers went through the windscreens.'

'Jesus.'

He will say the word because it is clearly what the man wants to hear, and the man will look pleased. He will not let on how close to the bone the remark falls – at how correct the man is to have situated his car in this part of the pound.

'Look really close you might see blood and guts stains on the bonnet.'

'There must be an exciting documentary here. You should get in touch with a TV company.'

He will speak more drily than he intended and the corners of the man's mouth will curl downwards. They will turn the corner and there behind a mountain of nuts and bolts as tall as he is he will spy his own vehicle, the familiar little air-freshener tree dangling behind the windscreen. He will approach it like he would a living creature, tentatively as if it might rear up and bellow at him for his abandonment. He will take out his keys and point them at the car, and the car's lights will duly blink on and a little squeak will sound from within, as if in recognition. He will reach out and gently touch the metallic surface with his index finger.

'It's all scratched,' he will say, more in wonder than accusation.

'How we found it,' the man will grunt. 'Good thing it hadn't been used for parts. Another month and we'd have started breaking it down. Should count yourself lucky.'

The man's tone will be a warning not to try and lay the blame on him. But he will know perfectly well how it got scratched, and in any case he will not care one way or another. The man will mutter something under his breath that sounds like a swear word and will tell him there's a form to fill in, and they will turn back down the path of crashed cars to the man's little shack of an office.

The next morning it is time for him to clean the stink house – the name the company affectionately uses to describe the toilets. After a single show they can be impressively filthy, but after a matinée and an evening show combined the filth is often nothing short of spectacular. Brown and yellow marks stain the toilet seats, and it is hard to tell if the surrounding muck across the floor is the result of mud from the field or excrement. But worst of all is the smell. He takes Marie's advice these days and winds a silver scarf from one of Vlad's old costumes around his face to protect his nose from the worst.

It takes over an hour to drive the sludge off the floor with the mop, swishing it out of the door and onto the metal steps where it splatters back down to the ground where it came from. Then it is time to do the toilets themselves, and even though he empties the buckets and pours bleach over every inch of the space the stench lingers around the holes. The walls are another matter. Over and over he dumps the sponge into the bucket and wipes at the filth, the icy cold numbing his fingers through the rubber gloves. As he thrusts the sponge at the cubicle wall a shadow falls across him and he looks up and sees the clown looking down, his hand clapped over his nose and mouth.

'Fuck-ing Jeez-sus,' enunciates the clown, removing his hand and waving it in the air. 'Un-fucking-bearable in here. How can you stand it?'

For once his expression does not seem to be twisted into its mirthless trademark smirk, though the absence of it makes it hard to tell exactly what expression the clown is wearing – or what he is thinking.

'I like it,' he says sarcastically, wringing the sponge of black water and dumping into the bucket once more. 'What do you want?'

The clown does not reply at first, and when he glances at him he looks as if he has been caught out.

'Fuck it!' snarls the clown finally. 'To say thanks. Happy?'

He is tempted to laugh at the clown but it is too cold to muster any real sort of amusement. He gives the wall a last swipe with the sponge, decides it will do, and stands up.

'No problem,' he says. 'Excuse me, I've got to get on.'

He pushes past the clown and goes into the disabled cubicle.

'Aw Jeez,' says the clown, peering after him and catching sight of a long thin turd that neatly lines the toilet seat. 'What the fuck is the matter with people?'

He uses the sponge to push the turd off the seat and into the bucket, where it lands with a comically dull thump. He wipes the seat and turns his attention to the walls. Still the clown hovers, until finally he starts to feel uncomfortable and throws the sponge back into the bucket.

'Look, I said it's fine. So don't worry about it.'

'Yeah, yeah,' mutters the clown. 'I know it's not fine. I've been a real cunt to you. I'm probably still acting like a cunt by standing here watching you clean up shit and not even offering to help.'

'There's another sponge over in the box by the door,' he says. The words are out before he has had time to think them through, and he does not dare to look at the clown's face to see how he reacts. The clown turns away and he regrets it, since it feels as if he has spat on his olive branch, but a minute later the clown returns, squats beside him, and half-heartedly dips the other sponge into the bucket.

'By the way,' says the clown, 'the name's Jethro.'

He forgot to give his mum the invitation that night and when he came across it the following morning, folded neatly into four in his pocket, he crumpled it up and tossed it in the bin without a second thought. That day he and Edward were going to the cinema and Paul was coming with them. He was already sick of Paul – of his sycophantic agreement with everything Edward said, and annoyed with Edward for tolerating him. He knew that with Paul along he and Edward would be unable to hold hands and get aroused, the best thing about going to the cinema. As he mulled it over it struck him that Edward had seemed cooler towards him of late, and less interested in fooling around, and this thought made his blood chill. Then he wasn't sure if it was true or something he was imagining.

Downstairs his mum was sitting in the living room looking about her, as if inspecting the place for specks of missed dirt.

'Where are you going?' she said as he pulled on his coat.

'To the cinema.'

'Oh.'

'With Paul,' he added, and thought he saw a pleased look on his mum's face as he went out the door. He wondered why she liked Paul so much and concluded it was because Paul was the son she would really like to have had – dutiful, clever, hard-working and polite. Probably she would not even mind that he was gay if he was like that. He felt a sudden flash of bitterness towards her, and was defiantly glad he was nothing like Paul.

When he got to the cinema Edward and Paul were already waiting in a queue for the box-office counter with *Interview With the Vampire* written above it. Edward had a satisfied look on his face, which he knew meant he had just made a joke, and Paul's expression was one of emphatic delight. He paused to take this in, curious at the way Edward seemed to bask in Paul's evident adulation. Then he stalked up behind them.

'Hi,' he said, startling them both. 'Thought we were going to see *Reality Bites*.'

'I'm too depressed for reality,' said Edward. 'Shall we see Tom Cruise and Brad Pitt bite each other instead? We can laugh and perve at the same time.'

He was about to grunt his assent when Paul piped up, 'I'm more in the mood for a thriller myself.'

He stared at Paul, suddenly hating him with almost violent passion. If Paul noticed the fury in his gaze he didn't show it.

Instead he smiled blithely at him and then looked at Edward, who was now studying a big cardboard display poster of a grinning Tom Cruise in period dress. The words 'Drink from me and live forever' were written in a caption above.

'Fine,' he said. 'Enjoy.'

He had the pleasure of seeing surprise register on both Edward's and Paul's faces before he turned and marched back out of the foyer. Only when he got outside did he realise what he had done, the gamble he had taken, and slow his pace. He felt dizzy and sick. He dared not look behind him, but he knew if Edward did not come after him it would mean he had elected to stay with Paul – that they would go to see the film together, without him. Every passing second created distance and made the nausea worse. He reached the corner of the building, the bus shelter, the traffic lights. Finally he could bear it no more and looked back. He took in the street, which was empty apart from a couple of kids with skateboards leaning against the wall of the cinema. He shuddered and breathed out.

When he got back he found Edward's mother seated at the kitchen table opposite his mum. They were both holding mugs of coffee and Edward's mother was in the middle of a dramatic gesture, her hand outstretched into the open space, the huge moonstone ring she wore on one finger winking in the light as if enjoying a private joke about the pristine surroundings. She was wearing a sky-blue dress with a long emerald-green sash wrapped around her waist, and looked somehow disproportionate and out of place against the beige and eggshell twin tones of the kitchen. In comparison his mum seemed small, nervous and bird-like. Her eyes darted towards him as he entered, the pupils large and fixed with alarm.

'Hello, you bad boy,' said Edward's mother. 'You didn't give your lovely mum that invitation to my shindig!'

On the table before his mother was another card featuring the painting of the frightened naked girl.

'Sorry,' he said.

'Oh, never mind about it! I thought I'd stop by anyway, since we've never met, and extract the promise she'll come. You are coming, aren't you? Please let's have no more of this "maybe" nonsense!'

She looked at his mum, whose pupils widened and who nodded quickly and brought her lips together in a self-conscious smile.

'Of course,' she said. 'Thank you. More coffee?'

'I'd love to, but I must make a dash. Have to get across town and sort out the space for my big debut.'

'How exciting,' offered his mother timidly.

Edward's mother beamed at her and stood up. His mum showed her to the door and stood there smiling manically until she had driven off. Then she turned, looking pale and drained.

'What a . . . an unusual lady,' she murmured.

She peered at him almost as if she didn't see him, and he wondered if she was about to faint and prepared himself to rush and catch her. But then she put out her hand and touched the wall, and used it to guide herself towards the stairs, murmuring something about taking a nap.

After the show that evening Vlad says he knows a cool place in the local town and whines and wheedles until he agrees to go out.

They catch a bus and get off in the town centre, where the aerialist takes him to the nearest cashpoint to get some money out. His bank account has depleted massively in the last two months – he has been paying for the food, drink and petrol while staying with Vlad, and he has not bothered to discuss the matter with the aerialist, who behaves as if his savings are inexhaustible and belong to them both.

'Come on,' says Vlad, tugging at his shoulder.

'Where is this place?' he asks, but Vlad merely puts a finger to his lips and smiles mysteriously. He follows him over the road, down an alley and across a car park to a gloomy-looking building where he sees a large door painted with zebra stripes. A mountainous bouncer with bristle-brush sideburns peers down at them.

'Fiver each,' he growls.

Vlad waits expectantly, and he digs into his pocket and gives the bouncer a ten-pound note. The bouncer nods and opens the door. From inside comes a blast of pounding disco music. He hangs back, suddenly nervous, for he has never been comfortable in clubs. But Vlad is already pulling him inside, down a metal staircase that looks like a fire escape, into a large dingy room full of men dancing ecstatically. The music is deafening and the air is thick with the scent of sweat, like a gym. Above the crowd a slowly rotating mirrorball sends shards of light spinning out over the gyrating limbs, which every now and then are hit by a strobe and turned into a bullet burst of staccato images, faces and bodies contorted in photographic stills that fade no sooner than the eye has absorbed them.

He follows Vlad down the stairs and they fight their way through the crowd to the bar, where Vlad orders two beers from a beautiful skinny boy in a tank top with a bleeding Union Jack symbol on the front. Vlad starts saying something to him, but he can hear nothing, can only see the aerialist laughing, and he has a paranoid premonition he could be telling him anything, something awful about himself, and he wouldn't know. He frowns at Vlad and shakes his head, cupping his hand to his ear to indicate he cannot hear. The aerialist leans in close.

'Let's dance!'

He shakes his head violently, but Vlad just laughs. The aerialist grabs his hand and leads him insistently to the dance floor. For a while he tries to emulate the fluid movements of the aerialist's body, but it is hopeless. His arms feel sluggish and his feet refuse to meet the beat. He feels tired, and his mouth aches already from the effort of smiling as if he is enjoying himself. After a couple of minutes Vlad seems to lose interest in him, concentrating instead on flinging his body back and forth to the beat, and he turns away, heading for the toilet. As he passes through the crowd he stumbles on someone's foot and receives a death stare from a powerfully built man in a leather waistcoat.

In the toilet he stands for several minutes before the urinal, putting off leaving the room again. He feels inadequate, as if at any moment one of the many men with their gym-built bodies might grab him and demand to know who the hell he is and what he thinks he is doing there. The door opens, causing him to jump, and he quickly goes to the sink, not looking up lest he should meet the eyes of whoever has entered and see some trace of scorn.

Returning to the dance floor he stands awkwardly at the side of the crowd, watching Vlad confidently jerk his body left and right to the music. The aerialist's tight T-shirt shows off his lean torso as if it were a trophy. Certainly he is not alone in watching him. The eyes of many men are centred upon Vlad, and a couple of other dancers circumnavigate the floor until they are grinding up and down beside him. He watches the crowd with a mixture of jealousy and fascination, the way in which eyes dart glances and lips pout to indicate interest. The flirting seems both theatrical and yet strangely perfunctory, as if he were watching the incomprehensible mating rituals of some obscure species on TV. Now and then he meets someone's eyes himself and flushes – the eyes sweep swiftly away, as if to mull over their assessment of his flesh.

He returns to the bar and orders two more beers from the boy in the tank top, who stares at him with apparent disdain while he takes out his money. The beer tastes watery and sweet in his mouth, and he winces as he gulps down a mouthful.

'Enjoying yourself?' says a voice in his ear. He is startled to see the clown leaning against the bar beside him, a beer in hand, peering at him with an arched eyebrow. His Mohican has been spiked up into a series of stegosaurus-like fins, and he looks like an apparition – a wicked genie that has been conjured out of nowhere by an absent-minded wish.

'Hi.'

He had not realised the clown was gay.

'So where's the unicycle?'

'Don't call him that!'

He realises he sounds stupid and looks back at the dance floor. The aerialist cannot be seen, lost somewhere within the battle-crush of bodies.

'Doing right by you, I hope?' says the clown, the corners of his mouth flickering upwards.

'Excuse me,' he says, picking up the beers. He pushes his way through the crowd, feeling beer slosh over both hands as arms and elbows lurch into him. Faces glance his way with annoyance as legs and shoes are in turn splattered with beer.

He gives up and decides to leave. Perhaps Vlad lost him too, he thinks, and has gone back to the caravan to wait for him there. But he knows this is unlikely. As he goes he catches sight of the clown again, admiring a boy twisting about obliviously before him, his eyes spinning in some alcohol- or drug-fuelled trance.

Outside the air feels wonderfully cool against his skin after the furnace-like heat of the club. The moon above is bright and full and casts silvery light across the car park. As he crosses it he hears something like a moan and turns quickly, his heart beating fast. It is coming from behind a large skip. Not quite knowing why, he walks towards the noise, flattening his footfall and shortening his steps so as not to be heard. Above the skip he sees a man's head, someone in his forties with a goatee and a silver earring, his hair shaved into a crew cut. The man's eyes are closed and his mouth is open wide, his tongue lolling about in pleasure.

He knows he should leave but he doesn't. Instead he takes a couple more steps for a better view. There behind the skip, beautifully illuminated by moonlight, almost as if someone had thrown back a curtain, the aerialist is revealed, on his knees sucking the man off.

He will park outside the home and take a deep breath. Then he will get out and push open the door and enter the small reception area. Instantly he will be hit by a familiar musty odour – the smell of old age. With it will come a wave of memory so arresting it will cause him to stop in his tracks. The woman at the front desk will look at him, puzzled, her natural smile of welcome wavering as she briefly debates whether he is a visitor or a crazy.

'Hello there, may I help you?'

In the corridor beyond her desk he will see carers coming and going with cups of tea – middle-aged women bustling about to rouse the home's residents for the survival of another day.

'Hello,' he will say. 'I'm here to see my mother.'

The woman will take a lot of time to verify the details he gives her, and when she does he will see she is even more confused, because he has not been before. She will look at him from time to time with expectation, evidently waiting for him to explain that he has been abroad, or ill, or kept from coming for some other reason. But he will give her nothing, will merely wait, stony-faced, until she calls a carer to take him to see his mother.

She will have been put in the Green Room, and he will want to tell them he knows where it is like the back of his hand, but he will resist. He will be glad that the home's staff is no longer made up of people he knows.

'She's not very responsive,' the carer will say as he follows her down the corridor. 'But you can tell there's life in the old girl yet,' she will add cheerfully as she pushes the door open, catching sight of his expression and seeming to judge it unnecessarily morose.

'Why don't I bring you both a cup of tea?'

But he will not hear her. She will not repeat herself and will discreetly exit the room. His senses will be numbed by the sight of the figure in the chair by the window. He will know it is his mother, yet at the same time it will be impossible to reconcile the slack-jawed face and the half-closed eyes with the image he has carried about with him all this time. It will be as though he is look-ing at a cruel parody of the woman he has known all his life – a drained and ravaged mutant version. He will understand it is the result of the two strokes he was not around for.

He lies balled up in layers on the little bed in Vlad's caravan listen-ing to the wheezing of his own breath in the chilly air and the rhythmic chugging of the nearby generator for the big top, which it was their turn to set up camp beside.

At about three o'clock the aerialist returns, opening the door and creeping in with a slapstick display of someone trying to be quiet. Vlad crashes straight into the little table, hisses a Romanian curse and turns, only to catch his forehead sharply on the overhanging shelf. Groaning, all attempt at quietness forgotten, Vlad switches on the light. Instantly the aerialist finds himself looking into his eyes, for he has been watching him all this time from his cocoon of cloth-ing and blankets. The aerialist lets out a small shriek of fright.

'Fuck!'

He doesn't say anything. Vlad drops his head and mutters some-thing else to himself in Romanian then turns to the little gas heater.

'Freezing in here!'

He watches him switch it on and then mutter to himself as it struggles feebly to light, over and over, repeatedly flicking the switch to make the heater grumble into a vague promise of life before it chokes out once again.

'Why are you staring at me like that?!' the aerialist demands finally, abandoning the task and turning back to face him with blazing eyes. 'What the hell is the matter with you?'

'I saw you.'

'What are you talking about?'

'I saw you with that man.'

'Saw what?'

'You!'

The aerialist's eyes narrow and he has a sudden premonition of how this will play out. He will accuse Vlad and Vlad will try to deny it, and they will shout and swear at one another and maybe even break something – for when the aerialist is in a temper, or drunk, things always seem to get broken – and then Vlad will finally admit it and glare at him and tell him that if he doesn't like it he can get out. And he will have to, because he doesn't like it, and there will be no other option.

'It sounds like you want to accuse me of something,' says Vlad threateningly, his voice deadly cold. He stares at the aerialist for a few seconds, then drops his gaze.

'It's nothing,' he says. 'I lost sight of you and felt lonely. I'm just tired. I'm sorry.'

Even as he says the words he feels the tension leave, and marvels at how easily a problem can be dealt with simply by ignoring it. The crease down Vlad's forehead gradually fades and he smiles soppily instead.

'Poor baby,' he croons, plopping down onto the bed beside him. The aerialist starts to unravel the blankets until he has found his skin. His fingers are icy but he does not complain. He lies still and rigid while the aerialist peels away the last layer so that he is naked and shivering before him on the bed, then yanks off his own clothes and throws them over his shoulder to join the mound behind him. Vlad lies down on top of him, kissing him sloppily, tasting of beer, chips and ash. The aerialist's fingers knead away at his buttocks, pushing and pulling, until his hands finally navigate his groin and touch his penis. There they pause, disappointed.

'Oh, baby,' moans Vlad in his ear.

The aerialist gives him a few pumps but nothing rises. Vlad wraps his fist around the shaft of his penis and gives it a last vigorous yank that makes him wince. Frustrated, Vlad collapses over him. A couple of minutes later he is snoring softly.

The gallery was off an alley behind the main road. The outside was painted white and it looked like a designer boutique, but inside it was cramped and teaming with adults in suits and ties and expensive summer dresses. He stood near the door with his mum, who looked around nervously with a frozen smile on her lips, clearly wishing she had not agreed to come.

'Well,' she said in a voice too bright, 'this is something.'

She was wearing a dark red dress with a navy collar, possibly the flashiest item of clothing she possessed. When she had come down the stairs in it, muttering worriedly that they were going to be late, he had told her she looked pretty and she had let out a giggle – a sound he had never heard her make before. In the car she had talked about how nice it was of Edward's mother to ask them, trying to convince herself that it was going to be a fun thing to do. But as soon as they were inside and she had seen the first picture, depicting a naked middle-aged woman forlornly fingering an apple that could have been a self-portrait of Edward's mother herself, she had stiffened. Now she wanted to go, and was looking for the artist so she could pay her compliments before leaving.

Meanwhile he was looking for Edward. He told himself that this was not the case – that he did not care whether or not Edward was here, but it was a flimsy effort at self-deceit, and he was carefully scanning each corner of the room.

'She's very popular, isn't she?' said his mum. 'Wherever can she be?'

Just as it seemed that neither Edward nor his mother were actually in attendance, the artist herself emerged from a group of well-wishers right at the centre of the space and bounded over to his mum, shrieking as she approached, 'You made it! Thank you so much for coming!'

It was obvious that she was drunk, a condition that evidently terrified his mum. But she smiled politely and allowed Edward's mother to put her arms around her and draw her close for a kiss on both cheeks.

'I don't know much about art, I'm afraid, but I'm sure it's very good.'

'Don't you look ravishing?' demanded Edward's mother, ignoring this stab at praise and looking her up and down with flamboyant admiration. She herself was wearing what looked like a translucent golden burka, combined with lots of silver bracelets on one arm. He turned away as his mum attempted again to say something nice but apologetic, and found himself looking straight into Edward's eyes from across the room.

It seemed to him as if some sort of electrical current shot between them, his entire body becoming fused with sparks and tremors. But no sooner had their gazes locked than another figure with a mousy crop and glasses passed between them, and he realised it was Paul. He shot his nose into the air and looked away. On the table near by was an abandoned beaker of white wine, and he reached for it and quickly gulped it down.

When he turned round again Edward was nowhere to be seen. But Paul was still there. He was here with his mum too, he realised, and Paul's mum and his mum had just seen each other and were exchanging greetings, palpable relief showing in both their faces at having located someone they regarded as sane and ordinary.

Something grabbed his ankle from under the table, making him jump.

'Psst,' hissed Edward from a crack between strips of white paper tablecloth. 'Come on!'

He hesitated. Then, as if he'd just noticed his shoelace was undone, he put the empty beaker down on the table and bent forward, then did a dramatic side roll under the table, where he bashed into Edward, his elbow connecting with Edward's head.

'Ow!'

'Sorry.'

He couldn't help grinning, and a second later Edward grinned back.

'Are you still cross?' said Edward, when they'd adjusted their positions so that they were sitting face to face.

He sniffed.

'How was the film?'

'A masterpiece.'

'Did Paul like it?'

Edward groaned.

'Oh God, he's driving me mad! He's like a fly you want to swat, but can't because it'd be inhumane.' Edward raised his voice and did an imitation of Paul: 'Oh yes, Edward, I do agree, oh yes, I am gay and I would like that too very much!'

Edward's impression was nothing like how Paul sounded, but he sniggered anyway. Edward sniggered too, then reached out and interlaced his fingers around his neck. At Edward's touch he felt his skin prickle with excitement, and he thrust his face closer to Edward's and closed his eyes. Their lips touched. A second later Edward's lips parted and his tongue darted into his mouth. He met it with his own tongue, sucking gently on it, and heard Edward let out a deep moan of pleasure.

Then someone yanked the tablecloth up.

'They're here!' Paul called in a loud accusing voice.

From behind Paul, his mum and Paul's mum were standing with a few of the other guests, staring at them aghast. The people around them seemed for the most part amused, and Edward's mother had her hands on her hips and a silly smile plastered over her face. But Paul's face was set in a deep frown, and he was glaring down at them, pale and shaking with anger.

He is on his break, watching from the top of a steep rise at the edge of the field as Big Pete, Midge and Benny take down the big top. It has already had the central rig removed, and sits on the grass like a giant collapsed lung.

'Hey,' says the clown.

'Hey,' he says, glancing down.

He waits for the clown to pass on by, but instead Jethro climbs the rise and plops himself down beside him, following his gaze over to the big top.

'Crap heap,' Jethro offers, fumbling in his pocket for his cigarettes. He locates his packet and withdraws one, then offers the packet to him. He is about to say no but hesitates, then takes one. The clown lights his own cigarette then tosses him the lighter.

'I gotta ask one thing,' says the clown then with the air of someone who's been waiting for a long time to speak his mind. 'I get that a person can be bored of his life and I get that a person can be so desperate he'd want to join the circus — even if it means cleaning up other people's shit and taking orders from some cunt with an anger-management problem. I get it, I do. But what I just don't get is how a person can have any self-respect slaving away for that man slut. I mean, it's just me, but don't you reckon you're better than that?'

He sighs, letting out a stream of pale smoke. It has been years since he smoked, not since he was a teenager, and the sensation of nicotine rushing into his blood cells fills him with nausea and an unexpected aching sense of loneliness.

'OK, OK,' says the clown, raising his hands as if he had reacted violently to his comment. 'None of my business, I know. And what right do I have to judge? No matter how fucked up you might be, I'm more fucked up. Got it, loud and clear.'

There is a pause. The clown seems to have ceased expecting anything from him and looks surprised when he says, 'It's not like he owes me anything. He let me come with him. Not the other way around.'

Jethro nods slowly, as if this was an excellent point worthy of careful consideration. The last poles of the big top that line the perimeter are coming down as Benny and Midge, under Big Pete's angry gesticulating, free the guy ropes. Jethro feels inside his jacket again, this time producing a large silver hip flask which he unscrews. The clown gives him a helpless look, shrugging as if to say life isn't worth the effort, and takes a swig.

'He's free to do what he likes,' he says.

Jethro smiles, smoky wisps emanating from between the gaps in his yellowy teeth. The clown holds out the hip flask and he takes it and has a gulp, the fiery alcohol surprisingly pleasurable as it sears its way down his throat.

'I'm just saying you're better, that's all,' says the clown. 'Take it or leave it.'

The body will not have shut itself down. If it were able to do this, it surely would. But it will have been preserved, taken care of, looked after where nature, cold and simple, would have demanded it be left to die.

'Mum?' he will say, experimentally. 'Mum?'

She will not respond, will not even look up at the sound of his voice. He will reach out for one of her claw-like hands and take it in his. It will be light as paper, the skin soft as cotton wool. He will swallow.

'Mum?' he will try again, more forcefully. 'It's me.'

Still there will be no reaction, not even when he leans over until he is inches away from that face with its downturned open mouth, staring right into her milky half-closed eyes. She will be like the husk of a human being.

He will think of the last time he spoke to her, on the phone outside a field in the middle of nowhere, of the fear and resentment in her voice and the magnitude of his betrayal will suddenly be such that he will struggle to breathe. The world will feel as if it is looming from all angles, an invisible force pressing in on him, and he will think it is a good thing he is sitting because otherwise he would probably faint. When he is finally able to draw in a gulp of oxygen he will see that his mother is shaking and for a few seconds he will gape in astonishment, for it will seem as if the sheer depth of his grief has somehow brought her back to him. Then he will realise it is because he is still holding her hand, and that it is only him transferring his own shudders to her fragile body.

'I'm sorry,' he will whimper.

The face before him will stare obliviously through him.

Then the door will open and he will sniff and sit back. A hand with a teacup and saucer will appear in his periphery and he will look up into the kindly face of the carer. In her other hand she will hold a plastic beaker with a funnel cap, and he will watch as she steers the beaker gently towards his mother's mouth. She will insert her lips around the funnel, expertly tipping the beaker back so that a small amount of tea washes against the mouth, and as if from some deep-seated instinct his mother will suck in a mouthful, and a couple of seconds later swallow it down.

'Good girl!' the carer will congratulate her.

It will sound to his ears like a sentencing.

★　　★　　★

In the caravan Vlad is on the bed reading a woman's weekly. Since he joined the aerialist it has been a continual source of amazement to him how he devours these thin cheery little publications aimed at housewives, chuckling to himself as he turns the pages, apparently fascinated by the articles on cooking, limescale prevention and home furnishing, and by interviews with C-list celebrities from the talk shows and soaps he loves to watch on his tiny portable TV.

'Big top's almost packed up,' he says. 'Ready to go?'

Vlad does not look up from the magazine as he comes in, and spits out his comment as if he is talking to the page before him.

'Been getting friendly with that arsehole, have you?'

He pauses in the doorway, confused.

'What?'

'I saw you out the window so don't try and deny it.'

'Try and deny what?'

'You and that arsehole – smoking!'

It dawns on him who Vlad is talking about.

'You mean Jethro?'

'"You mean Jethro,"' Vlad tries to mimic him, but it comes out just as thickly accented as usual. 'Yes I mean him! Did you talk about me? What did you say about me? I wonder. Did you have a nice good long laugh about the stupid aerialist who can't get it up?! Is that it?'

Vlad's face is dark as a thundercloud and his eyes are furious slits. He reminds him suddenly of a spoilt little boy who has not got what he wanted for Christmas and a laugh bursts out of his mouth before he can contain it.

'You can't be serious!'

'Oh can't I be?!'

He throws the coat over the chair and sits down on the bed beside Vlad. The aerialist pouts and busies himself petulantly with the magazine.

'He just wanted to say thank you to me for the other night. He was drunk and I went and fetched him, remember? That's all it was.'

Vlad turns back to face him, his eyes big and shining. The aerialist looks even more boyish with this expression and he wonders if he can really be jealous of the clown. He cannot prevent his heart from doing a little skip of pleasure at the idea.

'Don't trust him. He is an evil cunt who fucks over everyone.'

'Don't worry,' he soothes. 'I only accepted the cigarette because he was there. We're not friends.'

The aerialist humphs. He reaches out and turns Vlad's face slowly towards him. He looks into the aerialist's eyes for a minute, astonished by their beauty – here in this moment. Then, as if possessed, he grabs hold of his head and presses it against his face as if trying to smother him, thrusting his mouth against Vlad's lips with such force that a few seconds later the aerialist pulls back half laughing and half gasping.

His mum was silent all the way home, and when they got in she said she was shattered and could he make himself his dinner from leftovers in the fridge. She paused at the stairs and looked back at him, and in her face he recognised that old fear he had not seen for a very long time – as if she was thinking, who is this alien being, where is my real son and what has it done with him? She gave him a slight smile that was glassy and unable to disguise her troubled feelings, and then turned and went upstairs.

He was surprised to find that the look did not upset him as it used to. When his dad was still living with them, even though he had been away on business trips a lot of the time, such a look of fear and concern would have felt like an assault, a reproachful reminder of his failings. Now it was hard to believe he could ever have been bothered by it. The look was pathetic, a failing on the part of his mum, that was all, for the dreary little polite box she wanted to impose on the world.

He plonked himself down on the sofa and switched on the TV, taking care to keep the sound down since she developed a head-ache at anything above a whisper no matter which room she was in. All he could find to watch was a cartoon of *Tom and Jerry*, an endless cycle in which the cat connived and plotted to get the mouse that always outwitted and evaded him. It occurred to him that Edward would probably call the cartoon existential and he considered calling him to find out if he was right. Almost as if it had second-guessed his thoughts the phone began to ring.

'Hello,' he said, grinning because he was sure it was Edward.

'It's me,' said Paul brightly at the other end. 'That was so funny when I lifted up the cloth and everybody saw you two like that! But listen, I wanted to see if you felt like doing something tomorrow . . .'

As if in formation people get out of their caravans and trailers and come to stand in a huddle at the edge of the field, where they stare at the huge red big top with its swirly golden pattern of the solar system, rising up from the ground like the ornamental cupola of a

Russian palace. There is no denying that it puts their own tent to shame.

'Jesus, it's the commies,' mutters someone. There are sighs and groans and at the front of the huddle Benny sucks up a mouthful of saliva and spits out a giant lump of phlegm.

'Heh,' sniggers Midge. 'Looks like someone's already on the case.'

They watch as the livid figure of Big Pete marches across the field towards the red big top. It is like watching David approaching Goliath, and it almost seems as if the tent might suddenly come alive, prove to be an extraterrestrial blob and devour Big Pete's tiny form right in front of their very eyes. But Big Pete reaches the big top without getting eaten, climbs over some guy ropes and starts kicking at it furiously. They cannot hear him because of the wind and the distance but there is no doubt he is yelling and swearing. A few seconds later a flap opens and a tall man steps out and Big Pete squares up to him.

'Oh fuck,' groans Midge.

Big Pete is now pushing the other man, who does not react well to this and pushes him back, waving a threatening fist in his face. A couple more figures join them outside the big top and Big Pete begins to divide his anger between them, waving his arms furiously and turning round and round on the spot like a frenzied bull.

Vlad turns to him, yawning.

'I'm going for a nap,' says the aerialist. 'Tell me what happens.'

Vlad opens the door to their caravan, revealing to the company a brief glimpse of its messy insides, which turn to chaos no matter how frequently it is tidied and cleaned, before closing it behind him. Benny taps Midge on the shoulder and nods at the pickup that holds their own big top.

'Come on,' Benny says wearily. 'Everyone – let's do this.'

'Where're we s'posed to stake it?' demands Midge. 'The commies are right on our fucking patch!'

'Yeah, well, that's not our problem, is it?' Benny snaps. 'Big Pete pays us to set up the tent, and until he tells us not to, that's what we'll do. So let's move, eh?'

'Who died and made you emperor of cunts?' mutters Midge, but grudgingly he and the others follow Benny to the back of the pickup and crowd around to carry the big top out and lay it down on the grass rolled up like a colossal jumbo sausage.

'What now, genius?' says Midge. There is no space around them to unravel it, but to take it into the field would mean setting it up right next to the other tent.

'Now we wait,' Benny tells him.

'Brilliant!'

They do not have long to wait by the looks of things. Big Pete makes some final rude gestures at the rival circus, most of whom appear to have gathered outside to witness this crazy man who seems to want to take them all on at once in mortal combat, then spins on his heel and starts back. He trips on a guy rope as he leaves and sprawls forward on his knees. Even from a distance they can feel his rage, and for once no one even sniggers. Most look away as Big Pete picks himself up and continues his marching, fists clenching and unclenching as if in a parody of cartoon anger.

'What's going on?' he asks Midge quietly. 'Who are they?'

'The Red Circus,' Midge replies. 'Commies, we call 'em. They've nicked our patch.'

'Patch?'

'We don't just set up shop wherever we bloody well like, y'know. You think this itinerary of ours is random? Gotta have permission from the council, documents and shit. And there's the territory. Some towns, they don't support more than one circus a year. Others are shared territory. This one ain't.'

'Then what are they doing here?'

'Fucking us over. Dude who runs it obviously reckoned he'd set up and try and leave before we got here so we wouldn't know.'

Midge sighs deeply as if he had only managed to depress himself and pokes around in his coat pocket for his tobacco. Just then Big Pete arrives. Everybody falls silent, waiting for him to speak. The ringmaster looks slowly around the mêlée of trailers and caravans and takes in the saggy sausage of big top spread out on the ground at the centre.

'Put that away,' he orders.

Midge rolls his eyes as the company starts to heft it back into the pickup.

'All right, folks,' announces Big Pete. 'Looks like we're gonna be here for the night at least while this gets sorted out.'

'Hey,' calls out the contortionist, 'they taking our patch or what?'

There are a couple of stagy boos and sighs, but really everyone is on tenterhooks to know the answer. The ringmaster grinds his teeth at the ground for a few seconds, flecks of spittle flying out and catching the light before disappearing on the air.

'Me and them got some talking to do,' he says grimly. 'You lot stay out of it. And don't get too comfy, cos this ain't no fucking holiday.'

Big Pete waves violently to signal that any conference is over and people start to disperse, heading either for town to seek out the pubs or back to their caravans. He turns to go and join Vlad and as he does he sees Marie standing at the door to her trailer with a black shawl wrapped around her shoulders, watching with a bitter expression. She has lost a shocking amount of weight in the last couple of weeks, he realises, something he had somehow failed to notice in the intermittent glimpses of the ringmaster's wife he's caught while collecting and depositing keys for the box office. Her skin is pale and sickly-looking and her forehead looks prematurely lined from stress. She catches his eye but does not smile. Then she retreats inside.

'Useless bitch,' says Big Pete, coming up beside him to stare at his own little portable house. 'You'd think she'd do something about it, wouldn't you?'

'What do you mean?' he says, aware that any question carries the risk of having the ringmaster explode at him.

'Her bloody family, ain't it?' snaps Big Pete over his shoulder as he strides purposefully towards his trailer. 'Fucking red commie cunts!'

At school the word had got round. Somebody's mother had been at the exhibition, and she had told her daughter, and the news had travelled from person to person like a synaptic pulse until everybody knew. The entire room went quiet and then began to whisper when they entered the classroom that Monday morning. At the back of the class a boy called out 'Gays!' – it was hard to tell who because he immediately ducked his head down, as if not wanting to be the one to break the silence, an unusual thing given that they had been jeering at him and Edward for being gay since they had first become friends. But this was different, because now any element of doubt had been removed. He felt his insides turn to jelly as he realised this, but Edward merely looked around at the faces and gave an ironic laugh.

'Come on,' he whispered, trying to tug Edward to their seats.

But instead of sitting Edward cleared his throat and climbed up on his chair. The whispering ceased and everybody looked up in amazement.

'Attention,' Edward told them. 'We would like to formally come out to you, the good people of our class, easily the most deserving of our confidence. Thank you all for your unwavering support, for your refusal to give in to bigotry or prejudice, and for your cease-less commitment to the good fight.'

Edward bowed grandly. A couple of girls near the front started laughing and applauding, and quite a few others were smiling. He waited for the boys at the back of the room to start laying into them – they seemed to be conferring among themselves about the best line of attack. Edward reached down and grabbed his hand, and he was so surprised by the gesture he gripped back instinctively.

'Come on, Mavis,' Edward lisped, using him as a support as he climbed down. Edward sat and pulled him into the seat beside him. There was more laughter, followed by the words 'Fucking poofs . . .' from the back, and Edward gave him a sidelong, secretive smile, and as if then someone had flipped a switch, he felt his fear quite magically vanish. He smiled back at Edward, then turned, puckered his lips, and made a kissing noise to the girl sitting behind him, who grinned.

That night everybody assists with building a big fire. At first Benny, who has been left in charge while Big Pete is gone, shouts at them and tells them they will be caught by the council and fined, but then someone gives him a beer from one of the crates they brought back from town, and someone else hands him a spliff, and he calms down and decides he does not really care one way or another. The red circus has had a bad effect on morale – seeing its larger and far superior big top, and its trailers with their extra attractions that include a merry-go-round featuring rideable Disney creatures for small children and a darts and shooting range for adults has made the company restless and dissatisfied, and almost unanimously people have decided to get drunk. Someone even sneaks into the red circus during its matinée and returns to inform everyone in a despairing voice that it is really good. Several members of the company spit at this news, but mostly people shrug as if it was all they'd expected.

'Of course they're better than us,' mutters the clown. 'We're shit.'

Jethro gets a couple of dirty looks and Midge tells him to 'Shut up, you cunt', but he can see that basically everyone agrees with him. The general attitude seems to be that Big Pete's circus is on its last legs, and when someone suggests they use the big top for kindling the entire company cheers.

He seats himself between Vlad and the contortionist at the edge of the fire. The contortionist is already talking about next season, how she is going to return to London and get involved in the contemporary circus scene, maybe work in nightclubs and get on the books of some agents for corporate events. She says she will build a name for herself as a bendy burlesque star, as this is what everyone in the city wants to see. Vlad emits a short harsh snort and spits in the fire, leaving them in no doubt as to what he thinks of bendy burlesque stars, and the contortionist shoots him a glare. The clown skulks around at the edge of the circle, smoking and drinking and casting mean glances over at him and Vlad. Eventually he catches the clown's eye and looks at him askance, but Jethro immediately looks away and not long after he disappears.

It is late and people are starting to get very drunk. There is still no sign of Big Pete, but the lights of the red circus have gone out and music has been switched off, signifying that the other show is over. Midge suggests they get a crew together and go over to the red circus and show them what they're made of, but Benny just laughs and tells him they'd be eaten alive and to get a grip.

'What kind of a retard are you?' Benny demands. 'There're three times as many of them.'

The mood starts to dip once more. They have run out of beer and everybody is too stoned to think of going to fetch more. Over in Big Pete's trailer one of the lights is on, and he realises Marie must be home and listening to everything they're saying.

'Going to the gentlemen,' Vlad announces, standing.

'I'm coming too,' he says.

He stands but the aerialist gestures angrily at him to sit down.

'Can't I even take a piss without you holding onto my hand?' Vlad says.

He is hurt, but he hides it because people are watching. The aerialist climbs across people's laps and makes his way out of the circle. He notices that he is not going in the direction of the toilets though, or even heading towards the closest set of bushes, and his heart sinks. Vlad is off to the gentlemen all right, he thinks. But he does not get up and follow.

After about an hour he can stand it no longer. He thinks he cannot sit there drinking and affecting laughter when he does not know what the aerialist is up to, so he gets up and clumsily makes his way out of the circle himself. As he does he is suddenly reminded of the day he followed Vlad and first saw the company like this, gathered around a fire at the centre of a field, a pool of light and merriment closed off from the rest of the world. He remembers how impenetrable the group was and how impossible it seemed that he should ever belong, and now here he is exchanging nods and clinking his bottle against others' as he stumbles over people's legs and laps. And he thinks to himself then that no matter where the aerialist is or what he is doing, he is not in the slightest bit sorry for the way things have turned out.

From then on he will drive to the nursing home every day. He will go early, as soon as the home opens, when there are few other visitors and many of the residents are still being washed, cleaned and dressed. He will assist in this process with his mother, though the carer will always bathe her alone – 'Don't want to shock you, do we?' she will tell him with a wink. He will not inform her that he has plenty of experience in bathing old ladies who have lost the ability to move their own limbs after strokes and aneurysms. The carer will often ask him how the 'trapeze thing' is coming along, for she will have read about it in the local paper like everyone else. Indeed, he will be something of a celebrity at the home, and a couple of times he will find himself rushed at by two children, a boy and a girl, while their mother waves to him from the side of the old man she comes to visit. These children will beg him to tell them about the circus and what it's like to run away with it. He will be vague and embarrassed and smile a lot with the hopeful demeanour of someone who does not know how to talk to children. Young people have never been his speciality – it is old people in which he is expert. The children will chatter away over the top of him regardless, since in the end his presence is only a catalyst for them to voice their own ideas.

Sometimes he will try to tell his mother about it. He will explain about the excitement, the hardship, the ridiculousness, the strange allure of it all. Who he will really be trying to explain it to is himself, and he will never find a satisfactory way of doing so. He will always end up just sitting there with her hand in his and staring with her out of the window at the small patch of lawn that lines the building.

'Just as well you're in the home already,' he will say once, as a joke. 'If you could see what I've done to the house, it'd probably put you in here anyway.'

And she will stare blankly back at him and he will feel bad about the joke, suddenly wondering if somewhere inside she does understand after all. Then he will hear his voice taking on that same property of absurdly bright cheer that everyone uses to talk to unresponsive relatives, the one that he always used in the past too, and which his mother used to use when she worked here herself. Hearing this tone in his own voice will soon depress him back to silence. Sometimes the carer will walk in on the two of them with tea, sitting there quietly, and she will laugh uncomfortably and call them a pair of old waxworks.

There are voices shouting at each other – one of them belongs to the aerialist, it is clear from the way it is punctuated with Romanian curses. The other is someone he does not immediately recognise. He follows the direction of the voices until he sees them, not far from the road, dimly lit by one of the street lights. They are standing a metre apart and bawling insults at one another as if it is what they were born to do. The reason he did not recognise the clown's voice is because he has never heard him shout before. Jethro always speaks with a sneer, and his shouting voice sounds different, shaky and high-pitched, almost psychotic.

'You're a jealous fuck, that's all you are!' Vlad is yelling. 'Jealous, jealous, jealous! Because you're nothing but a sad old has-been! And you know what else? You're not even funny!'

The aerialist cackles manically and shakes his beer at the clown, producing a splatter of froth.

'Because you're such hot shit, eh?' the clown screeches back at him. 'Vlad the amazing poof! Who everybody knows can't even get it up – Vlad the amazing limp dick more like!'

The pair of them pause for a second, and it almost seems as if both have abruptly run out of ideas of what to shout next. Then, as if by mutual accord, they launch themselves at each other like two cats that have been waiting for the right signal to pounce.

They meet in the air, seemingly in a hug, but one which quickly develops into a wrestling match as they connect with the ground and begin to roll back and forth, each fighting to get on top of the other.

'Stop it!' he shouts, but neither so much as acknowledges his presence. He rushes up to them and then hovers behind the battle feeling strangely ineffectual and detached – almost as if he really were at the cinema watching it unravel on-screen. He sees the clown raise his fist and sees Vlad sock him in the jaw before he can bring it down and feels nothing, no sense of urgency or panic.

'Hey! What's going on here?'

It is Midge, running towards the fight from across the field. There is another shout from behind Midge and he knows that more people are coming, and this spurs him into action and he leaps towards the struggling duo and grabs the shoulders of the one on top, pulling hard. When this person snarls and turns to plant a fist square in his face he is so stunned that the image of Vlad realising who he is hitting seems to freeze-frame as he falls back into the mud beside them.

'Cunt!' Jethro screams.

He lies there, dazed, dimly aware that they are still fighting. Then Midge has reached them and is pulling them apart – but by this time it is unnecessary, as they are more or less done, panting and rubbing their respective wounds. Midge is shouting at them to go and cool off and someone else is crouching beside him and asking him if he is OK. He feels something wet on his lips and from the taste realises it is blood.

'I'm fine,' he says, sitting up.

His head swims but then the world settles and he focuses on the aerialist, staring at him from where he stands as if transfixed. Then Vlad turns on his heel and stalks away into the darkness. He looks around and sees the clown has already disappeared.

'What was that about?' asks Benny.

'Those two been wanting to fuck each other from day one of this detail,' says Midge sagely, reaching down to help him up. 'Come on, you need a beer, eh? I've been holding back a few.'

But he is not listening – instead he is running in the direction the aerialist went off in, bounding through the night and shouting Vlad's name. He turns wildly, but can see nothing, only the darkened field and in the distance the lights of the trailers and the bonfire, flickering red tongues that vanish into thin air as soon as they appear.

They swiftly developed a reputation, firstly for being gay and secondly for being out of control. In truth they were not out of control, but everyone seemed to prefer to think of them this way, and it was even how he liked to think of them too – though Edward declared that what they were really about was showing people how to think outside the box.

'A bunch of fucking drones, that's what this community is,' Edward would sigh. 'They need us to broaden their horizons before their minds close in on them entirely.'

It was a vocation, Edward claimed, to help the small-minded before it was too late, and they drew up plans as to how they would go about the operation. They photocopied the first pages of *The Communist Manifesto*, *The Female Eunuch* and *The City and the Pillar* and mailed them to random addresses in the phone book. They registered two after-school societies with the school secretary – one for the gay, lesbian, bisexual and transgender community and one for meditation, though neither society produced any members apart from themselves. Edward almost got into trouble one day when he asked the teacher if they could realign the classroom using the principles of feng shui to better aid their concentration, but after a few seconds of outrage the teacher saw the funny side and offered to raise the issue at the next staff meeting.

Paul was enthusiastic about sending the photocopied pages and even suggested making crack calls from a payphone, an idea Edward rejected as far too vulgar, but at school he maintained a cautious distance. Paul was in a separate class, a higher set, but still he only exchanged the briefest hellos with them when they passed in the corridor, and told them he couldn't sit with them at lunchtime because that was when he had music lessons. At first Edward's response was to hold his head high and turn it suddenly at an angle, as if he had just become aware of a bad smell whenever Paul greeted them.

'Not good enough to be seen with,' Edward sneered when Paul met them at the weekend, nudging him in the ribs. 'I suppose it's only understandable really – after all, we're just the help.'

Paul looked troubled and dropped his head.

'Look, I'm sorry,' Paul said. 'It's my parents. They're not like yours. If they had any idea that I was ... you know –'

'A raving fag?' Edward supplied.

'They'd never forgive me!'

'But, darling, that's the whole point of what we're doing!'

Yet Edward didn't push Paul beyond this, he noted, and at school the next day Edward did not do the thing with his head when they crossed paths with Paul during break time and Paul gave them his usual nod.

'The trouble with little Paulie is that he's clueless really,' Edward confided to him while they shared a cigarette behind the hedge that lined the playground. 'He's not got any real spine. Such a pity. But that's how it is with these mummy's boys.'

He sniggered. He was glad that Paul had created this distance between them. It was as if he had covertly agreed that Edward was his property and duly backed off to the sidelines.

'He just hasn't quite grown up yet,' he summarised, and Edward nodded.

Secretly he understood what Paul was feeling though, because when he was not with Edward his own confidence faltered. Each morning he would set out wondering if this would be the day that the head would summon them to his office for a long talk about their behaviour. He knew it would have to happen sooner or later from the outrageous things they were doing, and he dreaded it with a passion. Each time a boy from the lower years interrupted the class with a message for the teacher he felt sick with apprehension. But each time it turned out to be for something else, or the summons was for one of the boys at the back, and he would realise they had got away with it yet another time.

He stumbles into the caravan and finds the aerialist sitting on the bed holding a shot glass of vodka. The bottle on the table is already three-quarters down and Vlad's face is red and blotchy and set in an angry pout.

'I was looking for you,' he says. 'Didn't you hear me calling?'

'Yes,' replies Vlad. 'But I didn't want to be found.'

He closes the door. The little portable heater chugs forlornly in the corner, as if at any second about to give up the ghost. It is very warm and cosy in here but the cosiness and warmth feels all wrong to him, as if he has internalised the cold to the point that it has become part of him.

He waits for Vlad to say something, to apologise for hitting him and to tell him it was a drunken mistake and that he could not see in the dark. But Vlad just sits there sipping from his shot glass, glaring straight out ahead of him at the wall. He can feel his own anger now, swollen like a saturated sponge.

'So why didn't you want to be found?' he says finally, the words threading their way out between gritted teeth.

The aerialist drains his glass, leans forward, grabs the bottle from the table and pours in another shot.

'I just didn't.'

'But you hit me! You could have broken my nose.'

Without further ado the aerialist stands up.

'You want to hit me back?'

He spreads his arms wide, sending the contents of the shot glass shooting out over the bed.

'So hit me, pussy!'

His fist seems to throb, as if with yearning to make contact with that smug handsome jawline. He feels it balling up, and feels the surge of adrenalin pounding its way through him, imploring him to do it. The eyes before him blaze with challenge. But he resists.

'I don't want to hit you,' he says, slowly uncurling his fist.

'Well, you should!' screams Vlad. 'Because I'm sick of you and I don't want you any more! I'd like you to piss off where you came from. Go and annoy some other trapeze artist and leave this poor bastard alone!'

He punches the aerialist. The blow catches Vlad in the mouth and glances off to the side. But it is enough to send him stumbling backwards onto the bed, his eyes glazing over momentarily from the shock. He stares at the aerialist, trembling and amazed, unsure if he should beg forgiveness or launch another attack.

'You asked for that,' he says after a while, trying to sound firm.

The aerialist's body tenses as if he is going to fly at him. Then Vlad goes floppy – the fight seeming to leave him all at once. He lets out a long heavy sigh.

'You want to know something about that clown you're such good pals with? You want to know why he hates me so much?'

Vlad's eyes are droopy, as if he is on the cusp of closing down. He is completely and utterly drunk, he realises.

'Why?'

'Because he wants me.'

'Wants you?' he repeats.

'We fucked once. He never got over it.'

Vlad yawns then smiles bitterly.

'Go and ask him if you don't believe me.'

He stands there, confused and not knowing how to respond.

'Go on – ask your friend. He'll tell you all about it!'

As if he can take no more Vlad draws up his legs to his chest and curls his body into a protective ball, turning away from him. He waits a few seconds, then sits down on the bed and reaches out to touch Vlad's shoulder. But the instant his hand makes contact the aerialist jerks and shakes him off.

'Go away.'

He reaches out again, determined to make Vlad turn.

'I said fuck off!'

He withdraws his hand and stares at Vlad's back. But the aerialist does not relent. After a while there is nothing for it but to get up and leave the caravan.

One afternoon Edward had the idea that they would go to school wearing black make-up and silver jewellery like goths. He was nervous about the idea, but agreed immediately, not wanting Edward to pick up on it.

'Mother dear!' Edward announced, dragging him and Paul down to his mother's studio and barging in without knocking. She was dabbing at a new square of canvas critically, a Martini in her spare hand. 'We need your mascara.'

'Delicious, darling,' she murmured from behind her easel, not missing a beat. 'I've got extra thick and cry-proof in the box on my dressing table. Help yourselves.'

'Stupid womb,' muttered Edward after it had been located. He'd started calling her it again after her exhibition, which apparently had been a stunning success and had earned her several commissions. 'She'd smile and say hello to her own murderer probably.'

Edward seated himself in front of the mirror and he applied an experimental layer of black make-up to his eyebrows and eyelashes. He did not say to Edward that often he could be very like his mother, especially in the way he came up with ideas and made grand sweeping statements, as if he were a true connoisseur of all that was worth knowing in life. He knew that Edward's father called each month and asked to talk to him, and that his mother tried to get Edward on the phone, but that Edward always refused. He was sure Edward longed for his father though, and would give anything to have him back. It was completely the opposite to his own situation really: once a month on a Saturday he would take the train to see his dad in Swindon and stay the night in his shoebox flat, and they would eat a takeaway and watch some video which his mum had carefully instructed should not be above a 15 certificate. He hated the visits and could tell that his dad did not particularly enjoy them either. When he told Edward this his response was 'So why bother?' and he laughed because it was so simple and obvious. But when he told his mum he did not want to visit his dad any more she went pale and told him not to try and be funny, and from the way she looked at him he decided it would be better just to keep going than push the matter.

'You look like you're out of the Addams Family,' observed Paul.

'Well, well, well,' said Edward, examining his reflection. He nodded and batted his eyelids a few times. Then he turned to Paul and arched a darkened eyebrow. 'Your turn?'

'Uh,' said Paul, 'maybe not this time.'

Edward snorted to show this was exactly what he had expected of Paul, picked up the mascara brush and turned to him instead.

They timed it so that they would walk in just as assembly was about to start, so no one would be able to say anything until afterwards. Paul grudgingly agreed to be their lookout, and they hid in the toilets until he called them out when he saw the head on his way to the assembly room. They raced down the corridor and threw themselves into their seats just before he arrived. It felt as if they had taken position on a stage, and immediately a ripple of giggles and whispers spanned out across the room around them, only to be almost instantly quelled by the entrance of the head.

They did not get to first period before the head had summoned them to his office. They waited in the side passage opposite the school secretary, who kept looking over at them with round astonished eyes, as if she couldn't quite believe what she was seeing. Edward chattered away to her and offered to give her some of his beauty secrets, making her laugh. He tried to smile as if he thought the whole thing was funny and preposterous, but felt sweat trickling down his sides.

'Is this supposed to be a joke?' asked the head in an icy voice when they were standing before him. 'Should I be amused?'

The head looked almost hopeful that they might apologise and capitulate. Instead Edward made a show of clearing his throat.

'Apart from jewellery there are no regulations on what pupils can and can't wear,' Edward said, sounding like he had rehearsed it. 'That's the rules. You can confiscate the silver but we're entitled to dress how we please.'

He held his breath. For a minute the head stared. A vein pulsed on his temple and he looked as if he was going to physically pop in an explosion of righteous gore. He waited for the angry roar and

the tirade of grown-up outrage, but instead the head merely emitted a long breath as if he was in pain.

'You boys have been making quite a spectacle of yourselves
lately,' he said in a low voice. 'I've turned a blind eye to it because
it's not my place to interfere with people's lives outside the school,
no matter how immoral the things they get up to. But when you
bring it into the school then it does become my place. I'll be speaking to your parents.'

He paused and gazed at them each in turn for a few seconds.

'Is there anything more you'd like to say while you're here?'

For once Edward did not seem to have an answer ready.

'Very well. Leave the jewellery and get out of my sight.'

The head turned his attention to some papers, behaving as if
they had already left. They removed the rings and pendants and
piled them on the desk. As he was following Edward out of the
room the head spoke again, startling him.

'Didn't think I'd ever see you in here,' he said, still not looking up from his desk. 'Always thought you were a decent, hard-
working sort of boy. But now I see you're not like that at all, are
you?'

He swallowed, stunned by these words. Outside Edward let out a
loud cackle, producing another disbelieving giggle from the secretary, who was used to pupils coming out looking tearful and sorry
for themselves.

'We took on the system,' Edward crowed triumphantly. 'And we
won!'

But the words of the head reverberated accusingly in his mind.

★   ★   ★

As he wanders through the night he tells himself it is just another tempestuous episode, and that he will return later and that Vlad will be overcome with remorse and full of affection. It is the aerialist's nature – which often seems to him to be the nature of something larger than a mere individual, perhaps even the nature of the circus itself. He pictures the scene just a few hours from now: Vlad throwing his arms around him, him shrugging the aerialist off and insisting that he is leaving, Vlad shrieking apologies and then turning coy when he refuses to forgive him, and begging to at least be allowed to suck him off one last time. Embarrassed and excited by this image of the soon-to-be, he quickens his step. As for the clown, he thinks, what does it matter?

At that precise moment, almost as if fate had been listening in on his thoughts, he stumbles upon the clown himself, squatting on the knotted roots of a tree, repeatedly flicking his lighter and swearing quietly at it.

'Fucking piece of –'

Abruptly the clown becomes aware he is being watched and looks up at him, his shoulders squaring and mouth set in a defiant snarl, as if expecting an ambush. Neither of them says anything. Slowly the clown's face relaxes.

'How's the nose?' Jethro says.

'Great,' he replies.

'Caught you a bit of a blinder, eh? Fucking bastard. You wait till I see him next, I'm gonna –'

'Are you in love with him?'

The question launches itself into the air with all the grace of an elephant and causes the clown to drop his lighter in shock. Jethro curses and starts to fumble around in the darkness, but with a practically extrasensory instinct he knows this is just a ruse. The clown is trying to work out how to answer.

'Oh my God,' he says slowly, as the truth dawns on him.

The clown lets out a hearty guffaw.

'Don't be fucking stupid!'

'I don't believe it.'

Jethro catches his breath.

'Fuck off, OK?'

They stare at one another. He wonders if the clown is going to charge at him, and thinks he has had more than enough violence for one night. Then it occurs to him, as he holds the clown's gaze, that he has never seen so much violence in all his life as in the last few weeks, and this fact, along with the serious angry face before him, suddenly seems obscurely funny.

'You are!' he giggles. 'That's hilarious!'

The clown seems to teeter, unsure if he is being made fun of and how he should react. Then Jethro yanks open his jacket and wrenches out his hip flask. He watches the clown unscrew the cap and take a long deliberate swig, and thinks he has never known people who drink so much, or ever drunk so much himself. This thought, too, is for some reason funny, and he laughs again.

'Full of beans tonight, aren't you?' mutters the clown.

'I'm surprised, that's all!' he splutters. 'I thought you hated him!'

'I do hate him.'

'Does that mean you hate me too?'

The clown rolls his eyes upwards, so that only the whites remain. For a split second he is alarmed because it doesn't look like the pupils are going to resurface, but then they rotate back down and settle grudgingly upon him.

'Why should I hate you?'

'Because I'm with him.'

'So fucking what?'

The clown seems to be daring him to pursue this line of enquiry.

'You hated me when I first arrived.'

'That's just the tradition around here. Anyway, you've seen for yourself what a slag he is, haven't you? Sucking cocks in fields and car parks. Only strings you along cos you take care of him. Everybody knows it, including that fuckface ringmaster. Reckon you know it yourself.'

The clown's words hurt more than the aerialist's blow, and he takes a strained breath through his swollen nostrils. Yet as he watches him the malice in the clown's face seems to crumble away, his features untwisting into an expression that is astonishingly close to kindness.

'Oh – what the fuck? Don't listen to me, all right? I'm just some miserable alky. That rusty old unicycle is probably planning to fucking marry you for all I know.'

He leans towards the clown, who flinches, clearly thinking he is going to strike. But he is only reaching for the flask, which he snatches out of the clown's hand. A coughing spasm overcomes him as he takes a gulp. But when it subsides he feels warm and pleased. He smiles down at the clown, who waves his hands for the flask, which he tosses back to him with another giggle.

The centre of town will seem surreal and ominous as he drives through, suffused with the spectacle of normality at every turn

– people going about their business, running errands, pushing buggies, drinking coffee and talking into mobiles. No matter which direction he looks ordinariness will stare ferociously back at him, threatening to subsume him once more into its acceptable systematic process. Each breath will feel stertorous, as if all that prevents him from falling back into the old rituals and habits that once made up his existence is a thin strand of willpower, stretched to breaking point by the knowledge that he and he alone is crazy enough to have attacked his own home, to have reviled all human contact and installed a circus rig above the kitchen.

At the supermarket he will wait in the car until he has steeled himself for the task ahead. The prospect of entering the store and encountering the faces of people he might know will be almost enough to make him start the engine again and drive straight on home. But he needs too many things to turn back, and so he will force himself to get out of the car and head inside, keeping his gaze trained on the ground like a dog following a trail of scent.

The supermarket will be mostly empty, only a pensioner suspiciously examining tinned salmon and a cluster of teenage goths glumly inspecting the small selection of DVDs. The bored-looking girl behind the counter will ignore him as he hastily grabs a trolley and hurries down the aisle, filling it with everything he can think of as fast as he can. He will be silently congratulating himself on the success of his mission when he will turn the corner and run straight into Katy.

He will have seen her only a few times since they were at school together. Like him she will have remained in town, a local fixture, someone everybody knows and accepts. He will not have spoken to her in all that time though, and they will have only exchanged detached nods over the years, the fact that she was once a bully gradually giving way to the fact that she has become an adult who knows better. She will have filled out a lot over that time, and her wide-set eyes will seem even wider under a ragged fringe. Two small children will run back and forth around her as she considers a shelf containing packets of soup. She will see him before he has time to turn his trolley round and will exclaim his name loudly, causing the girl at the counter to look over with interest. He will try to pretend not to have heard, but it will be too late.

'But it's you!' she will call out, ignoring the children at her feet and wheeling her trolley over. 'I read about you in the paper!'

He will smile reluctantly.

'How've you been?' he will say.

Katy will shrug and jerk her head in the direction of her two kids as if this is all there is to say.

'I heard about your mother too,' she will say. 'That's awful. Is she . . . ?'

There will be an uncomfortable pause which will be punctured by her little girl screaming as the boy hits her in the chest. Ignoring them, Katy will lower her voice.

'I heard about . . . what you did too. Before, I mean. Going off with that circus show. Everybody was talking about it – caused quite the sensation around here, as I 'spect you can imagine.'

He will look at the floor, not caring how obvious he is making it that he does not want to talk to her. But Katy will not take the hint. Instead she will lower her voice even more.

'You know, after what happened with that boy you used to go around with everywhere . . .'

He will swallow hard.

'Edward.'

'Edward – that's it. Well, I just wanted to say that when I read that story in the local I thought to myself that you've not had an easy time of it. And that made me feel sort of bad, cos I know kids were pretty cruel to you way back when.'

He will raise his eyes and stare at her.

'What I mean is … I know I was pretty cruel to you. And I wanted to say that I'm sorry for it. For what it's worth.'

He will be lost for words. He will notice small warm lines around her eyes, tiny crow's feet, and will have a sudden flash of how her children see her – not as Katy the plain girl who made fart jokes and took the piss out of other kids to get attention, but simply as their mother, the person who loves them most in the world.

'It's OK,' he will say, keeping his voice as cool and level as he can make it. 'I never took you seriously.'

To this her attitude will change, almost imperceptibly, as if registering a slight. But then she will recover and nod as if to acknowledge this is exactly what she deserves to be told.

'In that case good. Well. Better be getting on then.'

With a small smile of goodbye she will continue past him down the aisle and her children will follow, whining in loud voices about some treat she has promised and failed to deliver. He will remain standing for a couple of minutes, pretending to be looking at the packets on the shelf and blinking back the tears that are pushing furiously against his eyes.

* * *

The sky is alive with streaks of fiery red when he stumbles out of the clown's caravan, his eyes heavy-lidded from tiredness and drink. The world is dark, but out of the gloom he can make out the edges of trailers and the mobile box-office unit, the patch of burnt-up ash where the fire was last night, and a minefield of tin cans and glass bottles twinkling in the half-light. His insides are swimming and strangely warm, despite the cold wind that bites into his exposed face and hands. In his drunken haze he is aware someone is shouting and swearing, and vaguely he realises the someone is Big Pete. To go over would be akin to running into the path of an angry beast, but the whisky has made him bold and reckless, and he jogs towards the sound, his feet crunching over the discarded trash.

'The fucking bitch!' Big Pete is howling and snarling as he staggers backwards and forwards outside his trailer, practically pawing the ground. It is obvious that he is not the only one who has been drinking all night. 'The fucking whore!'

As he approaches Big Pete bends down and plucks up one of the empty beer cans, which he hurls with considerable force towards the side of his own trailer, where it connects with a loud 'ding'.

'What happened?' he asks in a reasonable voice.

Big Pete does not seem to hear him. Instead he raises his fist to the sky and gives God the finger, before bending down to pluck up another piece of trash.

'I'll fucking kill her! Fucking kill her, I will!'

Big Pete hurls the object – a bottle this time – with all his might. There is the sound of smashing glass as it goes through one of the windows. The realisation that Big Pete is attacking his own property sobers him a little.

'What is it?' he says with more urgency. 'What happened?'

Big Pete turns, both fists clenched. He is easily within striking distance and although he cannot clearly make out Big Pete's face in the dark, he knows he is on the cusp of using those fists to hammer him into a pulp. Woozily he raises his own arms, which flop ineffectually into position before him like twigs. If Big Pete does decide to attack he stands no chance, so unsteadily he readies himself to run.

'Marie's gone!' snarls Big Pete. 'Left me for those commie fuckers! That two-faced know-it-all bastard and his dog-faced whore of a wife. Back to the inbred bunch of cunts she comes from!'

He struggles to decode what the ringmaster is saying.

'You mean . . . she's left for the other circus?'

Big Pete emits a great roar, stoops for another bottle and sends it speeding towards the trailer. It explodes against the front door. The ringmaster turns back to him, his eyes blazing red as a demon's as they reflect the fiery morning sky. For a second he is petrified, but then he realises Big Pete is looking through him, taking in the surrounding caravans and trailers, which are now showing signs of life as people open doors and windows to find out what their employer is raging about this time.

'You bunch of lazy-arsed motherfuckers!' Big Pete screams at them. He is met with derisive laughter and at least one person shouts back 'Fuck off!' and slams his door again. 'You stupid worthless talentless shits!'

Big Pete continues to scream, but suddenly he sounds small and pathetic, a drunkard, not worth taking any notice of – as if overnight his authority has dried up and gone. He decides to leave the ringmaster to his rage and turns and hurries across the ground to Vlad's caravan. He thinks how he will curl up beside the aerialist, who will be affectionate with sleep and will automatically put his arms around him, the difficulties of the night forgotten.

'Vlad?'

The door of the caravan is open. He pulls it and it swings out eerily from the dark compartment. Instantly he knows that something is up, even before he has stepped inside and fumbled for the light switch, revealing the room to be half empty and missing all of Vlad's most treasured belongings.

He turns and rushes back into the cold.

He listened carefully every time the phone went, creeping out from his room to the landing and squeezing his head between the banisters. He knew exactly when the head called to speak to his mum because of the way her voice dropped in shock when she realised who she was speaking to. 'Oh – hello,' she almost whispered, and he could feel the dread building up inside her as if preparing to gush forth like an avalanche as she waited to hear what was the matter. He heard her begin to apologise, and then stop as if she had been cut short, and then heard the words 'I see', and 'Of course', and finally 'Certainly'. Then she put the phone down and there was a silence. He went back to his room and waited for her to come up the stairs to talk to him, but the minutes dragged on and on and eventually he realised she was staying put.

When he could bear it no more he crept downstairs and peeped into the living room. His imagination was running wild with adrenalin and he almost expected to see his mum weeping with

her head in her hands, imploring the gods for mercy and demanding to know what she had done to deserve such a son. But instead
she was reading a magazine. She did not look up at first, but gradually, as if his stare was prickling her, she raised her head and met his
eyes. And he saw then that she was not going to say or do anything,
because she had no idea what to say or do, and because in any case
she had given up on him.

The red circus is nearly packed up when he reaches it. The big
top is gone and most of the vehicles are lined up at the corner of
the field, ready for the signal to move. One or two of the stalls are
still waiting for their owners to close up the flaps and put away
the bull's-eye targets and cut-outs of gorillas and dinosaurs with
holes where the faces should be for people to poke their heads
through while the vendor snaps them and then charges something
extortionate for a CD of the image. Roustabouts and members
of the company hurry back and forth across the space, all of them
ignoring him. No one is in costume or still painted, and the only
sign that last night there was a big top here is a small white canopy
supported by four poles, which might be the performers' dressing
area, yet to be taken down and standing despondently beside the
space where the towering swirly ice-cream cone of the tent was
previously erected. They have been striking since the show finished
last night, and are apparently in a hurry to leave.

He wanders through the activity, his eyes darting hopefully from
face to face. Now and then he stops someone, asking if they have
seen the aerialist, but they look at him blankly. One fat man in
overalls gives him a withering look and says, 'Aerialist? We got so

many frigging aerialists you'd think that's all there bloody was in the circus!' and walks briskly past him. He turns, over and over again, trying to guess which trailer Vlad might be secreted away in, but the whirr around him holds no clues. Hopelessness starts to set in.

'You!' says a female voice suddenly from behind.

Marie is supporting an old woman with skin so lined it is like a crumpled-up piece of tissue paper. The woman's eyes are dark concaves in her skull-like face, and her mouth nothing but a cluster of wrinkles badly coloured in with lipstick. She looks as if the merest gust of breath would blow her away.

'You shouldn't be here. You need to leave.'

'Marie!' he cries. 'Where's Vlad? I have to find him!'

'Who is it?' mutters the older woman, peering at him myopically and scratching some hairs on her chin. 'What does he want, eh?'

' 'S all right, Mum,' says Marie in a soothing voice. ' 'E's just a roustabout from Pete's circus come to check us out. 'E's just leaving.'

'Tell him to get away!' screeches the old woman, morphing without warning into a harpy. He half expects her to challenge him, fingers turning to talons and ready to scratch his eyes out, this being the way of the circus, but instead she raises an arthritic finger and points it ominously.

'Go back to that scumbag and his two-bit flea show and leave us well alone, you fucker,' she rasps.

'Don't worry, Mum,' says Marie, drawing her mother away. ' 'E's going.' She gives him a meaningful look. 'Ain't 'e?'

'I'm here to see Vlad,' he insists.

The old woman continues to glare in his vague direction, but Marie tugs her away and eventually she submits to her daughter, allowing herself to be steered over towards a large blue trailer. Marie glances back and raises a hand, warning him not to follow, and he watches, sick with heartache, as she assists her mother to climb inside, then shuts the door on her. She walks slowly back, her face unreadable.

'Is it true?' he demands. 'This circus is run by your family? You're leaving us for them?'

Marie takes out a stick of chewing gum from her pocket and pops it in her mouth. She chews and looks at him, as if reflecting. He has the feeling she is not taking him seriously.

'Big Pete's gone crazy!'

'If 'e sent you, you can just fuck off,' she says calmly.

'He didn't send me! Please, Marie!' He flushes, hearing the desperation in his own voice. 'I need to find Vlad!'

Marie inspects him for a few seconds, making no attempt to disguise her mistrust. Then she points her head towards the ground and spits out the gum. It lands in a clump of grass, a ball of unnatural plasticky pink. Then she sighs. She jerks her head and turns, indicating he should follow.

Because his mum no longer said a word, no matter how late he got in, he was able to meet Edward at any time he liked. Paul joined them at weekends, but Paul could never stay too late because his parents wanted him to be home by nine on weekdays and eleven at weekends, and despite some gentle teasing from Edward, Paul still obeyed their every instruction.

At school Edward continued to come up with new ideas about how to subvert the 'culture of mindlessness' which he said the rest of the world was intent on subscribing to. They started an anonymous newsletter in which they wrote essays that consisted of stringing together the longest words they could find, and also ones that comprised of no more than single three-word sentences. The content of the newsletter was deliberate gibberish, and they photocopied it and distributed it in the classrooms around school, though no one ever read it, and mostly pupils and teachers seemed baffled by the appearance of these nonsensical texts. Edward announced plans to start an orchestra purely for whistlers, and they almost got into trouble again when he upset the catering staff after launching a petition against the school lunches, claiming the mashed potato and rice pudding were not nearly lumpy enough.

One evening in the Easter holidays they met at Edward's house to discuss plans Edward had for a weekend away. Edward told them to go upstairs to the den while he fetched a surprise from his room, and he waited with Paul until Edward crawled into the space grinning secretively and holding something in his fist.

'You look like a maniac,' he said. 'What have you got there?'

Edward's grin widened epically and with a great flourish he opened his fingers. There was a small transparent bag containing what looked like a lump of mould.

'Ta da!'

Paul let out a horrified gasp.

'Drugs!'

Paul's prim reaction struck them as so funny they both burst out laughing. He rocked backwards and forwards on his ankles, lost his balance and almost knocked the precious substance flying out of Edward's hand. Paul smiled grudgingly, looking embarrassed.

'Relax,' said Edward drily. 'It's just pot. My dad used to smoke it all the time. The womb has a joint now and then too, when she thinks I'm asleep. Been pilfering minuscule amounts from her over the last few months, building up my own stash.'

'Have you smoked it before?' Paul wanted to know.

'Of course. It's not a big deal.'

Edward shot him a despairing look and he grinned back at him, though the truth was that he was nervous too. Though he had sermonised with Edward about the hypocrisy of legalising certain drugs like alcohol and tobacco and not others, a warning bell instilled from years of being told it was wrong was sounding, sending a tickle of fear and anticipation racing down his spine.

They watched as Edward carefully rolled the joint on the floor. He took an artist's pride in the process, sprinkling the weed up and down the paper as if it were a dish he was flavouring with some rare herb. Finally he judged there to be a sufficient amount and sprinkled tobacco on top. Then he picked the paper up, licked it along one side and rolled it between both thumbs and forefingers.

'There,' said Edward, proudly holding up a crudely misshapen joint. They all laughed, even Paul, and Edward shrugged and said, 'It doesn't matter anyway, it works just the same.'

Edward stuck it in his lips, lit it and took a long toke. He and Paul watched as Edward let out a moan as if it were what he had been waiting for his whole life. Then Edward leaned in towards him. At first he did not know what he was planning and looked at him questioningly, but Edward had his eyes half closed like a lizard lounging in the sun. Their mouths met and suddenly he felt Edward's lips part and a jet of hot cloud shoot up against his tongue. It had a heavy, almost sweet, cloying taste and when he breathed it in it tickled his throat like a feather. But he resisted the urge to cough or gag until his lungs were almost bursting. Finally when he could take it no more he let out his breath in a gust all at once.

'Whoa!' he heard himself say.

His head seemed to spin and he felt as if he were floating up towards the ceiling. He laughed and Paul, who had been scrutinising the process closely and evidently getting worried, looked intensely relieved.

'Something to take away the taste?' Edward suggested, reaching under a nearby chair and producing a bottle of red wine. 'Classic combination.'

On the trapeze he will begin to incorporate all the shapes he has seen. They will have names based on what they call to mind — gazelle, star, mermaid, superman, arabesque, layout, stag, angel, plank, around-the-world, bird's nest, swallow, eagle, foetus, hanged-man, cradle, coffin and crucifix. He will keep a log of all these moves and with each success he will tick them off — another accomplishment. Some he will get easily with his newly acquired strength and flexibility, but others will take hours and hours of practice. Occasionally he will lose his balance or misjudge the wrap and experience the weightlessness of falling before hitting the mattress below squarely with his back. When this happens he will shake himself off and immediately climb back up the rope and get onto the trapeze once more, for it is important to let the fear go immediately if he is not to be put off a move forever. The greatest challenge will be a fluid transition from shape to shape and he will experiment endlessly, trying to work out how one position might bleed seamlessly into another.

As he improves he will feel more comfortable on the trapeze and will start to take greater risks. He will teach himself how to balance on the bar on nothing but the small of his back, how to grip it with both fists and whip his feet down, pushing the bar into his body as he rotates, again and again in circles. He will be able to twist the rope around his calf and hang from one foot, to rotate around the rope while upside down, and to drop back into nothing only to catch hold of the ropes with his ankles. He will tie slings to the bar and use them to support himself while he presses the roofs of his feet over the bar and gradually applies more and more of his weight, repeating this same movement using just his heels, until in both positions he is able for a few seconds to let go completely.

The practising will be intense, difficult, exhausting work, which will make him pour with sweat and lacerate his body with welts and burns. But he will welcome each new challenge with relish. At times the pain will be excruciating and at times it will be invigorating, and at other times still there will seem to be scarcely any pain whatsoever.

There will be one trick in particular that will terrify and fascinate him – the signature move from the aerialist's repertoire. With this move the aerialist would stand on the trapeze holding the ropes and thrust his hips back and forth, creating a wave that would move the trapeze, eventually creating a swing. As the movement gained momentum, the aerialist would suddenly drop back and catch the bar on the height of the back swing, immediately beating his body up as the trapeze flew forward, to release as his legs flew over the bar and twist around, momentarily surrounded by nothing but air, only to drop and catch the ropes and trapeze with either side of his ankles.

Cautiously he will begin to experiment with making the trapeze move back and forth, creating a protesting squeak from his unsophisticated makeshift rig. Day by day his courage will grow, and the movement of the trapeze will increase, until at last he is flying up to an almost horizontal position above the floor on each swing, his body level with the first storey of the house. At the height of the back swing he will release the ropes and drop, catching the bar, and he will feel the momentum propelling his body forward as he clings with fingers so tight it is as if they have been soldered on. But he will not have the courage to attempt the next movement. It will be a trick that requires a harness and a safety line to practise and perfect. Without those things, it will be suicide.

The aerialist is sitting in the passenger seat of a brown truck, hidden behind the queue of trailers, gazing dreamily into space and drumming his fingers up and down on the dashboard. At the sight of him with Marie Vlad starts, looks furious for a split second, then resigns himself and climbs out of the vehicle.

At first he does not know what to say to Vlad and stands there looking at him as if struck dumb. The aerialist seems to be similarly afflicted, and Marie looks from his face to Vlad's and makes a humphing sound.

'I'll leave you to it then,' she says meaningfully. 'Vlad – we're hauling out of 'ere any minute so you better make it fast.'

She turns to him and nods, her mouth screwing up the side of her face in a wry smile. He thinks he sees a hint of sadness there, but then it is gone, along with Marie herself as she walks off towards the big blue trailer. Beside them is a giant red pickup which he knows must be where the big top is stored, with the image of a clown with his head thrown back laughing manically, and a busty flying-trapeze artist waving to the audience as she hangs off a bar with one leg. Several of the vehicles have started their engines, warming up for the journey ahead, and the atmosphere is suffused with the potential for movement.

'What's going on?' he says falteringly, as if the answer were not evident. 'What do you think you're doing?'

'I'm going –' Vlad jerks his head around him. 'Marie got me a good gig. Nice money. Cannot afford not to take it.'

'And what about your existing gig?'

It comes out like an accusation. The aerialist lifts his chin defiantly.

'What about it? That old bastard hasn't paid any of us for weeks. He tells us it is coming but everyone knows it's a lie – he's losing money! He can't even pay for a fucking cleaner. Why do you think he let you stay on, huh? Because of me? Ha!'

A thin man with long sandy hair and ginger stubble walks towards them, his shoulders hunched and his face dark, either from grouchiness or tiredness, it is hard to tell.

'We're off,' he says gruffly to Vlad.

'Coming!' snaps the aerialist. 'Give me a moment.'

'Thirty seconds,' replies the man, and walks over to the truck.

He stares at Vlad, who studies the grass and kicks at it self-consciously, like a kid who has been caught doing something naughty and knows he is about to receive a lecture.

'How could you just leave like that?'

'I don't need that old pile of junk,' replies Vlad. 'You can keep it.'

'I wasn't talking about the caravan. I meant me.'

He says it softly. Vlad does not look up.

'You didn't even leave a note!'

'What difference would a note make?'

The words seem to slice into him, severing some mystical cord that exists between hope and reality. Tears blur his vision and he feels them tracing hot pathways down his cheeks. He gulps, struggling to swallow down the urge to fall on his knees and weep.

'Can I come with you?'

He doesn't care how it sounds, if it is pathetic and desperate.

'Please.'

The aerialist bites his lower lip and moves the pressure of his stance from one foot to the other. This is his answer.

'Why not?' he implores.

What he really means is, How could you do this to me? He can't say so but it is in his voice, in his eyes, in his tears. Slowly the aerialist lifts his head and meets his gaze. Vlad has a soft expression. It is the one the aerialist wears when he is touched by something he has done and thinks he is being cute. But even as he looks at him Vlad's face seems to change, to melt under his stare into something harder, colder, wizened. It occurs to him that he is seeing a truth about the aerialist he has never acknowledged – that beneath Vlad's childish antics, petulant outbursts and drunken declarations there lies a person who is hard and strong, someone who understands the importance of survival above all other things.

Behind them the truck splutters into life. The man winds down the window and sticks his head out, turning it at an uncomfortable angle until they are in his line of vision.

'Oi! Hasta la vista time!'

He feels the blood pounding in his temples.

'Look,' says Vlad, 'we'll meet up again in the future, OK? Once the season is finished.'

But the words fall on his ears like a joke, and the aerialist seems to know it because he lets out a tiny pitying laugh as if at the futility of what he has just said. Then Vlad darts forward and presses his lips hard against his mouth. He inhales the familiar salty sweaty smell of his lean body and shuts his eyes. The smell disappears and so does the pressure on his lips, and when he opens his eyes again the aerialist is climbing into the truck.

He stays standing while the man backs up and then, presumably at Vlad's instruction, sounds the horn – which has the effect of making the other trucks all toot their horns as well, as if taking up a rallying cry. Then, one by one, they turn off onto the road. The aerialist looks back once and waves, and then, just like that, he is gone.

Paul held the joint between his thumb and forefinger as if it were a poisonous grub. They watched as ever so slowly he brought it towards his lips, which he pressed tightly together. He rested the joint against them for a fraction of a second, then inserted it and the end flared orange as he sucked in. Almost immediately he opened his mouth and let out a great cloud of smoke.

'Wow,' Paul spluttered, passing the joint back to him.

'It doesn't work if you don't inhale,' he said pointedly.

Paul shot him an angry look and thrust out his chin.

'I did inhale.'

'No you didn't.'

'What's your problem anyway?'

Paul said this lightly but there was an edge to his voice. He was tempted to reply, to say how pathetic he found Paul, confident that Edward would back him up – or at least not disagree, which amounted to the same thing. But something, perhaps conscience, stopped him, and he contented himself with a knowing smirk.

'You know what?' Edward announced. 'I'm bored. Let's go out.'

'Brilliant idea,' he declared, grabbing the bottle of wine and leaping to his feet. 'Let's go to the park.'

'I'm not sure,' said Paul. 'It's getting late.'

But he followed them as they wriggled their way sluggishly through the mesh of furniture to the door, and trailed along behind as they trooped down the stairs and retrieved their coats. As they passed the door to Edward's mother's studio opera could be heard from within, as well as something that sounded like a cross between weeping and howling, as if the artist were baying at the moon. Edward rolled his eyes.

'Oh my God,' Edward sighed. 'You see what I have to put up with.'

Outside it was freezing and he felt instantly wide awake and stone-cold sober. It was only when Edward took his arm and pointed out with a giggle that he had his coat on inside out that he conceded the effects of the joint hadn't quite worn off. Paul meanwhile insisted that he was completely stoned and loving every minute of it.

'Ha!' was all he said. Paul shot him a glare and Edward squeezed his arm.

It took twenty minutes to walk to the park and they made the journey in relative silence, each lost in his own thoughts. When they reached it they heard voices and laughter, recognisable as other kids from school – rougher kids who lived on the shabby side of town, like Katy. Kids he and Paul knew they didn't want to run into in the dark. He was briefly afraid that Edward would insist they continue and even go right up to them, simply out of principle. But after a moment of consideration Edward shrugged and suggested they wander somewhere else instead since he wasn't in the mood to deal with delinquents. He and Paul readily agreed and they turned round and went in the opposite direction, towards the church.

The smattering of caravans and trailers that makes up Big Pete's circus looks pitiable when he returns. People are starting to emerge, and a few are splashing water on their faces from buckets heated on the hob. Most look hung-over, and conversations are stilted. Nobody knows what is going to happen and the excesses of last night have given way to uncertainty about the future. As he passes he overhears someone saying that Big Pete has slashed his wrists and another person claiming he has drunk himself into a coma – but no one has enough courage or concern to actually knock on his trailer, go in and find out. As he passes Franka and Griselda's caravan, Franka, who is drinking a Coke on the step, calls out to him, but he does not answer. He reaches Vlad's caravan and goes inside, shutting the world out.

He lies on the bed for a long time, hugging a pillow and watching the light at the corners of the curtain grow bright and white as day advances. He feels numb. Nothing quite seems real, as if he had had a terrible accident and is now trapped in the aftermath cycle of shock. He can hear the company coming and going on the site. People are talking, shouting and laughing, groaning about hangovers and muttering about the cold. There is a whiff of smoke in the air, meaning that someone has built up the fire again, and the smell of weed. He squeezes shut his eyes, trying to block out all sensations.

Sometime towards evening there is a knock and the door is pulled open. It is Franka, her pretty blonde hair tied back beneath a patterned shawl.

'Hey, you,' she says gently. 'I heard about Vlad.'

As if her words were the incitement he had been waiting for, the tears come pouring out. Franka hesitates then drops to the bed and hugs him, gently rocking him back and forth like a baby.

'Oh dear,' she says from time to time. 'He isn't worth it. He really isn't. Anyone'll tell you. We're all amazed you put up with him for so long.'

He doesn't say to her that what he is crying for is more than this. The aerialist was his reason to be here, and without him he has nowhere. He simply cries on and on, drinking in the strange pleasure of letting go completely.

Finally Franka pulls back.

'Come on,' she says, and through his tears he suspects she is wishing she had never come in to check on him. 'Big Pete wants a meeting. It's what I came to tell you.'

He says he'll be out in a minute, and Franka nods sagely and tells him she'll see him out there. After she is gone he looks for the little mirror that usually hangs on the back of the door, sees that it is not there and realises Vlad has taken it. He thinks he is going to start crying all over again, but it seems that there are no tears left in him, and after a couple of chokes he gets a hold of himself, blows his nose and goes out.

Many of the company are now sitting around the fire amid the glittering detritus from last night. He knows everyone is watching him as he makes his way over, and that like him they are wondering what he will do now, and if he will stay on with the circus. He sees Franka and Griselda and sits with them, and Franka passes him a mug of lukewarm tea. She tells him that the contortionist has left with the Red Circus as well, and that Griselda wants to ask Big Pete to terminate their contract.

'He hasn't paid us a penny yet!' snaps Griselda, as if he had condemned this idea. But Franka is worried that if they do it he will not pay them at all.

'How did we get involved with this lame show anyway?' she sighs.

Griselda has other ideas already, and talks enthusiastically about a theatre company in Manchester that's looking for chorus girls who can perform tissu.

'If we could get it, the gig lasts all summer,' she says.

He nods and says of course, but it seems to be happening too fast, this abandonment, and there is something bewildering about it. He wants to tell them not to give up so easily. But it is not his place. Instead he takes a sip of the tea, which is refreshing but disgustingly sweet, and looks around, trying to find the clown. But Jethro is nowhere to be seen.

'I mean, where do you get off running a show if you can't even guarantee payment on –' Griselda starts to say, but at this moment the door to Big Pete's trailer bursts open and he emerges in full costume and make-up, his right arm held high and outstretched in welcome as if they were the audience for that night. The sight is such a surprise that there is a smattering of clapping from the gathered company, though most of it ironic.

'My dearest companions!' booms Big Pete in the deep ominous voice he puts on for the ring, the one in which he announces death-defying feats of aerial spectacular, twisting contortionism and side-splitting hilarity. 'As many of you will already know, we have an enemy out there, and that enemy has bent us over and shafted us right up the arse!'

He holds both hands out as if in appeal, and there are a couple of boos. But mostly the faces of people watching are unreadable. 'What does he think we are?' mutters Griselda. 'Stupid or something?'

'But what that enemy doesn't know is that I for one am sick of bending over!' Big Pete continues.

Someone at the back applauds, and a few heads turn to see who. But they stop before anyone can catch sight of them.

'So we've lost a couple of people. So we've fallen on hard times. So we're in a tight one. Does that mean it's time to give up?'

Big Pete pauses for dramatic effect and drops his chin as if he's been struck, only to lift it nobly up to the sky again.

'This circus was built on blood and sweat and tears – I built it, and I'm not about to let it all fall apart. Not without a fight. So I want you to understand this – you're all in my employ and you're all under contract, and you will all be paid. I promise. So let's stop pussying around and pull ourselves together, eh?'

Another pause. The ringmaster looks around at the faces of those assembled.

'What do you say?'

Silence. The spectacle of Big Pete trying to rally them as if they were his troops is excruciating, yet at the same time no one can tear their gaze away. It is almost hypnotic, a car crash of epic proportions.

'This show ain't over!' Big Pete proclaims. 'Not by a long shot!'

A couple of members of the company let out small cheers at this, including Midge, but the cheers peter out when it becomes clear that the majority are not going to join in. Big Pete glares at them, his shoulders squared and his fists clenched as if ready to take them all on at once. But just as Big Pete seems set to lose it his shoulders slump and his chest, so proud and puffed, turns concave as he exhales a long weary sigh. Finally the ringmaster raises his hand again and waves it at them. But this time the gesture is not theatrical, only dismissive.

'Come on then,' he snarls – it sounds as if he is choking – 'piss off and get packing. We've got a date to make in Lonsdale.'

People start to disperse. He hovers uncertainly, and in doing so accidentally meets Big Pete's gaze. The ringmaster's eyes lock on to him and he feels himself being assessed and inspected. He waits for the news that he is dead weight, useless, that it is time for him to fuck off and annoy someone else.

'As for you' – Big Pete says – 'there's cleaning up needs doing.'

Edward and he were giggling, but Paul walked a few steps in front, his arms folded tightly across his chest and his posture hunched like he was trying to ward off bad spirits. As they passed by the vicarage Edward gave his arm a squeeze and, trying not to laugh outright and give themselves away, they both quickly vaulted the small wall to the churchyard. Paul did not turn, and they ducked down behind it. Leaning against the wall and panting from the sudden spurt of energy, he kissed Edward hard on the mouth and felt him respond with equal force. Emboldened by alcohol and the effects of the joint, he reached for Edward's crotch and squeezed the swelling he found there, and thought he heard Edward gasp as he reached out to return the pressure.

'Hey, guys – where are you?' called Paul from somewhere up the road.

They peeped over the edge of the wall and watched Paul return, looking furious, his arms still tight against his chest as he looked from one direction to another. When he turned away from them Edward reached down, picked up a clod of earth and flung it. It connected beautifully with the back of Paul's neck.

'Ouch – hey!' Paul cried, whipping round. 'Look, where are you, OK?'

'Woooh,' he called, making a ghostly sound. 'Paaauliee! Come to me!'

Paul approached.

'Look, this really isn't —'

'Boo!'

He stood up and Paul let out a shriek and raised his hands as if to defend himself. He burst out laughing, but even in the dark he could see Paul was livid.

'You think you're so great, don't you?' Paul screamed at him. 'Just because he lets you go round with him. Well, I've got news for you, you're nothing but a sad hanger-on! And that's all you'll ever be!'

Paul panted, apparently exhausted by this outburst. He stared back at Paul for a few seconds, then smiled cruelly.

'If I'm a sad hanger-on, what does that make you?'

Paul looked as if he was about to explode.

'Children, children,' said Edward in a mock-motherly voice. 'Calm down now. It was my idea to hide, Paul dear. And it was me who threw the earth. I thought it would make a good joke. I'm sorry. The last thing I wanted to do was get you all worked up and bothered.'

Paul said nothing but fixed his glare on Edward instead. Looking contrite, Edward held out the half-finished bottle as a peace offering. For a few seconds he thought Paul was going to turn and run, and on the one hand he was pleased because it would leave him alone with Edward and on the other he was sorry, because they were getting such good sport out of him. But then Paul snatched up the bottle, wrenched off the cork, threw back his head and started to gulp it down. 'Steady on,' murmured Edward, but Paul did not stop until the bottle was empty. Then, looking exhilarated, he hurled it overarm in the direction of the church. There was a loud tinkling as it crashed against something made of stone.

'That's desecration,' he said. 'You hit one of the graves.'

'So fucking sue me,' Paul replied.

Paul took hold of the wall and vaulted over it with a sprightliness that surprised him, then started purposefully towards the church. He sniggered.

'Oh dear,' he said. 'He's become a rebel.'

Edward gave him a disapproving look, and he suddenly felt a little ashamed, as well as annoyed with Edward since just a moment ago they had been in cahoots and so now it was a bit rich for Edward to act as if he was the only one picking on Paul. He realised his bladder was aching and his head felt cloudy and light. He wasn't sure if it was caused by the joint, by the wine or by shame.

'Come along,' said Edward.

They set off after Paul and found him standing before the church gazing up at the tower, which looked rustic and quaint by daylight, but now, by the light of the moon, seemed ominous and eerily Gothic.

'Doesn't it just make you want to don a habit and sing hymns?' said Edward. He was talking to Paul, but Paul did not answer. Edward dug in his pocket and produced something that he handed to Paul with a lighter.

'Here,' said Edward. 'A little something I made earlier.'

It was another joint. Wordlessly Paul took it and lit it. He watched as Paul went through the same farce of taking in a mouthful of smoke and then letting it straight out again. Edward glanced at him as if to warn him not to say anything, then took the joint and had a long toke himself.

He looked up at the tower, at the spire that tapered into a cross atop which the moon seemed to be balanced like a precarious pearl, luminous white against a black mantle. Against the tower was a trellis, upon which a wandering rose had climbed almost to the tracery of the cross-shaped window beneath the spire.

'If you loved me, you'd fetch me that moon,' he said dreamily.

Edward peered up at it.

'Absolutely,' said Edward. 'Just wait here.'

Edward handed him the joint and made a movement towards the trellis, putting his foot on one of the wooden slats and making as if to climb. He laughed and Edward let out an exaggerated yawn.

'Well – perhaps in just a minute.'

He nodded, suddenly incredibly tired – too tired even to laugh any more or continue with the joke. He put the joint in his mouth and sucked on it then passed it to Paul who plucked it off him without looking at him. He felt another pang from his bladder.

'I'll be back,' he muttered, stumbling across the graveyard towards the hedgerow. Here he saw what seemed to be a large hole in the bushes, and he went through and found himself in a small enclosed bit of woodland, with several old beer cans lying around – which meant that other people must come here too. Pleased with his find, he unzipped and let out a long stream of piss, watching the white steam rise and then evaporate into nothingness in the dark.

At Lonsdale they do not go down well. Travelling in the opposite direction, the Red Circus has already been through here just a week before, and there is still a frayed corner of the gaudy poster advertising them on the town hall noticeboard. The smattering of audience they get look unimpressed – everyone knows they are being compared to the Red Circus and that they do not come off well in the comparison. Big Pete swears and shouts at the company more than ever before, and people avoid entering the big top until the very last minute, driving him almost to a frenzy. Pierce and Imogen's balancing act is now pushed to the headline spot, and backstage Pierce becomes angry when he hears Big Pete building them up to impossible proportions. When Big Pete returns backstage Pierce starts towards him, but Imogen stops him, putting a hand on Pierce's shoulder and whispering 'Don't.' Their act is met with polite applause, and people start to leave before Big Pete has even brought everyone back for the final bow. Afterwards there are complaints to the box office because Vlad the Vampire, prominently displayed on the posters, made no appearance, and Big Pete tells him to unravel each poster and insert over the image of Vlad a white sticker carrying snippets of praise for the circus from local newspapers. He spends a whole afternoon sitting cross-legged in the box office, pasting over the aerialist. With each poster his heart receives a wrench, for it is as if he is deleting the aerialist's very existence. After it is done Big Pete inspects the posters and grunts his satisfaction, but everyone who sees it is horrified by the white box and how ugly it makes the poster, and how uninviting it renders the circus.

The fact of Vlad's leaving is oddly distant to him, as if it has not yet properly set in. At night he misses the aerialist's body and the warm and salty smell of his skin, yet it is also peaceful not to have to worry about Vlad and what he will think and say. Not to have to be afraid when the aerialist fails to return at night, of where he is or what he is doing. The matter is no longer in his hands, and there is something soothing about the reliable throb in his heart when he returns after each show to the empty caravan, or when he wakes in the morning and traces his hands over the scattering of belongings Vlad did not see fit to take with him. He wonders if Vlad is already performing for the other circus, and he wonders if he has already got his eye on someone else, has already slept with them, perhaps even shares their bed on a regular basis. He wonders these things but they do not add to his suffering. It seems to him as if all along it was Vlad who was the adopted one and not he, and that deep down he knew eventually the aerialist would leave without him. He is grateful still to have the circus, such as it is.

On the morning they are due to leave Lonsdale Pierce and Imogen pay Big Pete a visit in his trailer. They are in there for five minutes. Shouting is heard, and then they emerge – Pierce red-faced and Imogen wide-eyed. Without a word to anyone, Imogen starts their car while Piece attaches their trailer, and, with no good-byes, they drive off.

He could hear a strange noise, but it wasn't until he had almost reached Paul that he realised it was Paul sobbing. He realised too that Edward had not gone off somewhere, but was lying on the ground, and that Paul was doing a sort of mad dance over him, as if he was having a fit. It was hard to make Edward out exactly, but as he got closer he saw Edward wasn't moving and his eyes were open and staring skywards.

Paul met his eyes and froze, his mouth opening ridiculously wide and his eyes round and shining in the moonlight. He pointed down at Edward.

'We have to get an ambulance ... We need ...'

He laughed and Paul gaped at him. Edward was being kind to Paul, trying to make him feel he was one of them again, because they had hidden from Paul and given him a scare. But Paul was such a bad actor that it was hard not to feel sorry for him.

'Oh no,' he said flatly. 'He's dead.'

He prodded Edward with his foot. Edward's face rolled to the side, revealing a crest of red foam that seemed to be bubbling up from a crack behind his left ear. Edward's brains oozing out of his head.

Time seemed to freeze and all he could hear was the steady thump of his heart. He saw that Edward's leg was twisted at an impossible angle, and despite the darkness he could make out something white and sharp jutting through the knee of his jeans, something that shouldn't be there at all.

'Not . . .' he heard himself say.

'He was climbing!' wept Paul, resuming his mad dance. 'He was climbing up to fetch the moon, he said, for you! He slipped . . . he hit his head on the ledge — he just bounced off it!'

He stood over Edward, thinking that he must check his pulse, try to remember CPR, must try to stop the bleeding. But he could not seem to do any of those things. All he could do was stand and stare at the bone protruding from Edward's knee. He swallowed.

'Go and find help,' he said.

His voice came out calm and ordinary. Paul stared at him for a few seconds. Suddenly Paul took off down the path, screaming at the top of his lungs, leaving him and Edward alone.

He tore his eyes away from Edward's leg and looked at his face. It didn't seem like Edward at all, but rather like a waxwork with

Edward's likeness. His eyes were empty and fixed on some undefinable point behind him, as if whatever substance it was that made Edward who he was had been sucked out through those glassy pupils.

He swallowed again, and the swallow turned into a shudder. Then it seemed as if something truly extraordinary was happening – the world was turning upside down and its contents were draining away into the endless darkness that now lay beneath his feet, glittering with stars like a jet black carpet flecked with shards of diamond.

It wasn't until much later, after the vicarage lights had come on and the vicar and his wife had followed Paul back to the churchyard to find out what he was raving about, and he had shaken his head unable to answer their questions, and the vicar had carefully draped his coat over Edward's face while his wife went to call the ambulance, that it occurred to him he must have fainted.

By now he will relish the aching in his muscles after each set of exercises – the deep shrieking pain in his tendons after each stretch, the pins and needles in his shoulders as the strength ebbs out of them, the soreness in his palms and fingers, and the flood of endorphins to his brain as he lies still on the mattress afterwards, gazing up at the trapeze.

Each night after he has eaten he will go to his room before he bathes, take off all his clothes and stand naked in front of the full-length mirror – the mirror salvaged from his mother's room. He will inspect the effects of his regime. The slight belly acquired over the years will have receded as a wall of muscle tightens around it like a girdle, forcing it to diminish almost entirely. His biceps and forearms will now carve themselves out of his arms in artful bumps and bulges. His back will have grown broader, bulkier, and his pectoral muscles will swell out from his torso like slabs of paving stone. He will admire these changes to himself, this sheath of strength growing out from his body, not from a sexual point of view – though he will be undeniably pleased with his new looks – but as if they were a trophy, one that grows incrementally more valuable. It will feel proof of the work he has done, medals from the ongoing battle to discipline his flesh.

But the real triumph will be his achievements with the stretching. By increasing his leg span in minuscule amounts each session, he will for the first time in his life be able to raise his leg above his head and kiss his own foot. It will be a point of pride with him now that he can slide into the splits from standing, and that every day he grows closer to a box split – letting his legs slide out on either side of him until he is sitting in straddle, his torso ever inching towards the floor.

When he looks at himself in the mirror his predominant impression will be of his body as a weapon, a missile created out of human tissue, one he has been honing with a single-mindedness of purpose such as he has never felt before. It is the power of despair, he will understand, that is the secret ingredient in this process. He will stare at his new body from every angle and he will feel as if he is ready for something. Though what that something is, he will not yet know.

After Lonsdale the company moves further south. At the next town they draw a moderate crowd for the first night and then only a handful of people for the follow-up shows. Big Pete holds a meeting in which he again tries to raise morale, telling the company he is advertising for new acts, and that there will be auditions once they reach Newquay, in which he will want to know what everyone thinks – for they are a family, he claims, and in his family everyone's opinion matters. But among themselves people are dubious: they are not falling for it. The discontent has spread like a disease, beyond the point of a cure. He overhears Griselda again talking about the theatre in Manchester that is looking for tissu girls, and this time when Franka replies she is openly enthusiastic.

He is hosing down the mud-splattered plastic covering on the outside of the entrance to the big top when the clown appears. He has seen him only briefly since the night Vlad left – coming out of his caravan to use the facilities and at the shows, in which he wanders drunkenly towards the stage entrance and gives a half-hearted half-inebriated performance, sometimes even falling over unintentionally. At the last show the little girl he picked on to caper with screamed and shouted to her mother about his stinky whisky breath. In other circumstances Big Pete would have said something, perhaps even threatened to fire the clown, but here he has no choice, and the ringmaster watches him stumble about the ring without a word, his jaw bulging as he grits back his anger.

'Bit early for you, isn't it?' he says, not glancing up. 'Sun's still up.'

'Watch,' Jethro says with a chuckle. 'Magic!'

He looks at the clown, who folds his arms and then unfolds them. From nowhere during this manoeuvre he produces two cans of beer. The clown holds one of them out to him. He shakes his head.

'Suit yourself,' shrugs the clown, pushing it into the pocket of his baggy jogging bottoms and opening the other can. He takes a slurp. 'So . . . how's life at the circus without the unicycle around to suck you off?'

Without pausing to consider whether or not it is a good idea he lifts the hose and aims it full blast at the clown, who is so shocked as the rush of cold water hits him that he drops his beer can and topples back against the canvas, sliding down to a choking heap on the grass.

'Arsehole!'

It is impossible to tell from the way the clown convulses if he is outraged or laughing. He does not care anyway. Invigorated by his own action, he lifts the hose and attempts to blast the clown again. But this time the clown is too fast for him and catches the nozzle, forcing it back on him so that he gets a fountain in his own face. He takes a mouthful, coughs and knocks the hose away. Still grappling with Jethro, he falls forward on top of the clown.

All at once they are no longer choking, laughing or fighting, and it seems inevitable that they will kiss. He sees the clown's face up close, takes in the lines around those cynical eyes, his dirt-speckled pores and the skin of his nose laced with red veins from alcoholism. The clown smirks at him, and a frisson of disbelief that he is actually going to do this runs down his spine. Then, at the last possible second, they both turn their heads, and he rocks backwards onto his haunches.

The clown wipes his face with his sleeve, gives him a rueful look and then reaches for the beer. He watches Jethro knock back a gulp and catches sight of something behind the clown – a ripple of movement in the window of Big Pete's trailer. The clown turns and follows his gaze.

'He's daft not to have folded, you know,' Jethro says. 'Stark fucking in-your-eyes bonkers.'

He nods. It is what everyone is saying.

'Are you leaving too?' he says.

The clown turns back to him, actually looking self-conscious for a split second, as if he has been caught out. Then he brushes a hand back over his sodden Mohican and smirks again.

'Gotta jump ship or else get dragged down with it. That's how it goes. Best start making some plans yourself.'

'Big Pete's not jumping ship,' he replies quietly.

'Yeah, well, he's the fucking captain. He's gotta go down with it.'

He stares at the grass. He wants to tell the clown that he doesn't have a choice either, but it will only sound soppy and Jethro will make fun of him, he is sure. When he looks up he finds that the clown is not smirking any more but watching him closely. He feels himself blush under the clown's inspection, for it is as if Jethro is looking right through him and seeing whatever there is to see inside. He picks up the hose and stands, turning his attention back to the muddy canvas.

'Time to face the real world,' says the clown, not getting up. 'Whatever it is you got waiting out there, this episode is over, my friend. Time to get on. That's the way the bitch goes.'

In those first days after the accident it was as if he had fallen into a trance. Everything was unfocused and fuzzy around the edges, and time drifted by inexactly, almost as if it no longer had any purpose, whether it went forwards or backwards or remained frozen still. He slept a lot, sinking into a daze in which he dreamed of nothing in particular, opening his eyes to find with surprise that he was still himself, lying on his bed in his room. Sometimes it would take a few seconds for him to remember what had happened, and he would sit up in bed and woozily think about calling Edward. Then his stomach would knot tightly as it all came back to him in a sickening rush, together with the knowledge that he would not be calling Edward ever again.

When he was not sleeping he would stare at the ceiling or the wall, or else find an object on his shelf which he would study so intensely its dimensions would eventually blur and cease to make sense. He would tell himself that he was looking for a way through to a parallel universe – a door between this reality and the next, one in which Edward might still be alive and well with new ideas about how to overthrow the established order of things. He felt that if only he could concentrate hard enough, stare at a door or a book or a lampshade long enough, the way would be revealed and he could slip through into that other world where things were yet to be ruined.

At other times he would go over and over what had happened, combing through the evening detail by detail, who had said what and in what order. He would scour his memory for missing pieces, desperately seeking the forgotten information that would make sense of it. But he soon discovered that nothing would make sense of it, because it was death, and death refused to make sense no matter which angle you examined it from.

At mealtimes he would fork into his mouth the requisite amount to appease the worried eyes of his mum, then return to his room, from which he would not resurface until it was time for the next meal. One morning at breakfast his mum broke the silence to tell him Edward's mother had invited him to go to Edward's funeral, and that it was being held that afternoon. But the mere words made him choke on his mouthful, coughing his food back up over the plate. Then he slammed his hands over his ears as if he had heard a secret that could kill and fled from the table, and his mum did not ask him again.

At dawn he is woken by the sound of an engine being revved, and wheels scraping over the uneven ground outside. He gets up and opens the door. In the weak morning light he sees that the clown's caravan is gone. There are a couple of people out who have also been woken by the noise, smoking reflectively as they stand or squat on the steps of their trailers. He looks over to Big Pete's trailer, but all is dark and quiet within.

Once news spreads that the clown has left, the circus seems to dissolve all at once. One minute they are a company, the next everyone is saying goodbye to one another, hugging and high-fiving, packing up his or her things and preparing to move on out. He accepts embraces and handshakes and assurances of goodwill with a frozen smile, trying to hide the despair he feels. Franka is tearful and cannot stop sniffling, and she holds him tightly, making him promise to stay in touch. Griselda just looks cross and tight-lipped, and hugs people one by one in a perfunctory manner, as if she cannot wait to get out of there. Midge suggests a final drink to everyone, but most are too busy packing up to accept his offer. Throughout it all Big Pete remains hidden. Everyone seems to be expecting him to come out, to try one last time to rally people and get them to give the circus a final chance. But he does not even come to the window. The lights stay off and people take it as a sign that the ringmaster has given up too.

'Bah,' mutters Midge. 'Let him rot. Come on.'

'What about the big top?' he says.

It is still up, looking strangely unimpressive, even forlorn, in the wake of its abandonment. Midge launches a glob of spit in the direction of Big Pete's trailer and swipes his hand across the air.

'Not a fucking penny he's paid us,' Midge mutters. 'Let him take it down himself.'

'Listen,' says Benny, coming up behind, 'we're heading to Leicester if you want a lift.'

He shakes his head. Benny glances between him and the big top and Midge rolls his eyes and jerks his thumb towards their truck.

'Come on, if he wants to stay with that old motherfucker then let him!'

Benny shrugs. Midge has already started to walk away.

'Ignore him,' Benny says, sticking out his hand. 'So long.'

He shakes the roustabout's hand and Benny turns and follows Midge to their pickup. They are the last ones to leave, tooting their horn at him as they turn off up the road.

He wanders across the field into the empty big top and takes a seat on the bleachers at the edge of the ring. Outside the sun has broken through the grey cloud and it is shaping up to be a beautiful day. Yet there is something tragic about the glimpse of golden light through the transparent covering over the entrance.

'What're you still here for?' bellows Big Pete from behind him, making him leap. 'You waiting for pay? Cos there ain't any! And even if there was, you'd be the last one to see it – I got a line of people what want money crawling right up my arse!'

Big Pete pauses, draws a deep drag on the cigarette dangling out of his mouth.

'I'm not waiting for pay,' he says.

The ringmaster emits a great whoosh of smoke.

'Then what you still doing here, eh?'

'I just . . .'

'You just what?'

He bites his lip and looks around. He thinks of the first time he set foot inside the big top and how the excitement seemed to course through him as if the circus had been injected straight into his veins. Now it looks like nothing – its contents, that which makes the circus what it is, have evacuated, leaving only this great blue shell behind. It is no longer even a big top really, just a giant canopy stretching over him obscuring the sky. He looks at Big Pete and takes in the challenge in his eyes, the refusal to show defeat. Without another word he turns and walks towards the exit. 'Go on then – fuck off!' he hears the ringmaster snarl to his back as he passes out and into the daylight. He wonders briefly what Big Pete will do, now that he has lost everything. But he does not pause or turn back. He walks past the caravan, which he wants nothing from, and carries on walking to the edge of the field.

A couple of days after the funeral the school guidance counsellor made a house call, either on her own initiative or at his mum's request, he did not know which. His mum sent her up and she stood in the doorway to his room while he lay on his bed with his back to her, asking questions which he did not have the answers to.

'If there's anything you want to talk about, anything at all, it's OK,' she told him. 'I'm here simply in order to listen. Nothing else.'

He ignored her. She paused, then tried a different tack.

'I understand from talking to Paul that you had something of a relationship with Edward. That you were special friends. Perhaps you'd like to talk about that?'

Still he did not turn.

'It can be very good to talk about things, even if you don't feel you want to. Letting it out is always better than keeping it bottled up. I know there've been times when I've just wanted to crawl under a rock and hide, but afterwards I always regretted it, because the more I crawled away the harder it was to crawl back. It's important you understand that no matter what you tell me, I'm not going to judge. Only listen.'

She continued in this vein for some time, now and then lapsing into silence before starting up again, until finally he did turn and told her in no uncertain terms that what he'd really like was for her to fuck off. But after she'd left his room he grew curious and crept out to the landing to listen to her conversation with his mum. He overheard her saying his behaviour was completely standard in light of what had happened, and that she wouldn't be surprised if he felt guilty. He should come for regular sessions with her, she said, as soon as he went back to school, something he knew he had no intention of doing. In the meantime perhaps he should spend a few days with his father? His mum agreed. Eventually, promised the counsellor, he would return to being the boy he was before. He listened to his mum saying that she hoped as much, and almost laughed for the first time since it had happened, because he knew that really she did not want him back the way he had been before and if anything preferred him this way. He thought to himself that he didn't want to be the same again either. His mum hadn't liked Edward and had told him to keep away from him, perhaps knowing with some hidden psychic sense that it would end in disaster, and now he wished more than anything that he had obeyed her. At least if he had kept away Edward would still be alive.

They will seem to him preposterous, an invading posse consisting of two men and a woman, all dressed in smart clothes and wearing rosy ingratiating smiles. No sooner will he have said a cautious hello than the woman will have begun to gabble at him. Her name is Sue, she will say, and the two men are called Daniel and Bob, they are all from the local council and are delighted to meet him.

'OK ...' he will say cautiously.

Sue will widen her smile to reveal lots of perfect white teeth that may or may not be dentures and will extend her arm towards him and regally offer him her hand. Not knowing what else to do, he will take it.

'We want to commission a performance!' Sue will say grandly.

'Pardon?' he will say.

'A performance! For the town fête!'

Sue will extract her hand and gesture into the air, like a magician conjuring up an illusionary spectacle.

'You see, this year we've been desperately wanting to do something that everyone can enjoy, not just the old folks. We don't want to finish with the town band doing their usual repertoire and sending everyone off to sleep. Boring!' – she will perform an elaborate mime of someone yawning and falling asleep – 'So we sat around and racked our brains at the meeting the other night, and then someone said, "Eureka! What about that fellow in the papers who does the trapeze?" Well, we all agreed it was a simply marvellous idea … But then it was a matter of trying to get in touch to see what you thought about it – nobody could get through on the phone! So I said to them last night – I said, "I'm going to go down there myself and put it to him in person!" Bobby and Dan decided to come along for muscle, so to speak –'

'Look,' he will interrupt, 'the thing is –'

' – and I can't tell you how exciting we all find it,' she will interrupt back, trying to peer past him at what he has done to the house. He will automatically pull the door towards him to block out any sight. '… and there's a gentleman from the TV station who's interested in potentially filming the event! Maybe even making a sort of feature out of it! He's asked if it would be all right for him to call around later this afternoon, to have a chat –'

'I'm afraid that's –'

'Before you make your mind up, do you suppose we could come in and have a peek? Maybe you could even show us a couple of things that you do? We'll be needing to get some idea for health and safety, since it'll have to be done in the school field as usual – obviously we can't hold it in your house!'

She will let out a girlish laugh and make a move forward, as if expecting him to dematerialise. But he will stand firm as a sentry, forcing her to stop inches from his face, the ghost of a frown rippling across her forehead.

'Look, it's very kind of you,' he will say. 'But it's not something I'd be interested in. Thank you very much for taking the time to come and see me.'

Sue will look astonished for a second.

'Oh, but think of how proud everyone will be of you! To have someone from their very own town putting on a proper circus show. People'll go mad for it, I tell you. And it'd make you ever so popular! I do sometimes think' – Sue's frown will deepen and she will lower her voice to almost a whisper, as if afraid of being overheard – 'I do sometimes think that there are people who don't realise community is about giving as well as taking, and that if you have something worth sharing, something that you can share at no expense to yourself, you do have a certain duty. I mean, that's the essence of what a community is.'

'Really –'

'And in case you were to consider it' – she will hold up a hand – 'in case you were, we'd take care of all the expenses. The council's got a fund specifically put aside for this kind of thing. And Bobby's already done some investigation into how we can get a rig set up. They can put it up above the stage, easy, if you could provide the trapeze – they just clip on and off, isn't that right? With the little thingumajigs? And we'll make sure to see it gets filmed and put on the town website. I mean, I really don't see how you could possibly say no!'

He will laugh, it will all be so ridiculous. But this will be a woman who does not give up. She will continue to plead and wheedle, delivering her arguments with the consistency of a battering ram, while Bob and Daniel stand silent and knowing behind her, smugly certain of his eventual submission.

'After all,' Sue will almost screech at him, her voice rising to a crescendo and her hand lifting to the heavens as if calling on the gods to bear witness, 'what on earth is the point of it all if you're not going to show off what you can do?'

He walks through the town, following the signs to the station. At a cashpoint outside he stops and withdraws as much money as he can. He is overdrawn to the maximum now, and for the first time it occurs to him how mad it is to have been scrubbing toilets for the last four months for no pay and he smiles grimly to himself. At the station he buys a one-way ticket to London and waits on the platform for nearly an hour, until a slow train crawls to a halt before him. He gets on and takes a seat opposite two old women who try their best not to look troubled by his presence and only end up making a display out of the fact they obviously are. He is dirty and unkempt – on the road the dirt has a way of getting into the skin and hair and refusing to come off. He watches the countryside and towns roll past his window and gradually a hypnotic calm settles over him. He starts to feel impossibly sleepy. The two old women eye him suspiciously but he does not care. He gives in to the need to close his eyes. When he wakes up they are rolling into Paddington and the women are gone.

He gets out and is startled by the crush of people. It has been years since he was in the city and he has not prepared himself for the sheer quantity of human beings all pressed together in one place. He feels a rush of fear and alienation, compounded by the myriad bodies flailing against him, and by the sensation that he is the only person who does not know exactly what he wants or where he is going. He has an urge to drop to the ground and huddle himself up into a tiny ball. He pushes his way through the people towards the Underground station and buys a ticket. On the Tube journey he is pressed up against two businessmen who stink of cheap cologne, and after they get off a woman in full black hijab who smells powerfully of body odour and who stares intensely at his feet. It is so crowded that he misses the stop where he is supposed to change, unable to get off before the doors close, and has to ride back on himself to get to King's Cross. By the time he reaches his station and climbs the stairwell up to the city, the sky is dark.

When he reaches his destination it turns out to be a nondescript, faded red-stone building, stained by splatterings of pigeon shit, the façade weathered in parts to the point of crumbling away. He climbs the broken steps and presses the button for the top flat, creating an electric buzzing sound which is followed by eerie silence. He waits with trepidation, suddenly suspecting that it will all have been for nothing, until the tannoy abruptly crackles into life. A voice he recognises, despite the static distortion, says, 'Yep – who is it?'

He clears his throat.

'Paul?' he says.

He returned to school the following week. 'It'll be good for you,' declared his mum, in a voice that brooked no refusal. He didn't refuse. Whether he was in his bedroom or the classroom it would make no difference. His exams were approaching, and he knew she was worried that he would fail them because of what had happened, and he knew that she was right to be worried because he probably would. Certainly he did not care about passing them. But the next morning he took his backpack out and got his books together, and went downstairs at breakfast time.

'Oh – you're ready!'

She sounded surprised and pleased, and she smiled at him and hurried to pour him a cup of tea and put on some toast. Eat up, she told him brightly, and she would give him a lift on her way to work. He saw she was relieved, and had taken his readiness as a positive sign.

At school he hovered for a few seconds in the doorway to the classroom, overcome with horror at the sight of where he used to sit with Edward, at the empty seats – the unthinkable knowledge that one of them would remain empty. But then the bell went and a press of bodies propelled him inside, and before he could sit there someone else had claimed the space, and he found himself instead forced to sit at a desk close to the back, not far from where Katy sat. He could feel himself being studied by the others – their eyes combing over him, awed into silence by the knowledge of what had happened even as they were galvanised by their curiosity.

'Oi, gay boy,' hissed a voice from behind him finally. 'Who you gonna hang round with now your bum chum ain't around?'

The boy followed his comment with a giggle. He did not turn.

'Shut the fuck up,' he heard another kid say.

The teacher arrived before the other boy could retort. He saw her looking at him and knew from her expression she had been briefed about how to handle him. The teacher did not pick on him once throughout the lesson, or ask him to do any reading out loud. He was the last to leave the classroom and on his way out she cast him a look and a sympathetic smile, and there was something so awful about it that he could do nothing but duck his head and hurry out of the room.

In the corridor he ran straight into Katy, who had been told to stay behind along with two boys because they would not stop whispering while the teacher was talking. He tried to go past them but Katy stood in his way.

'So,' Katy said, stabbing his chest with her index finger. 'We heard you killed your boyfriend. Nice work – murderer.'

He stared at her.

'How come they let you back to school anyway?' she continued. 'Shouldn't you be in prison or something getting arse-raped? I bet you'd like that though, wouldn't you? Is that why you did it? So you could go to prison and get arse-raped?'

She wore a huge grin, the faces of the boys behind her had mirroring grins.

'Fuck off,' he said, sounding dead to his own ears.

Katy shook her head from side to side in an exaggerated style.

'Murderer!'

'I do beg your pardon!'

The teacher had appeared at the door with her arms folded and a scowl on her face. Instantly Katy lost her grin and looked at the floor.

'Get inside – now!' the teacher barked.

He took off down the corridor before the teacher could give him another of her looks or say anything about how he should just ignore the others. He hurried up the stairs to the room where the first set, the brainy kids, were taught. They were just coming out, and he waited for Paul to surface, but soon everyone had gone and he had not emerged. He peered inside through the little window in the door in case Paul was still packing up his things, but the room was empty.

He skipped the rest of school and went walking around town instead, avoiding the places where he might run into people who knew him. He came back towards the end of the day and waited on the climbing frame in the playground, watching the main doors intently. When the bell rang both doors opened and kids streamed out in a torrent. Soon it had slowed to a trickle and within half an hour nobody but the staff was leaving the school. Still there was no sign of Paul.

Once Paul has got over the shock of seeing him and has accepted his vague muffled explanation, something that requires Paul to perform a sort of dance around him and prod him and then pinch himself, he tells him he can stay as long as he likes.

'I just don't believe it!' Paul keeps exclaiming. 'Blanket silence for months and suddenly here you are! I mean, talk about taking a walk on the wild side. You ran away and joined a fucking circus!'

Paul's flat is much nicer than the outside of it suggests. It is small but expensively decorated, with red fleur-de-lis wallpaper, leather upholstery and art deco mirrors etched with traceries of leaves and soulful Grecian women. As he shows him to a tiny guest room that contains nothing but a skylight and a single bed, Paul tells him proudly that he will be the owner by the end of the year.

'Sorry,' Paul apologises, as he sits down on the bed, 'I haven't finished doing it up.'

'Thank you,' he says. 'It's wonderful.'

'It's a dive,' corrects Paul. 'But you're welcome. Hey – did you have a bag with you?'

He shakes his head, and watches Paul's mouth drop open again as he explains he does not have any belongings.

'But . . . your clothes?'

'I borrowed someone else's while I was – on the road.'

'OK,' says Paul, obviously struggling with this concept more than the idea of him joining a circus. 'Well, darling, those rags need to be darned, or else maybe burned. I'll dig around my wardrobe and see if I've got some old thing that's your size.'

Paul vanishes and he sits down on the bed with a heavy sigh. He has all but forgotten the luxury of a proper mattress. He realises he wants nothing more than to lie back against the pillow and close his eyes again, to sink into blissful oblivion. He thinks about Big Pete and wonders what he is doing – if he is still there, in the big top, sitting huddled at the centre of the ring with a case of beer, getting drunk and reflective. Then he thinks about the clown and where he might be – already drunk no doubt, and probably getting drunker, perhaps in some bar, or else in his caravan parked at the side of a field on the edge of some obscure town. Finally he thinks about Vlad, imagines him in the air at that very moment, swinging back and forth on the trapeze, releasing his hands and catching the ropes with his ankles to breathless applause from below. He tries to imagine someone like himself watching the aerialist from a hole in the curtain backstage, waiting with water and to rub his sore muscles and assure him that he was amazing. The image is strikingly clear.

'Here you are, my lovely.'

Paul stands in the doorway brandishing two glasses of red wine, a bundle of clothing over one arm which he somehow manages to toss onto the bed without spilling a drop. Paul sits down on the edge of the mattress beside him and holds out one of the glasses.

'Come along now,' says Paul in the manner of someone taking charge of a situation. 'Time for you to give Paulie the whole story.'

The weak morning light created pale shadows over the carpet as he crept along the landing and then, very carefully, began to descend the stairs. From the sitting room he could hear static from the radio and the telltale sounds of Radio 4, and his mother chewing her breakfast and the local paper rustling as she turned its pages. He went to the table and opened the drawer for the phone book. Fumbling he opened it and ran his thumb down the list of names until he found the number he wanted. Then, with a shaking hand, he lifted the phone.

It rang for a few seconds.

'Hello?' said Paul.

Suddenly he couldn't bring himself to speak.

'Hello? Who is this please?'

Paul sounded completely normal, as if everything was right with the world.

'Paul?'

There was a pause. It seemed to him he could almost feel the shock settle over Paul as he realised who it was.

'I'm not supposed to talk to you,' Paul said eventually. His voice had changed to flat and mechanical-sounding – empty of any feeling. 'Mum said.'

'What are you on about?' he cried. 'Paul, where have you been? I waited for you at school . . .'

'Why?'

'Because –'

He did not know. He only knew that there was something he needed, and that for some reason Paul was the only one who could give it to him.

'I don't go there any more. I've moved to St John's.'

'What?!'

'I'm not supposed to talk to you,' Paul repeated in his dull voice.

'Why did it have to happen?' he heard himself demanding. 'Why?'

He sobbed, and felt a stunned silence permeate the line. For a while the whole world seemed to have gone quiet, and all that remained was the sound of his own grunts and gasps. Then there was another voice in the background, one which said, 'Who is it, Paul?' He heard the phone being transferred and Paul's mother came on the line.

'Hello? Can I help you?' she said.

He sniffed, sucking back up his outburst, microscopic shudders running through his body from the effort of not collapsing.

'Don't call here again,' said Paul's mum quietly. 'He's got nothing to say to you and neither have I. You should deal with your own conscience and leave Paul alone.'

With these words she put the phone down. He stood there in the hall for a long time listening to the dialing tone.

'Sweet mother of all that's holy,' says Paul eventually, after he has given him a short rundown of all that has happened to him in the past four months. He smiles. It feels as though he has been talking about someone else, as if he is telling his story from an outside perspective. It is edited of course, does not and cannot contain all the information. The emotions have been censored, as if they were merely by the by and not the crucial underlying element that dictated the various chapters of his tale. He takes a sip of the wine and wonders if Paul believes him. It has all sounded incredible to his own ears, too incredible, and sitting there in Paul's nice flat he could almost believe it never happened.

'Darling!' Paul declares. 'You have outdone us all. I salute you.'

Paul raises his glass and he raises his glass in return and they clink them together. He cannot help his face flushing, partly from pride and partly from the simple bolt of happiness that comes from being praised for his adventure.

'So why, darling?'

'Why?'

'Why did you do it? What was the straw that broke the camel's back?'

He is pulled up short by the question, and glances up to find Paul is not smiling any more but peering at him intently. Paul genuinely wants to understand, he thinks.

'I suppose maybe I was having some sort of a nervous breakdown,' he hears himself say, grinning stupidly at the words as they come out of his mouth, for they sound like a line from a play or a film, not something you openly admit to in an ordinary conversation. 'I saw the circus and I chased after it. At the time it seemed like the only thing I could do.'

Paul nods, but now he is frowning.

'And what about your dear mama?'

He swallows. The mere mention of her creates a fissure of guilt, one that threatens to become an abyss.

'I haven't spoken to her since I left.'

Paul absorbs this information seriously. For a minute he almost expects Paul to start admonishing him, telling him what he already knows – that he is selfish and thoughtless and that his mother must be half out of her mind. But instead Paul lets out a short sharp laugh.

'So you finally severed the old umbilical cord!' he crows. 'We must celebrate immediately!'

He will pass the night badly, waking up in hot sweats and tearing off his T-shirt, only to find himself shivering and clammy just moments later. His breathing will become unnaturally heavy and stilted. Eventually he will rise and wander the house in the darkness, feeling his way from room to room like a blind man. When he comes to the kitchen he will reach out and take the rope and then, almost as if in his sleep, he will feel himself begin to climb, and then he will be sitting on the trapeze, swaying gently to and fro in the gloom.

He will sit there for hours, adjusting his position now and then as the bar digs into his buttocks and thighs. The sun will begin to rise and with it will come the realisation that he has indeed been waiting for something, and that furthermore the time for that something has finally come.

He will descend from the trapeze and pull the lid off the dustbin. There on top of the rubbish will be the torn fragments of the piece of paper on which Sue wrote her number, and he will fit them back together as if they were a jigsaw and lay them out on the table. Satisfied, he will go upstairs and sleep soundly until midday.

When he wakes he will feel warm and contented, almost euphorically at ease. He will rise and go immediately downstairs and collect the pieces of paper. He will go through to the hall, plug in the phone and dial the number.

She will pick up almost immediately.

'Hello, Sue speaking.'

At the sound of her high-pitched sing-song he will feel a spear of doubt, and will stand there deliberating over whether or not simply to put the phone back down again. Then, remembering his difficult night, he will take a breath.

'I'd like to do it,' he will say.

Dusky orange lights swirl against dark walls, illuminating the people sitting around the various booths so dimly they are turned into ghostly clusters of moving shadow. Only when someone walks to the bar is he lit fully, a face flaring up out of the darkness as if someone has struck a match beneath it. He has an uneasy thought that the atmosphere is almost like being in an abattoir, surrounded by strung-up carcasses.

'I think I'm going to call it a night,' he says.

'What?' Paul stares at him, the whites of his eyes shining in the gloom. 'Don't be ridiculous, we just got here!'

'I have a headache.'

'Darling, that's because you've hardly drunk anything.'

'No – really,' he says uncomfortably, but Paul is taking his arm, motioning to a friend over in the corner talking to a series of homologous shapes, a homologous shape himself.

'Come along now,' says Paul coquettishly. 'We need to find you someone. You're not getting any younger and a fact is a fact – no one loves a fairy when she's forty.'

He submits and allows himself to be led back to the bar where Paul orders two beers and two tequila shots, takes his hand and squeezes lime juice on the knuckle followed by salt and makes him lick it, do the shot and wedge the lime rind into his teeth. His mouth prickles, his head swims and his throat smarts – but it is a good smarting. Paul is right, he does feel better, like someone who has had the sense slapped back into them.

'Over there. He's looking,' says Paul. 'Show some teeth.'

He does but it is a sheepish smile, and the man seems to be turned off by it because he looks away and resumes his conversation with the silhouette beside him.

'Prick,' Paul supplies.

Paul leads him back to the table where his friend is and he finds himself inserted between the friend and a skinny man in a white vest with beautiful big eyes. Both ignore him and continue talking to one another, something he feels is just as well as he can hardly hear anything over the music, and is amazed they are even able to conduct a conversation. Every so often Paul catches his eye and smiles at him, and he is touched by his concern and tries to make an effort to look like he is having a good time. But really he wishes he was elsewhere, and if there was anywhere else for him to go, he knows he would leave.

They are joined by more people and everyone squeezes up into the booth to let more bodies sit down. He finds his thigh firmly pressed against the skinny man's, but the skinny man does not acknowledge that they are touching. He concentrates on drinking his beer and before he knows it the bottle is empty and Paul's friend is asking if he wants another. He nods and mouths the words 'thank you', and the friend glances at Paul, as if agreeing on something they have previously discussed. While the friend is gone the skinny man finally notices him and asks him something he doesn't catch.

'Sorry?'

The man repeats himself.

'I'm sorry, I'm deaf, I didn't catch that!' he bellows.

The skinny man nods, seemingly amused and leans over. For a second he thinks he is going to kiss him, but then the man cups his ear and says, 'You're the guy from the circus, right?'

'Right,' he says.

'Cool. What was it like?'

He is going to tell him but at this point the friend returns with their beers and the skinny man loses interest. He smiles to himself and looks away, and finds that he is being checked out again by the man who was looking earlier. This time the man grins at him. He is thickset and has a shaven head, and even at a distance and in the murk of the club his teeth look flawless and unnaturally white, almost like the teeth of a vampire. He ignores the instinct to look away and stares back. Then he nods at the man, and the man nods too. As if in harmony they both rise up from their tables.

As the days went by he felt himself go through the motions of living – eating meals, going to school, doing homework, watching television, going to bed, and without it costing him any effort he gradually settled into a routine. In lessons he never spoke up unless spoken to first, and he avoided the other kids during break by staying inside. At home he ate his meals quietly while his mum chatted about the day as if everything was back to normal – and in a way it was. Not the normal it had been while Edward was around, but the normal as it was before he had met Edward, back when he had been the reticent and polite boy his parents had always intended for him to be. He listened to his mum's bland talk about the old people's home, about his dad who was due to come for a visit at the weekend, about the state of the garden or some slice of town gossip, and he discovered he felt no disdain or scorn. The mediocre details of the week ahead, the impending empty conversations with his dad over cups of tea, the overgrown hedges and the stories about childless old women whom nobody wanted to visit were even soothing. He understood finally why someone might want to shield themselves from the wilder aspects of life. It was comforting to pretend they were not there, that if you ignored violence and danger and death and anything that signified these things they would go away and leave you alone.

A month later he sat his exams and to everyone's surprise received decent marks. The teachers congratulated him and said it was amazing under the circumstances that he had managed to take them at all; his mum smiled proudly and his dad, who was down from Swindon especially for his results, put his hand on his shoulder and allowed it to rest there for a few seconds. They spoke about what he would study in the sixth form, if he might want to go to college and what sort of a job he might go on to have. He saw his future being mapped out – a future of ordinary people and ordinary places, of careful steps and calculated decisions, of safety, security and above all comfort. And as his parents discussed his options while he sat there in front of them listening and not saying a word, he discovered that these things were exactly what he wanted.

He feels the man's tongue pushing into his mouth, his hands over his body, kneading his back, his buttocks, his thighs, their groins tightly pressed together. He thinks of Vlad, of his smile and of his furious needy kisses. Then he sees again Vlad's face as he left, smells the departing scent of his body and hears the flippancy of his good-bye. It is too much and suddenly he is sober and unaroused.

'What's wrong?' says the man. He has a high nasal voice very much at odds with his near hyper-masculine appearance.

He pulls away.

'I'm sorry,' he says. 'I don't think I'm up for this.'

The man stares at him. He feels his hands and arms dropping away from his waist and shoulders. Then the hand returns in a sudden last-ditch assault, snaking down his chest and fastening onto his crotch. He reaches down and pushes it away.

'I'm sorry.'

'Whatever – fuck off,' mutters the man, walking away, leaving him to his pocket of darkness at the corner of the club. His head is starting to pound in time to the ceaseless beat of the music, which seems almost to be mocking him.

He staggers through the club looking for Paul, pushing past the crowd of hot, half-clothed bodies, naked glistening torsos and huge saucer-like eyes. He catches sight of Paul at the centre of them, his T-shirt wet and flat against his body, his limbs jerking around as if in the throes of a violent orgasm.

He reconsiders. Turning round, he heads for the cloakroom where he collects his things. Then he walks quickly up the stairs, past the bouncers and out into the night.

He never intended to be a carer. It felt to him that it had just happened, as if it were something predestined and beyond his control. The truth was that it was the most logical path to take, and to deviate once he had embarked upon it would have been to invite uncertainty into his life. After he finished school his mother got him a proper job working with her at the home over the summer, and he spent long hot days changing bedpans and bed sheets, helping old men to their baths and commodes, helping wheelchair users take walks and fetching an endless cycle of cups of tea and digestive biscuits. The head carer told him she thought he had a special aptitude for caring and suggested he get himself a formal training. His mum liked the idea: she was proud of him at the home and frequently told him how happy he made the residents. He applied to the local college and was accepted for a course in domestic care. Two years later he had his qualification and two caring placements, one in town and one just a few miles away in the next county, both with elderly men who had difficulty using the stairs and strongly resented having to depend on anyone else. They had been through a number of carers, finding something to complain about in each one. But they liked him, because he was quiet and polite, and because he did not answer back when they got frustrated. Though neither ever said as much, he could tell they were pleased and knew the agency was happy with the work he was doing, and he thought that it must be true: that he really did have an aptitude for caring, and it was what he was meant to do with his life.

Years later he began to understand what a cruel joke this was. The title carer was misleading, he realised, because he didn't actually care, he only behaved as if he did. One elderly person was much the same as the next, and if anything he had desensitised himself to the anguishing sight of human helplessness, something he witnessed day upon day at all his placements. He found himself adopting the same exaggerated cheer as his mother, making the same overly bright greetings and offering the same inane observations about inconsequential things which he had always secretly hated. But now he understood why it was done – not for the sake of the patients, but for the sake of the carer and the relatives. Not in order that they did not have to face up to the helplessness of those before them, but so that they did not have to face up to their own helplessness, in the presence of time as it marched unstoppably over the human body, ravaging and pillaging until there was nothing left but for it to surrender.

His mum never mentioned the fact that he was gay, not even when they were watching television and the subject came up on talk shows or the news. She did not talk about him settling down, or meeting a nice partner, and he did not talk about it either. From time to time he would mention plans to move out of the house, pretending that he still had ambitions of going off to lead a more independent life one day. But the subject made his mother turn pale and look so frightened that he was soon overcome with guilt and fell silent.

He rarely met people his own age, and when he did they were usually other carers – big-boned, round-faced girls from New Zealand and Australia, for few British people under the age of fifty seemed to aspire to be carers. Once in a while he would drive to the next town to visit its one gay club, where he would sit slowly sipping at a single pint of lager and watching the room. He was very rarely approached by any of the men he liked, the ones who went to the bar to pick up, and he never got up the courage to approach anyone either. The older men, the ones who routinely propped up the bar, tried to draw him out in conversations laden with innuendo, and with blunt questions about his sexual preferences, but he was terrified of them, though most looked as if they would soon be in need of care themselves. He responded with the same blandness as he used on the people he looked after, it was as if he was unable to speak in any other way, and when they went too far trying to get a rise out of him, saying something shocking or indecent, he would give a light laugh and ignore them as if that was all there was to it. Eventually they became used to him and stopped bothering, and he discovered he could sit there for hours completely ignored, until it was time for him to go home.

He often had the sense that he ought to be leading a different kind of existence, that the way he lived was no life for a gay man in modern times. He fantasised about being the sort of person he saw on TV or in films, a guy who went out clubbing with his friends, sharing with them a stock of witticisms he could trawl out whatever the occasion, yet someone who also knew when to stop being witty and how to fall in love, and more importantly how to make someone else fall in love with him in return. But he knew in his heart that he was not this fantasy person, if indeed there really was such a character, and moreover he never would be.

It will be a warm and sunny morning and he will be practising his beats with the back door open to let in the breeze, when he will become aware of a presence and look down to see Mrs Goodly waving at him from right underneath, her head inches away from his swinging feet.

'Sorry to barge in!' she will shout, oblivious to her peril. 'I tried knocking and calling but you didn't answer. But I knew you were here!'

He will reach for the rope and slide down to the floor.

'Gosh, look at you,' she will say as he stands waiting to get his breath back.

'You shouldn't walk underneath me like that,' he will pant. 'I could have kicked your head off.'

Mrs Goodly will giggle coquettishly.

'Come to think of it,' he will say, 'if I don't answer the door you shouldn't let yourself in. This isn't your property.'

'Oh – you!'

Her giggling will increase and she will reach out and slap his shoulder as if he is being a naughty tease. Then she will open her eyes wide with mock excitement and give his bicep a proper feel.

'Well I never!' she will exclaim. 'Would you look at that, like one of those Mr Universes. I tell you if I was thirty years younger ... you'd have to watch out!'

He will be so surprised to see this side of Mrs Goodly that he will be rendered almost speechless. But he will remember how not so long ago she stood in this same spot with the other women from the neighbourhood and tried to tell him how to organise his life, and will pull away and give her a cold stare.

'Is there something I can do for you?'

Mrs Goodly's mirth will simmer down to a light chuckle.

'Well, I heard you're doing the fête –' she will begin.

'How did you know that?'

'Because it's in the paper, silly! Anyway I wanted to come round and say that I – well, we really, since I'm here on behalf of the girls – we all think it's marvellous and a real step forward ...'

She will pause then award him a gigantic smile.

'What I mean to say is, what's in the past is in the past, and we just wanted you to know that we're proud of you. Hope you understand we've only ever had your best interests at heart.'

He will continue to stand there gaping at her, something Mrs Goodly will pretend not to notice. She will let out another peal of giggles and will pat his arm again. Then she will see herself out of the back door, and he will watch, still rooted to the spot in amazement, as she waddles off up the garden. From his lips, as if independently, there will come a blast of noise – a short bitter laugh.

One day, not long after he'd turned thirty, he was on a train on his way to a new placement, when he became aware that the person in the seat opposite was staring at him and twitching his features excitedly. This man had blond hair and a ring in one ear, and wore a T-shirt so tight his nipples stuck out of it like studs. He turned his head away quickly and pretended not to have noticed, but he could tell the man was still looking from the reflection in the glass.

'Oh my God – it is you!' breathed the man all of a sudden.

He turned back apologetically to tell the man he had the wrong person. Then he took a breath of recognition himself.

They talked awkwardly at first. Paul was a stylist now, he told him. He had dropped out of university, much to his mother's horror, and gone to work for a fashion magazine where one thing had led to another and he'd been given a lucky break with a minor celebrity. He'd just broken up with his boyfriend, Paul said, but he wasn't particularly sorry because the guy had been a selfish prick and only interested in reflective surfaces, and Paul had his eye on somebody new anyway, a guy who worked for one of the agencies that booked him. Paul claimed he was saving up, and almost had enough money for a deposit on his own flat. He listened in silence as Paul went on, nodding and smiling and emitting the requisite 'Oh's and 'Ah's at what he felt to be the appropriate places. Paul chattered on endlessly, seeming to take it for granted his life was fascinating to him – and indeed he was right. He listened in amazement, taking in the gossipy, stylish and uninhibited creature the pious and quiet do-gooder he'd once known had become.

'And what about you?' Paul wanted to know finally, when he'd finished detailing the disaster he claimed was his love life. 'My God, I've just gone on and on about me! What are you up to now? Where do you live? Are you seeing anyone? Fuck me – it's been so long!'

He tried to evade Paul's questions but eventually it came out, and he swallowed his sense of shame and watched Paul digest the fact that he still lived in that little town, still with his mum, still in the same house. He watched it dawn on Paul just how differently their lives had turned out and felt an embarrassed silence develop, pitted only by the sound of the train rushing over its tracks.

'Oh,' Paul murmured finally, as if he had admitted to having a debilitating illness or psychological condition. 'I had no idea.'

'It's OK. I'm a carer now.'

'Well – that's great!'

He laughed out loud, for it was clear Paul could think of no fate worse, and he remembered how he used to feel this way himself. His laugh broke the tension, and Paul grinned and knocked his fist against his forehead.

'I'm sorry. You must think I'm a total arsehole.'

'Don't worry,' he reassured him. 'You're quite right. I'm a loser.'

Paul let out a laugh of his own. They chatted more easily after that, for it felt as if they had got rid of all pretence, and neither cared any more for a comparison between their lives. He told Paul how his dad had died the year before after a heart attack, and how his mum had retired and never left the house any more, relying on him to shop and tend to any problems. He told him how he had been secretly saving up with a view to one day moving out and buying somewhere of his own, and then admitted that he was not seeing anyone and saw a shadow pass briefly across Paul's face. He knew he was wondering if he had ever seen anyone after Edward, and was very tempted to come out and confess that he hadn't. But then they pulled into his station.

'Well,' he said, putting out his hand, 'good to see you again.'

'God! What is this, *Brief Encounter*?' cried Paul, standing up and throwing his arms around him.

He was pleased by the embrace, it made his day, and just as he was getting off Paul ran down the aisle screeching at him for his email address, and he wrote it down for him on the back of his ticket. Paul blew kisses as the train pulled away, and watching it disappear he felt a sweeping sense of nostalgia. He really did not expect to hear from Paul.

Almost a month later he received a short email in which Paul apologised in capital letters for not writing sooner, explaining he had lost the ticket with his address. It had been handed to him by the woman who collected his dry-cleaning, Paul wrote, together with a raised eyebrow and a knowing look. He laughed out loud at the message, attracting a suspicious glance from his mum who was watching television in the same room and who had an instinctive resentment towards the Internet.

After that he and Paul got into the habit of emailing one another regularly, until gradually he came to feel that he knew this daring new adult version of the awkward boy he had once hung out with.

*   *   *

He is sitting in the dark, on the ledge of the open window, looking down and watching the shadows cast by people under the seedy orange glow of street lamps as they stumble drunkenly on their way from bars and clubs. The chilly night breeze washes over his face, bringing with it the smell of traffic, grime and pollution, the essence of the city. He hears Paul unlocking the front door and then coming into the room, but he does not turn. The light comes on.

'Darling – don't do it!'

He lets out a mirthless laugh.

'You left,' says Paul. 'You could have said something.'

'Sorry, I couldn't find you.'

'So send a text.'

'I don't have a phone.'

There is a disbelieving pause while Paul tries to envision just what this must be like, then finally, with the air of somebody giving up, Paul says, 'Darling, what's really going on here?'

The change in Paul's tone strikes an unexpected note and he has an almost insurmountable urge to break down. He bites his lips and resists it with everything he has, telling himself he has cried too much recently and it is time to get a hold of himself. Gradually the urge subsides.

'Are you thinking about him?'

There is no question who Paul is talking about. He has a gulp of air, taking inside him the ugly molecules of the city.

'Sometimes it's like I'm always thinking about him,' he says.

He hears Paul moving behind him, the sound of keys clinking as they are set down on the table and of a coat being removed and thrown over the sofa. He knows Paul is using the time to think of what to say and wants to tell him not to bother saying anything, because there isn't anything to say.

'It wasn't your fault. You know that.'

Yes, he knows. He was just a child. It was not he who made Edward do it, climb the trellis, nor was he the one who made Edward slip. It was an accident, a tragedy that has no motive and nobody behind it to carry the blame. One of those senseless, meaningless, purposeless things. But the guilt is just one of those things too, that's what he wants to tell Paul. It might not be logical, it might very well be the construct of grief – but once it has got inside you and taken hold there is no getting rid of it.

Paul clears his throat.

'I don't just mean . . .'

'It's OK,' he finishes for him.

'No – you don't understand!' says Paul with sudden urgency.

'Look –'

But Paul bounds across the room to his side, with a force that could easily have sent him over the edge were it not for the way Paul clutches at him, as if the world were trying to rip him away. He sees pupils large and dark, the thinnest band of colour around them, the white expanses beyond laced with delicate tendrils of red.

'If you need to blame someone it should be me!'

He twists and stares at Paul. Then he chuckles, suddenly reminded of Vlad, the only other person he knows who is such a drama queen. Paul is out of his mind because of whatever substance he has taken.

'It must be bedtime,' he says.

'It was my fault,' says Paul. 'He said he was going to get the moon for you and started climbing. He was laughing because he said it was so easy. He tried to get me to come up too, but I was so angry with him for throwing that dirt . . . I watched him climbing up and I wanted that little fucker to fall and break something – I wanted to see that smug face in pain for once! He was always so full of himself . . . I . . . I reached down and I picked up this stone and I took aim and I threw it! I didn't think . . . I didn't think I'd . . . It hardly even touched him!'

The pupils seem to grow even wider, so that they blot out the irises all together in miniature eclipses.

'Do you hear what I'm telling you?' demands Paul, his voice high and hysterical. 'I'm saying I killed him! I threw a stone and it got him on the side of his head amd he let go and then he fell off!'

Paul's voice wavers. At any second he might start shrieking or maybe collapse. And it occurs to him that the only time he has ever seen Paul overcome with emotion before was on that very night.

'If it wasn't for me he wouldn't be dead!'

Abrupt as a thunderbolt, Paul's words hit home. Suddenly it hurts to look at him, and he yanks his gaze away, back to the street. He can still hear Paul though, sobbing manically, and feel him, his fingers digging painfully into his arm. After a long while Paul's panting turns to wheezing and then slows almost to normal, and his grip relaxes.

'How could I have hit him?' Paul asks, his voice now soft with an almost childlike wonder. 'I mean – me, who never so much as kicked a football in my life. Who couldn't even hit the ball in rounders. How is it even possible?'

'It doesn't make any difference,' he hears himself say firmly. 'It was just an accident.'

He is right too, this is something he knows rationally and so he forces himself to turn back and take Paul in his arms. But even as he holds Paul, he knows he is lying. Deep down, in a place so buried its whereabouts have long been forgotten, it does make a difference. It makes all the difference in the world.

Sometimes when he thought about his past, it would seem to him as if it had not really happened at all, but rather as if he was still waiting for it to take place. As if he had drifted through it in a walking, talking sleep, one that made each year merge indistinguishably into the next and turned existence into one long cycle of rituals and patterns. Breaks, holidays, trips abroad stood out like islands in the endless nothing, yet even they looked flat and dull if he closely examined them – the time when he had walked around a small town in France all on his own, unable to speak the language and feeling that everyone was whispering about him, or the occasion he had taken a train to Cornwall and found himself stranded in a miserable bed and breakfast with no idea what to do with himself.

Time sipped at him like the sea lapping against a peninsula, weathering it down imperceptibly, inexorably, until there came a day when it was ready to crumble entirely. He felt the effort of carrying himself through the days like a great weight, the burden of having merely to be, that grew heavier and heavier until finally the knowledge that what lay ahead was only more of the same, stretching on until his consciousness saw fit to close down on him, became more than he could stand.

It is early afternoon when he rises. He goes to the window and looks out, and sees the sun winking over the shiny glass surfaces of office blocks. In the bathroom he mechanically goes through the motions of using the toilet, brushing his teeth and showering. He has a coffee in the kitchen and smokes a cigarette from the packet Paul has left out on the table, admiring the way the smoke trails from the tip and curls skyward, becoming more and more translucent until it is gone altogether. Simple things can still be beautiful, he thinks.

On his way out of the flat he runs into Paul, staggering out of his room in a set of pyjamas that have a pattern of robots warring with angels on them. Paul looks at him bleary-eyed, and he notices bags under Paul's eyes and for the first time thinks how old he looks.

'Are you OK?'

Paul's voice sounds rough and at least an octave deeper.

'Just off for a walk.'

'About last night . . .'

He pauses, curious to see if Paul will apologise, say he was off his head, maybe even try to take it back. But Paul does not say anything in the end, just leaves his desire for some ungrantable pardon floating unsaid in the atmosphere and stumbles groggily back to his room.

The roads of the city are deserted – almost phantom-like in their emptiness. He wanders aimlessly, turning up streets and crossing squares, getting lost and not caring, feeling increasingly like a phantom himself. He does not think about Edward. The ground is too sore, the knowledge that he has based his entire way of living on unnecessary guilt too frightening to examine. Instead he thinks about his mother, and experiences a sharp pang of longing. He wonders what she has been through since he left and if she will have changed, if she will just be the same frightened mouse-like creature as before. He suddenly needs to see her again. It occurs to him that despite spending his life with this woman, really he knows so little about her – about her upbringing, where she met his father, or what she dreamed of for herself when she was young. She has never spoken about such things, and has never expressed an interest in speaking about them either. Now is the time to ask questions, he realises – now, before it is too late. He resolves that he will call and tell her he is coming home. And when he gets home he will not pretend the last few months did not happen, will not act contrite as if he regrets what he has done. He will tell her every last detail and then he will demand details from her, about who she really is. Somehow, he will make things right between them.

When he returns the door to Paul's room is ajar but the curtains inside are still drawn. The lights are off and the figure in the bed has not moved. He goes to Paul's phone, lifts it and dials. There is no answer at the other end and so he hangs up and dials again. But the phone rings and rings and still no one picks it up.

On the day of the town fête he will drive down to the school field to inspect the rig they have set up over the stage, and to attach the rope and trapeze. It will have been erected by a company who usually set up lighting scaffolds, and the two men who have pieced it together will be standing examining their handiwork looking baffled, as if confused as to what anyone could possible want with such a structure in the middle of a field.

'You the circus guy?' one of them will say, a lanky man with thick black stubble lining his jaw.

'That's me,' he will answer, surveying the truss, which stands at seven metres height. The men will have driven the base stakes into the ground on either side of the stage, securing the truss with long ropes that anchor it down from the very top.

'You really gonna hang a trapeze from this thing?'

He will jiggle the shoulder over which he has draped the trapeze, and pat his bag which contains the rope. The man will lose his suspicious expression and look impressed.

'Thinking of popping by later. Ain't never been bothered about these fêtes before. Boring, ain't they? But my girlfriend's mad keen on gymnastics and stuff. Reckon she'll want to see you.'

'Great,' he will say.

He will climb up and attach the trapeze with a karabiner on each rope, and then hang the rope half a metre to the side of it. The two men will watch wordlessly, one of them footing the ladder. Over at the edge of the field, in the playground beside the school, a group of children and their mothers will also be watching, and he will wave to them from his vantage point, and a couple of the kids will wave back.

'Ah – there you are!'

As he descends the rope Sue will materialise from round the back of the stage with a couple of other women in tow, fellow council members she will introduce with such speed that he will miss both their names. The women will smile and one of them will raise an ironic eyebrow behind Sue, as if sharing a private joke. Sue will look up at the trapeze and clap her hands together.

'Oh! Isn't it just the most exciting thing you ever saw? I can't tell you how much interest we've been getting – I've had people asking all sorts of questions! I just know this year is going to be the best ever. We're going to put you on right after the Mayor's speech. People tend to switch off a bit when he talks so it'll be a great way to keep them listening!'

She will pause to laugh delicately as if she'd made a witty little joke, and he will grasp the opportunity to give them a polite nod and excuse himself.

'Two o'clock sharp!' Sue will trill from behind him as he leaves. 'Don't you forget about it now!'

He will wave back at her, knowing there is little chance of that happening.

He woke to the familiar sound of his alarm and the dull sense of the impending day ahead. But as he climbed out of bed he knew there was something different. He showered as usual, cleaned his teeth and dressed as if it were an ordinary morning, but as he was combing his hair he noticed that the hand holding the comb was quivering with minute spasms. He held it up to the mirror and observed it with surprise – it looked as if an electrical current was running down his arm and into his fingers. He put the comb down and peered at his reflection. He looked the same as ever, pale and serious, but there was a new light to his eyes, something about them he couldn't quite define. He knew then – perhaps not consciously, but in his heart and in his bones – that he wouldn't be going through this Sisyphean ritual again.

Downstairs his mum was already up. She was always first to rise, and if he woke early he would often hear her pottering around in the kitchen, tinkering with plates and pans as she examined drawers and cupboards for stains and dust, endlessly polishing and repositioning items about the room.

'I'm worried about the dishwasher,' she said as he sat down at the table. 'I think it needs someone in to look at it.'

She had been worried about the dishwasher since he bought it for her at Christmas three years ago. She had grown increasingly insomniac as she got older, and claimed it made a howling noise that kept her awake. She had never liked the look of it, and refused to believe it cleaned anything more efficiently than washing items by hand. Six months ago they had got rid of the television because she said it emitted a shrill buzzing that made her skin itch unbearably, even when switched off. Lately she had become even more suspicious of the Internet, which she denied served any useful purpose and insisted caused bad eyesight.

'Then don't use it,' he said simply.

She drew a short breath, shocked. He reached into the collection of cereal, bowls and milk she had arranged perfectly on the table and poured Bran Flakes into a bowl. His mother crossed her arms.

'I want someone to come,' she said.

'Fine,' he replied. 'Call someone up.'

She didn't like to make phone calls any more. She said it made her nervous not being able to see the face of the person she was talking to, and she had once read an article in the local paper that suggested excessive use of phones was linked to cancer. He was the one who dealt with such matters.

'What's wrong with you today?'

He lifted his spoon and noticed that his hand was still trembling. With great care he inserted a spoonful of Bran Flakes into his mouth and crunched down. They tasted of nothing. Robotically he chewed and swallowed his mouthful.

'Answer me!' cried his mother. 'What is it?'

'You wouldn't understand,' he heard himself say, and was surprised by the bitterness in his voice.

'Understand what?'

He drew a breath. It was not true that she wouldn't understand, he realised, but it was true that she did not want to. He felt her eyes demanding that he apologise, that he stand up and say he was very sorry and that he had got out of the wrong side of bed that morning, that it was down to nothing but an unpleasant mood. He felt her willing him to do it, felt her need him to so strongly it was almost stupefying. But he couldn't. He couldn't apologise, smile, alleviate her fear. He dropped his head.

'I don't feel well.'

'You look perfectly fine to me!'

'I think I might be having a breakdown.'

There was silence – silence and the gentle rattling of the dishwasher pounding water against the crockery inside it. If you listened ever so carefully you could hear a thin sound that resembled a screech, just like his mother said, and the realisation she was right penetrated the fog in his head like a laser beam. Suddenly he was filled with the urge to tell her all the things she didn't want to hear or know about – to make her listen, whether she liked it or not.

'I get up day in and day out and I go and help someone else get up. I help them have a bath and I help them take a crap. I help them eat food and I help them drink tea and I help them to sit in the garden or watch TV. I help them do all these things with no aim other than for them to survive another day. And most of the time all I can think is that they'd be better off if they just lay down and died and were done with it. What's more, lately I've been thinking the same thing about myself. That I'd be better if I just lay down and died and was done with it too.'

Her eyes were round as pennies.

'Why are you saying these awful things?'

'Because I'm tired!' he cried, sounding louder and deeper than ever before. His mother flinched. 'That's all there is to it!'

She quivered and he felt her gather her strength.

'How dare you? What the devil's got into you? Now I know' – his mother stabbed the air with a finger and lifted her chin haughtily – 'I know that you're embarrassed because you still live at home and because you think I'm stupid and don't understand technology and such, but you should show me some respect. I cook for you and I clean for you and I don't expect anything in return. And what's more I've never said a word about –'

She stopped herself abruptly and looked away. He shut his eyes and for a few seconds he saw only black, a black that pounded with blood and anger and mindless frustration. When he opened them again she was clutching her head, as if to protect herself from a migraine.

'About what?' he said.

'Do you think I don't know what you get up to? Where you go when you don't come home until late? And do I say anything about it? Do I make a fuss, tell you how to live your life?'

He stared, unable to reply. All he could concentrate on was how much she had shrunk over the years. She had grown so thin and stooped she was now no more than a wisp of a human being – half a person at best. And it seemed to him in that moment that she had diminished deliberately, as if trying to lessen her presence in the world and thereby reduce the likelihood of it noticing her, of it coming after her, demanding anything of her. Without another word he pushed his chair back and walked out of the room. 'Where are you going?' he heard her cry, but he didn't stop. He went out the front door, letting it swing shut behind him.

She will be sitting in the armchair by the window when he enters, the place they always put her. The armchair itself will seem enormous, like a great maw of cushions preparing to devour her. His mother's head will rest against a pillow that will have been propped up behind her neck, and her eyes will stare vacantly towards the wall, ignoring the window. Her mouth will be slightly open and tiny drops of spittle will glisten on the lower lip.

He will stand in the doorway, his heartbeat quickening as he gathers his resolve. Then he will look back down the corridor. The home will seem unusually silent and empty – almost as if it has fallen into a ceremonial hush.

He will step softly into the room and close the door. He will resist the need to pull up a chair, to talk to her one last time, to give himself the chance to change his mind. Rather he will go straight to the bed, pick up the remaining pillow and approach the armchair keeping his eyes levelled on the carpet. Only when he reaches it will he lift them and take one final look at her face. But he will not falter. He will raise the pillow and bring it down over those withered features, pressing with all his might. She will make no sign of resistance. A great sob rising within him, he will twist his face away to the window, forcing himself to stare out at the small strip of lawn and the yellowing hedgerow. His hands will feel numb, as if they belonged to another body in another time. The world around him will seem to diminish, grow distant, as if whatever strange fabric it is made from has lost its sheen, its essence of reality. Sound will fade until it is gone altogether.

All at once he will pull back the pillow and hurl it to the corner of the room. The faint throbbings and hummings of the home, of radiators and electrical appliances, will come rushing back into his ears like thunder. Colour and detail will flood into the room. He will sink to his knees, grasp the body before him and bury his head in its lap. He will remain this way for a long time, letting the blanket covering her spidery legs grow sodden with his tears.

When he looks up her face is as before, slack-jawed and staring. He will take in the almost imperceptible rise and fall of her breast and he will be filled with strange emotion. It will not quite be gladness, but something beyond gladness – a kind of awe for this used-up old vessel, the body that gave him life, and its unbreakable will to continue, even with a future of nothingness opening out before it.

He will take her hand and set it gently in her lap. Then he will quickly leave the room.

He drove directionlessly around town for a couple of hours, passing up and down the high street, the old shops with their familiar display windows which never changed, turning off into cul-de-sacs and doing circuits of the town hall. Finally he headed towards the church and parked on the road outside.

He walked across the graveyard slowly, heading in a roundabout way towards the building. He hadn't been there for years. After it happened, up until he was in his mid-twenties, he had avoided the place, taking care not even to drive past it, making detours into town when necessary. But one day when he was twenty-six he had forgotten to do this, had driven past without thinking and had found he was not filled with anguish at the sight of it. Every so often after that, when he finished work early but did not want to go straight home or drive to the bar in the next town, he would go there to walk around. He had never visited the place where Edward was buried – some other churchyard off in Kent near where he'd been born. He knew that place would not hold the same mean ing for him. It was here, where the accident had happened, that Edward's memory clung – an invisible shadow over the ground before the porch, where people walked every day without the slightest notion that a boy's life had once ended there.

He stared at the space now, struggling to remember, to see again the shape of Edward's body and to feel again that boundless horror combined with the instinctive understanding that the world would never be the same again. But time had worked its sleepy magic on his memory so that he saw nothing but an impression of what had transpired. He was not even sure how much of what he remembered was really memory, and how much just his imagination.

As he stood there straining to recall the details, he became aware of a sniggering, and looked up to see a trio of teenage boys lazily making their way to him. They were passing back and forth a cigarette, obviously playing truant from school. He waited for them to pass, but as they reached him one of the boys, the tallest, who had a shaggy fringe that fell artfully across his left eye, called out to him, 'All right, mate, you a necro?'

The other two giggled furiously, their eyes wide and alive, waiting to see if he would react. He dropped his head and stared at the spot where Edward had fallen, willing them to leave.

'You waiting to pick up kiddies or something?'

He continued to ignore him. Edward would have had a good retort ready, he thought. Edward would have known exactly what to say to this kid to put him in his place. Edward would have said . . . but he suddenly had no idea what Edward would have done.

'Leave him, he's weird,' suggested one of the other boys.

The one with the fringe sniggered.

'Freak,' he muttered.

With these words the kid took the cigarette from his lips, which was now almost a butt, and threw it. He felt it bounce off his chest. He looked up in automatic fury, wanting to pound the boy's head into the nearest gravestone. But screeching with laughter the boys took off down the path and out of the churchyard. The cigarette lay on the gravel, directly where Edward had once lain, a thin stream of smoke emanating from its tip.

Back in his car he took out his mobile and dialled the head of the agency.

'There you are at long last!' she answered him. 'I've left two messages. Mr Piers has been calling to ask where you are!'

'I'm sorry,' he told her. 'I'm not coming in today.'

'But you should have been there an hour ago!' she said crossly. 'What's Mr Piers supposed to do?'

He wanted to break down then and tell this woman he'd never even met all the things that were wrong in the world, then beg her to help him. He wanted to warn her that he was probably going to do something stupid if she didn't help. He wanted to hear her express concern for him and not for Mr Piers.

'I can't make it. I won't be in. You should send someone else.'

The woman made a tutting noise.

'This is very last minute . . . I don't know who else is going to be available at such late notice. It's not going to look very good on your record, you know.'

Fuck the record, he thought.

'I'm not sure I can condone –'

He brought his finger down on the button to end the call and closed up his phone. There was no going back now, and the knowledge of this fact, clear and indisputable, drove all the despair from his mind. He plugged the key into the ignition and started the car.

A crowd of people will have gathered on the field before the stage and he will see somebody beneath the rig is talking into a microphone. There will be stands displaying cakes, bric-a-brac, flower arrangements and a tombola, and a pink-and-blue bouncy castle will be swaying under the weight of numerous youngsters. He will see Sue looking around distractedly and nodding at something one of the locals is saying to her, and he will know she is wondering where he is. He will pass the field and turn into the school's car park, which is almost full. Immediately he will see the caravan, parked in the disabled space up against the school diner. The space next to it is free so he will pull up alongside and get out the car. He will rap on the side of the caravan, and from within will come a familiar voice cursing.

'I told you it's only for half an hour so piss off!' the clown will snap, throwing the door open and presenting the outside world with a ferocious grimace. When Jethro sees it is him his face will slowly untwist.

'Oh,' the clown will say. 'Hi.'

'What are you doing here?' he will ask.

Jethro will look momentarily embarrassed.

'What do you think? Came to see your show, didn't I? See what this cockshite is about you turning yourself into a trapeze artist.'

His vision will blur.

'You came to see me?'

Jethro will look cross for a second, as if he is going to start snarling or shouting. Then the clown will suddenly grin. Jethro looks better than before, he will notice – his skin is an almost healthy pink and the dark circles under his eyes do not seem as prominent. As if he knows what he is thinking the clown will say, 'Stopped drinking, ain't I? You're looking at a fucking saint here!'

He will smile at him, a sad smile, and the clown will jump down from the caravan and start walking around him in a circle, inspecting his body. Jethro will reach out and poke his thighs and then his buttocks.

'Huh!' the clown will mutter. 'Been busy, ain't ya?'

He will nod, choking a little.

'Jethro . . .' he will start to say.

But he will get no further. The presence of the clown is both wonderful and awful, so much so that he will be scarcely able to draw breath, never mind form a coherent sentence. 'It's good to see you,' he will finish lamely.

'Yeah?' the clown will say. 'How come you never emailed or nothing?'

He will swallow.

'Things have been . . . difficult.'

'Fuck off!'

'My mother, she was ill . . .'

The clown will stare at him mistrustfully and he will meet the stare head on. They will look at one another for a long time, just holding one another's gaze and not speaking, and it will be as if an understanding has arisen between them, of all the suffering they have ever been through, and of all the suffering to come. He will want to drop to his knees and confess everything he has done, to hear Jethro tell him it is OK. But there will be no time.

'I have to start . . .' he will say. 'I'm late.'

He will turn and hurry across the car park.

'Hey!' the clown will bellow after him. He will stop and look back at Jethro standing in front of his caravan with his hands on his hips. The clown will roll his eyes towards the heavens, heave a great sigh, then roll them back.

'Good luck, eh? We'll catch up after?'

The danger of losing control will be too great. He will run across the gravel towards the crowd. Ahead of him, towering over the stage, stands the trapeze rig and for an instant it will resemble gallows silhouetted against the sun.

He drove through the woods that lay on the opposite side of the common and took a small turning that was easy to miss if you didn't know it was there, signposted only by a rusty metal notice marked 'Private'. Forty yards on he parked the car in front of a steep incline, which led to a large ditch in which various pieces of old furniture, clapped-out cookers and broken-down refrigerators were strewn, a purgatory for household items that had outlived their desirability.

He switched off the engine and sat for a long time studying the dashboard, not daring to look above it – for he felt that if he did he would have no option but to execute his plan. But eventually his gaze drifted up and he looked out at the surrounding trees and then over at the ditch, which seemed like a great mouth that had opened up in the earth, a passage to the underworld such as from an ancient myth. The sun beat down powerfully on the windscreen, burning his scalp, and his bladder ached for relief. He felt his stomach rumble and remembered he had not eaten since breakfast. He thought how pleasant it would be to free himself of these human sensations, and he thought it was probably time. But still he did not move.

Bit by bit the heat of the sun declined. The air began to grow cold and shadows crept across the earth like ghostly fingers stretching out to touch one another. The faraway sounds of cars roaring past on the motorway that lay on the other side of the forest could be heard and nearby the tooting of birds as they saluted the end of the day. All at once he removed his seat belt and slung it to the side, reached down and took off the handbrake. He started the engine and he held his foot over the accelerator. Then, like a slap, it hit him what he was about to do – the momentous reality of it, and he let out a spontaneous gurgle of fright. In a flash he understood that this was not what he wanted.

It was then that he heard the distant sound of music. A twisting gypsy-like melody with fiddles and tambourines, that snaked its way through the air and to his ears and seemed to wind itself around something inside him. He looked over his shoulder and saw distant lights through the darkness, winking pink and blue through the trees like the auras of faerie folk. The source of the lights lay past the woods, on the common.

He shifted gear to reverse and brought his foot down, backing the car up the trail, clumsily taking out bushes and branches in the process. When he hit the road he turned round and drove until he reached the common. Here he pulled up the car and gazed in wonder.

On the field before him, surrounded by a cluster of caravans and trailers and decorated with strands of coloured lights, sat a big top, the word 'Circus' decorated in silver spangles above its entrance, the sinewy music emanating from within.

At the station he uses the payphone to call a taxi from the local cab company. It arrives ten minutes later. He thinks of his own car, abandoned in some random field north of town, and it occurs to him that he ought to work out where he left it, and set out to see if it is still there.

'All right?' says the driver, peering at him closely after he tells him the address. 'You from round here?'

'Sort of,' he replies, not wanting to be drawn into a conversation.

The driver continues to peer at him and for a tense few seconds he wonders if he knows this man, or if the man knows him. Then the driver nods without any apparent further interest and they drive out of the station. His heart begins to hammer as he takes in the familiar surroundings of the town, and some inner sense shrieks like an alarm bell, telling him to get the driver to stop and turn round, take him back to the station where he can get on the next train out of there and never return. Yet there is also a leaden feeling of finality that gradually subdues this shrieking, as if it were always inevitable he would return. As if for better or worse this is where he belongs.

Even so, when they turn onto his street he almost changes his mind. The sight of the house intensifies his feelings to such an extent that he wonders if he is going to faint. The first thing he notices is how the front garden is overgrown – for years it has been his job to hunt for weeds and uproot them under his mother's watchful eye, but without him it has gone to seed. Shakily he climbs out of the cab and offers the driver his money. Then he stands, staring at the house idiotically, unable to take another step, still wondering if it is too late to turn back. But then it is too late, as the cab removes this possibility by driving off, leaving him with no option but to open the gate.

He has just set foot on the front path when he hears a shrill cry from behind. Alarmed, he spins round to see Mrs Goodly hurrying over. A cleaning smock is draped over her dress and her face is pale as if she has just seen a ghost.

'Oh my Lord – you're back!'

'Hello, Mrs Goodly,' he replies, making an effort to sound calm.

But she seems unable to get over the fact, looking him up and down and wrinkling up her forehead.

'How is everything?' he asks carefully.

'Oh dear, oh dear . . .' fusses Mrs Goodly, flapping her arms up and down like an agitated bird. She turns her head around as if to look for assistance, but there is none to be found and so she turns back with a fretful smile. 'Oh dear. What am I supposed to say, I wonder . . .?'

He decides he does not have time for this ridiculous woman.

'It's nice to see you too,' he says with a brisk nod, and then continues up the path to the door. He takes out his keys and breathlessly fits them into the lock. As he opens the door he kicks over a small mound of post, which slides across the floor all the way to the table. It is dark in here, and he can see the blinds to the kitchen in the next room are closed.

'Hello?' he calls out.

The silence booms back like a gong. Even before he has taken another step he understands that no one lives here any more.

As he climbs the rope he will be stricken with panic. All eyes below will be upon him, absorbing his every movement. His hand will shake as he reaches out for the trapeze and his body will rotate away from the bar, so that he will miss and have to make a second attempt to grab it. But the instant his fingers close around it he will be filled with a great soaring sense of triumph. He will climb confidently beneath the bar and raise his legs in front of it, then thrust his torso forward and swing back into a dramatic beat. The crowd will begin to applaud as he rotates around the bar, and there will be screams and whoops when he whips himself up into a sitting position only to drop instantly backwards and catch the ropes with his ankles. He will feel wild, elated and free, his body alive with joy, as if a long imprisoned spirit has finally been released.

'Well, would you look at that, ladies and gentlemen?' he will hear the Mayor saying into the microphone, and there will be another burst of cheering. As he propels himself from shape to shape, he will catch a glimpse of Sue beaming, flanked by well-wishing members of the public. Over by the cake stall he will see Mrs Goodly, clapping away delightedly in the midst of a small throng of old women.

Suddenly he will be like a god, and there will be nothing he cannot do. Up here, perching in the sky, anything will be possible. He will climb to a standing position and take hold of the ropes, thrusting his hips back and forth. Slowly his movements will begin to move the trapeze. People will start a slow clap, as the swings get higher and higher, until he is rocketing back and forth across the air. Now he will be able to see Sue frowning – they will have gone over his repertoire and this will not be something she is expecting. There will be other looks of concern too, as the karabiners holding the ropes let out pained screeches each time the trapeze passes beneath them. Then there will be a collective gasp of amazement as at the height of the back swing he suddenly lets go of the ropes and hops off the trapeze, dropping down to catch the bar with both hands. As the crowd begins to applaud he will feel the wind roaring in his ears and it will feel as if every care he has ever had is falling away beneath him.

Then, as he soars forward and raises his legs, he will find himself looking straight into the eyes of the clown, standing at the front of the audience beside a group of wide-eyed toddlers. Once again he will have that sensation of understanding, as if the clown can somehow see right inside him. Jethro will be shouting something, he will realise, but whatever it is it will be lost to the wind and the applause. He will break his gaze away, tensing every muscle in his body, and concentrate on his arc towards the sky.

At the height of his swing he will drive his body up and over the bar and release it, feeling himself fly through the air, propelled as if by sheer force of will. He will hear a collective gasp from below, and a burst of whoops and screams. He will twist violently to his left and will feel the ropes against his feet for a split second before one of his ankles fails to catch and he begins to fall. Somewhere in the spiralling vista he will glimpse the bar and will reach for it. Even as the trapeze disappears above him he will reach, straining every muscle in his body, fingertips clawing at air, refusing to admit defeat.

ACKNOWLEDGEMENTS

THANK YOU TO my agent Peter Buckman for his boundless enthusiasm and perseverance.

Thank you to my editor Michael Fishwick for his incisive notes and suggestions, and to Anna Simpson, Katherine Fry, Alexa von Hirschberg, Alexandra Pringle and everyone at Bloomsbury.

Thank you (as always) to Mum, Dad, Tamsin and Seraphina for their support.

Thank you to Dawn King, Hannah Barton and Jackie Le for all their advice and encouragement over the time this book was written.

And thank you to Raphael Smith – you helped me more than you know.

A Note on the Type

The text of this book is set in Bembo. This type was first used in 1495 by the Venetian printer Aldus Manutius for Cardinal Bembo's *De Aetna*, and was cut for Manutius by Francesco Griffo. It was one of the types used by Claude Garamond (1480 1561) as a model for his Romain de L'Université, and so it was the forerunner of what became standard European type for the following two centuries. Its modern form follows the original types and was designed for Monotype in 1929.

ALSO AVAILABLE BY WILL DAVIS

MY SIDE OF THE STORY

Winner of the Betty Trask Award

'A coming-of-age tale that combines the coolness of *Queer as Folk* with the tenderness of *Adrian Mole*'
ELLE

So what if your parents hate each other and want you to have therapy?
So what if your holier-than-thou sister (aka The Nun) and her posse have decided you're going to hell?
So what if the school tyrant and his goons are hunting you down, or if your best friend has just outed you to a neo-Nazi?
Jaz isn't planning to lose any sleep over it – at least until he meets the guy of his dreams at the local gay bar. Suddenly things are a lot more complicated . . .

'Will Davis is a witty writer who effortlessly conjures up the frenetic detail of Jaz's sixteen-year-old world'
INDEPENDENT ON SUNDAY

'The dialogue fizzes with savvy one-liners . . . Davis's observations of the dysfunctions of family and school are as sharp as his prose is fresh, and his debut is intriguing, touching and entertaining'
TIME OUT

BLOOMSBURY

DREAM MACHINE

Four girls. A thousand desperate dreams. One shot at stardom . . .

Across the country wannabes are auditioning to be part of mega-girlband Purrfect in a new reality TV series. Among them are ice-queen Louise, who thinks she's got God on her side, foulmouthed Joni, desperate to hide the fact that she's got a baby, mousy teen Ella, obsessed with her stepmother's boyfriend, and cocky Riana, a stripper with a naughty penchant for coke. Each one is determined to be the new Purrfect girl. But as the show progresses it seems someone has a very different sort of agenda in mind – someone who's not afraid of things getting deadly . . .

'A clever contemporary tale which shows that sometimes what you dream of isn't what you really want . . . A great beach read'
BOOKSELLER

'A sharp, witty novel . . . More salacious than you could ever hope for'
GAY TIMES

ORDER BY PHONE: +44 (0)1256 302 699; BY EMAIL: DIRECT@MACMILLAN.CO.UK

DELIVERY IS USUALLY 3–5 WORKING DAYS. FREE POSTAGE AND PACKAGING FOR ORDERS OVER £20.

ONLINE: WWW.BLOOMSBURY.COM/BOOKSHOP

PRICES AND AVAILABILITY SUBJECT TO CHANGE WITHOUT NOTICE.

WWW.BLOOMSBURY.COM/WILLDAVIS

B L O O M S B U R Y